TANGLING WITH TROLLS

HAVEN EVER AFTER - BOOK TWO

HAZEL MACK

COPYRIGHT

© Hazel Mack Author 2023

EBook ISBN: 978-1-957873-47-3

Paperback ISBN: 978-1-957873-47-3

All rights reserved. No part of this publication may be reproduced, stored or transmitted in any form or by any means, electronic, mechanical, photocopying, recording, scanning, or otherwise without written permission from the publisher. It is illegal to copy this book, post it to a website, or distribute it by any other means without permission.

This novel is entirely a work of fiction. The names, characters and incidents portrayed in it are the work of the author's imagination. Any resemblance to actual persons, living or dead, events or localities is entirely coincidental. However, if I get the chance to become Ever's newest resident, I'll take it!

I don't support the use of AI in book, book cover or book graphic creation. If you love human generated books, please feel free to learn more at my website here.

Editing - Mountains Wanted

Proofreading - Marcelle | BooksChecked

Cover - Anna Fury Author

Cover Art - Linda Noeran (@linda.noeran)

❀ Created with Vellum

(Seal: THIS BOOK WAS WRITTEN BY A HUMAN · I DON'T SUPPORT AI BOOKS OR ART · HUMAN GENERATED)

AUTHORS ARE NOW FACING AN UNPRECEDENTED CHALLENGE · ARTIFICIAL INTELLIGENCE (AI).

AI-based "books", which are computer written, rather than human, are flooding the market and reducing our ability to earn a living wage writing books for you, our amazing readers.

The problem with AI as it stands today? It's not capable of thinking on its own. It ingests data and mimics someone else's style, often plagiarizing art and books without the original creator or author's consent.

There's a very real chance human authors will be forced out of the market as AI-written works take over. Yet your favorite authors bring magical worlds, experiences and emotions to life in a way that a computer can't. If you want to save that, then we need your help.

LEARN MORE ABOUT THE HARMFUL EFFECTS OF AI-WRITTEN BOOKS AND AI-GENERATED ART ON MY WEBSITE AT WWW.ANNAFURY.COM/AI

SYNOPSIS

WREN

A month ago, I had no idea that monsters lived in hidden towns. Surprise! The tiny New-England town of Ever is a haven for them. Vampire brothers run the coffee shop. Werewolf bikers will fix your car. I can sort of wrap my mind around that.

But then I meet Ohken Stonesmith, bridge troll and all-around badass. He's way older than me, crazy confident, and he owns the town's only flower shop. In short—he's my ideal man.

The second surprise? I'm a green witch! But when I struggle to use my newly-discovered magic, Ohken offers to teach me, although his methods aren't exactly conventional. He's a big fan of teasing me and making me crazy enough to get out of my own head. As our lessons grow more heated, I realize I'm falling for not only this wacky little town, but also the quiet male who's my biggest cheerleader.

Unfortunately, not all monsters want to live in peace. When evil sneaks past Ever's protective wards, I want to help. The problem is I keep blowing things up instead of fixing them. I've got to get control of my power fast, or Ever—and my budding romance with Ohken—will be in deep trouble.

GET THE FREEBIES

WANT SPICY EPILOGUES?

Sign up for my newsletter at www.annafury.com to access the FREE bonus epilogues to every Hazel Mack book I write.

CONTENT NOTICE

While this book is very sweet and lighthearted, there are a couple heavy themes to mention. In particular, there's light reference to recent parental death by accident, as well as one scene with slight gore. Like…one sentence of gore. I promise it's not much, but did want you to be aware!

If you have any particular questions, feel free to reach out to me at author@annafury.com!

To my incredible beta and sensitivity readers. You made this book better with your thoughtful commentary and realistic interpretations of my words. I am endlessly grateful to each of you: Brittney, Meg, Deysi, Geraldine, Jes and of course, Mr. Fury himself...

My deepest heartfelt thanks go to Marcelle, who has been a tireless friend, confidante and basically the best proofreader ever. ILYSM...

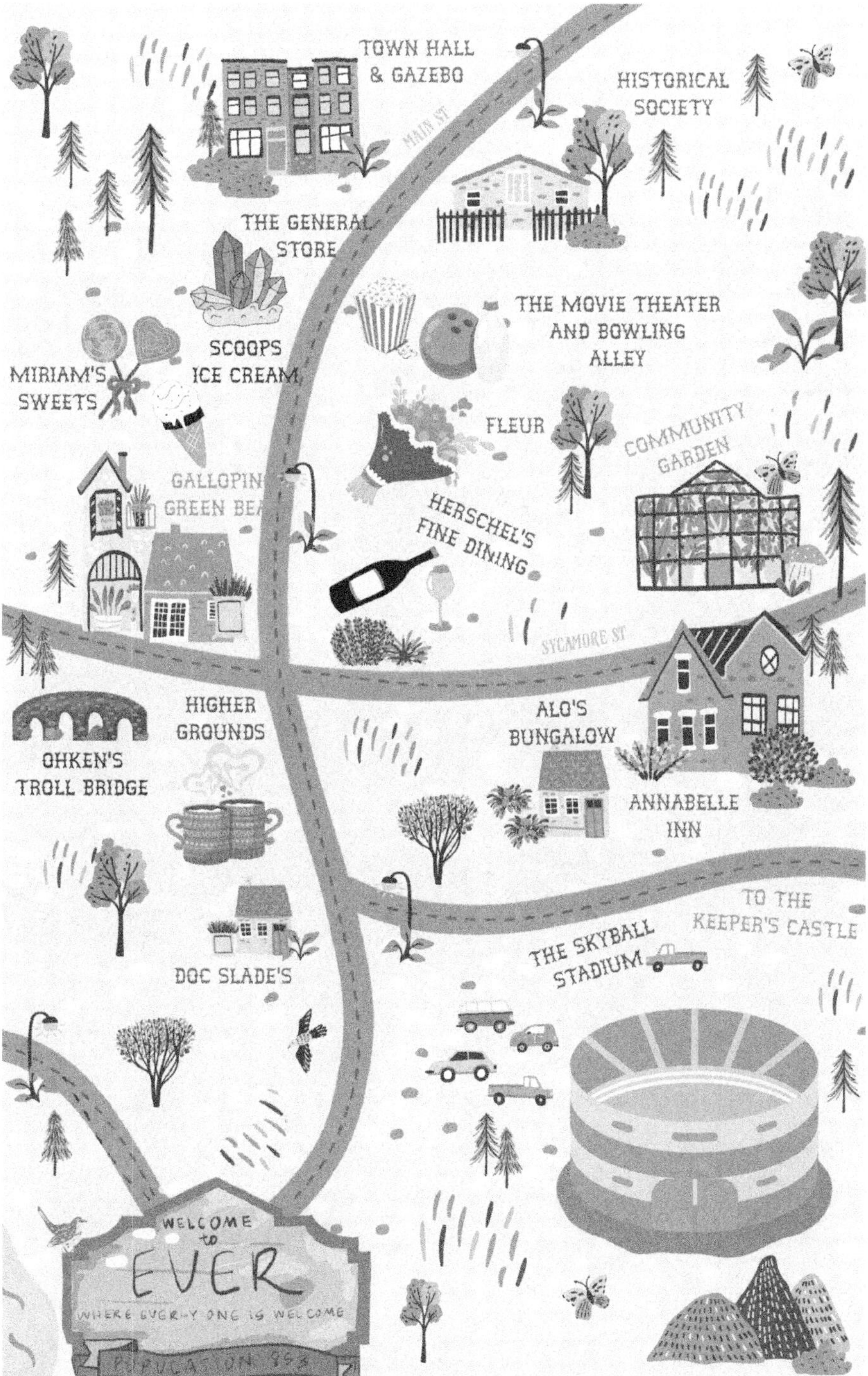

TOWN HALL
& GAZEBO
HISTORICAL
SOCIETY
MAIN ST
THE GENERAL
STORE
THE MOVIE THEATER
AND BOWLING
ALLEY
SCOOPS
ICE CREAM
MIRIAM'S
SWEETS
FLEUR
COMMUNITY
GARDEN
GALLOPIN
GREEN BEA
HERSCHEL'S
FINE DINING
SYCAMORE ST
HIGHER
GROUNDS
ALO'S
BUNGALOW
OHKEN'S
TROLL BRIDGE
ANNABELLE
INN
TO THE
KEEPER'S CASTLE
THE SKYBALL
STADIUM
DOC SLADE'S
WELCOME
to
EVER
WHERE EVER-Y ONE IS WELCOME

CHAPTER ONE
WREN

I stare out the window of my mermaid-themed room at the Annabelle Inn, looking at the empty stone perch where a gargoyle sometimes sits. Alo, one of Ever's two gargoyle protectors, told me he sits there in stone form when he needs a minute away from his rambunctious five-year-old, Iggy. I wonder where they are today? Probably up at Miriam's Sweets on Main getting candy, or maybe at Scoops getting ice cream.

Sometimes I wonder if they go to Miriam's so much because of Iggy, or if Alo's just coming around to the idea of Miriam being head over heels for him.

They'll sort out their love story, if they're meant to have one.

Or not.

That used to be my mother's favorite advice—*it'll either work out or it won't*. Which isn't advice at all, but more like a statement of the obvious. Thinking about her sends a stabbing sensation through my stomach, my heart clenching in my chest.

I miss her so much.

I look down at the journal resting on my thighs, wondering what my mother would think of the turn my life has taken, if she could see me.

I can almost imagine the conversation now. If cell phones worked here in Ever, and time didn't pass at the speed of a bullet train, I'd call her.

Hey Mom, the girls and I took a road trip, discovered a hidden monster town, and now Thea's dating a gargoyle!

She'd look shocked, and then she'd cackle, and then she'd make me my favorite caramel latte and we'd talk it out.

We can't talk it out anymore, though, so I'll journal it instead. It's what my therapist recommended after Mom and Dad died.

Thea and Morgan are handling our parents' deaths in different ways, and it's okay to grieve however one needs to. I can hear Morgan working out through the Annabelle Inn's thin walls. That's how *she* deals…

Reaching over to the window, I stroke the glass softly and grin. "Let Morgan know I'm up?"

The house creaks and groans, and the window in front of me opens and shuts three times. The Inn's telling me she'll help me out.

Two seconds later, there's a loud crack and a thud, and Morgan shrieks.

"Annabelle! What gives?!"

I laugh, and the window next to my leg vibrates a little bit. The Annabelle is laughing along with me.

Houses laugh here in Ever, Massachussetts. It's not weird, it's totally fine. No matter that three weeks ago I had no idea there was a town where monsters lived in hiding from humans and that houses came alive to pick their owners.

Footsteps stomp up the hallway and my bedroom door, which is painted with iridescent scales, flies open and hits the wall.

The Annabelle's pipes creak in warning.

My triplet, Morgan, stomps in with her long arms crossed. Auburn hair is piled high on her head and she's sweaty as fuck. She's gorgeous, though, even when she's pretending to be mad.

"Wren Elizabeth Hector, did you send the Annabelle to trip me?"

I scoff indignantly. "Trip you? Hardly. I simply asked her to tell you I was up."

Morgan narrows her gray eyes at me then kicks my door shut and glares up at the ceiling. It's painted with a stunning scene of mermaids frolicking on a beach.

I follow her gaze up and sigh. "Isn't she lovely?"

"Isn't she wonderfullll…" Morgan mutters, crossing the room to flop down on the bench seat across from me.

The reading nook windows flutter open and closed quickly in greeting. Morgan reaches out and strokes the thick, paned glass affectionately. Her eyes drop to my journal.

"I haven't seen you journal in a few weeks." Her voice is soft when our eyes meet.

I give her a saucy look. "Two weeks ago we were living in New York with normal jobs, totally unaware that Ever existed. Two weeks ago, Thea wasn't mated to a goddamn gargoyle. And two weeks ago? I didn't know all three of us were witches."

Morgan puffs air out with her lips and sits forward, picking at one of my Converse laces. "Do you miss the outside world? I mean when our 'weekend' here is done, do you think you might wanna go back even though Thea's staying?"

It's on the tip of my tongue to say 'hell no,' because Ever and its monstrous inhabitants are fucking fascinating to me. But I miss my job as a botanist. And to say I'm not great at being a witch is the understatement of the century.

When I hesitate to answer, Morgan frowns. "That's what I

thought." She crosses her arms after she unties and reties my shoelaces. "I know we all agreed we'd stay once she and Shepherd got together, but I feel like my opinion on that changes by the day."

I give her a grim look. "Would that have anything to do with the Keeper?"

Morgan stands and scowls. "He's part of it for sure, but more than anything I don't really feel like I have a place here."

I stand and tuck my journal behind a pillow in the window seat. Even the Annabelle is quiet after Morgan's pronouncement. Pulling my triplet in for a hug, I squeeze her crazy hard.

"We might find places here and we might not, and it's okay either way, right?"

"Yeah," she grumbles into the side of my head.

"Plus we've basically got the best brother-in-law ever, and that's worth something too, right? Wouldn't you miss being constantly drowned in snacks?"

Morgan lifts her head at that and smiles. "I do fucking love Shepherd."

"He makes the best baked goods," I agree, gesturing down at my fluffy belly. I look back up at Mor. "My fat rolls agree as well."

She laughs and shakes her head. "I guess the whole gargoyle mating tradition of feeding his mate's family has worked out pretty well for us. I swear he shows up every day with some kind of food."

On cue, the doorbell rings, and the floor beneath our feet shifts and ripples. The Annabelle shoves us toward the door to my room, and the door itself opens politely. Morgan wraps her arm around my waist and we head out into the plush, carpeted hallway. Beautiful paintings of lush gardens, happy gargoyles, and enchanting mermaids line the halls. They're all done in the same style. I don't know who painted them, but they're incredibly detailed, almost realistic.

Downstairs, a big shadow covers the entire front, glass-paned door.

Shepherd.

He peers in, grinning broadly. Our triplet Thea stands in front of him with her face pressed to the glass and her eyeballs crossed. She's goofy as fuck on the best of days, but I think he's brought that personality characteristic out even more.

Morgan opens the door with a wry grin. "Ya know, I think Thea is already hooked like a prize fish, you don't have to keep feeding us every day." There's no actual chiding in her tone though, she adores Shepherd. Best I can tell, everyone in this damn town adores Shepherd.

Thea strides inside and hands Morgan a box. I can already smell freshly baked cookies. Shepherd ducks in after her, dark purple horns nearly hitting the doorway.

I reach for the cookies with a smile. I've always been the fat sister, and I'm fine as hell with that. I'm healthy, happy, and gorgeous. But since we met Shepherd, my diet consists of 90% cookies and 10% his great-grandmother's lasagna recipe.

Which is bangin', by the way. I'm not complaining.

Shepherd just winks at me, because he has no intention of stopping the steady flow of treats.

"Snack up, shack up, Wren. It's a gargoyle male's motto, remember?"

I roll my eyes, but I grin because he seems to have taken it to heart.

Shepherd's grayish-purple tail wraps around Thea's waist. It must comfort him, because he often does it in quiet moments. It's fucking cute—she's basically tied to a giant monster like a cute little puppy on a leash. The spade-shaped tip lies flat against her stomach. His enormous wings are tucked up behind his back like a cape, so he looks like a badass gargoyle hero from that '80s show I used to love.

Which he literally is.

I do find it a little interesting that my sister, the former detective, is now mated to a monster whose job it is to protect this town. Like calls to like, I suppose.

"Are we ready for witchy-woo lessons?" Thea claps excitedly, her long, blonde braid swinging freely.

"Yeah!" I deadpan. "Can't wait to blow up more shit in the garden that literally powers the wards that keep the town safe. Goodie!"

Shepherd and Thea give me matching looks of warning.

He's the first to speak. "Wren, you've known you were a witch for all of two weeks. Discovering this is a monster town was a huge shock. Be kind to yourself and eat more cookies, it'll help." He glances down at my shirt, which says "Fat and Feral," his grin growing wide. He waves a hand at the text. "It would be a shame if you couldn't wear that proudly anymore."

I snort at that. Monsters don't get my fat-pride shirts at all. I've tried to explain what they mean to Shepherd and all it's resulted in is him upping the flow of snacks lest I stop being fat. It's kind of hilarious. And also very heartwarming. And incredibly affirming.

Thea rubs her mate's big arm, smiling up at him with hearts in her eyes. Morgan clears her throat and slips her arm through mine. Thea grabs Morgan's hand, and we leave the Annabelle's cozy front entryway to head outside. Like every other day, it's somewhere between sixty-five and seventy degrees. The weather doesn't change in Ever; it's like this year-round because of the protective wards over town.

This town is just about perfect.

I sigh as I look ahead. The view outside the Annabelle never fails to amaze me. Right across the street from the inn is the community garden. It's surrounded by a seven-foot-tall hedge, but as soon as you step through the open gate, it's like being in the secret garden from my favorite childhood classic.

A long A-frame support runs the length of the garden to my right. Giant gourds hang down in rows on the inside of the frame. It almost looks like a hallway dripping with pumpkins. That's where the town's pixies live when they're in small form. Which makes me wonder if Miriam is joining us today. She's become one of my closest friends since we arrived.

Moments later, a tiny green glow exits a hole in one of the gourds. It expands from being a mere dot until there's a quick flash, and Miriam stands there in her human-sized form. She's built slight like Thea, but taller, almost six feet like me. Her green pixie cut sticks up wildly in the front, and it matches the green-and-pink dragonfly-esque wings fluttering at her back.

She eyes the box of cookies I'm carrying and claps her hands, trotting over excitedly. Without asking she rips open the top of the box and grabs a chocolate chip cookie, shoving it into her mouth. Her fuchsia eyes roll back into her head as she moans.

"By all means," I croon sarcastically.

Miriam slaps my shoulder. "You love me. You'd never deny me snacks. That's why we're soulfriends."

That does pull a real smile to my face. The first time I met Miriam she pronounced me her 'soulfriend,' and it's honestly been our thing ever since. I think it miffs Morgan a little bit that she didn't get included in the title.

Unfortunately, Morgan has gotten the shit end of the stick about everything since we arrived in Ever. She's got the weirdest monster situationship. She's got the hardest witch power to master. And the Annabelle picks on her relentlessly, almost like she's trying to drive her out.

Oh.

Maybe she is. The houses in Ever do pick their inhabitants, after all. That thought hadn't occurred to me until now, but I make a mental note to talk to Catherine about it. The inn seemed fine with all of us until we decided to stay. Hmm.

"Catherine's at the table," Miram chokes out around a mouthful of cookie, jerking her head toward the round table in the far corner of the garden. It's where we do most of our witch lessons.

"Ugh," I groan. "I suck so bad at this." My eyes flash to the edge of the table which is still burnt from my last attempt to control my green magic.

"Yeah, you really should be growing things as opposed to blowing them up," Miriam chirps helpfully. "But you'll get it."

"Thanks," I grunt as I snap the top of my cookie box closed. "No more for you Miriam."

She gives me a salty look and sticks out her tongue, reaching out with one veined, green-and-pink wing to slap me on the back of the head.

Before I can holler about it, she pushes off the ground and flies up into the air, zipping over the gourd structure.

I sigh and follow her. My sisters and Shepherd are already seated at the round wooden table. I shoot Shepherd a pointed look. "Staying for today's show?"

He grins back at me, a dimple appearing on one side of his dark gray lips. "Wouldn't miss it for the world, sis."

Thea nudges him in the side and gives me a quick nod of solidarity.

Next to Shepherd, a cough draws my attention.

Catherine, the Annabelle Inn's owner and our current hostess, smiles at me. Salt-and-pepper waves hang in an elegant half updo, framing her round face. Her smile is genuine, and just like every other day, she's wearing a beautiful wrap dress that accentuates her buxom, hourglass figure.

God, she's more put together in her sixties than I've ever been. She's elegant as fuck. And nice. She's the sexy single grandmother I never knew I needed in my life.

Her lips purse and she looks over at Shepherd. "Friend, I think it might be easier if you don't stay and observe today. Would you mind giving the triplets some space, please?" She bats her eyes exaggeratedly.

He groans and sticks his tongue out at me. "No fun. I wanted to help put out another fire."

"Rude," Miriam snorts, grabbing my box of cookies and opening it back up to steal another.

"Hey," Shepherd starts, pointing his finger at each of us in turn. "I brought her that box of cookies you know. The Hector triplets are mine now. Shouldn't I get to be here for the downs as well as the ups?"

"Honey," Thea says with a laugh. "Get outta here."

I watch Shepherd purse his lips, but he leans over and nuzzles Thea's cheek, growling playfully. He looks up to wink at me and then stands. I'm pretty sure we all stare at his ass as he crouches down and then rockets up into the sky, spreading his wings wide as he catches an air current and shoots toward Main Street.

Thea sighs and grabs one of my cookies, shoving the whole thing in her mouth.

When he's gone, Catherine sets a giant, tall purple crystal in the center of the table. I hate this damn thing. Thea immediately grabs it, smiling when the crystal glows a bright purple, lit from within by a billion tiny dots. I watch in awe like I always do. Morgan sits stone-faced next to me. Thea grabbed ahold of her magic from day one, it seemed, and she's getting better by leaps and bounds.

"Excellent, Thea!" Catherine chirps. "I don't think you'll even need the crystal soon."

Thea beams, then gives Morgan and me a baleful glance. "I was able to envision the ward yesterday for a few moments before it faded. I'm definitely starting to be able to focus on my power. I'm thankful, just in case something happens again." Her smile falls, and the table grows silent. Ever's cute as shit, but it's got its cons—most notably the soul-sucking thralls who constantly try to break through the wards to attack us.

You know, normal small-town monster things.

Catherine looks over at me, gesturing at the crystal. "I don't know that Ohken will be able to join us this morning, but he said I should tell you to come find him later if you'd like to practice outside the garden." She doesn't grin super huge, but I know she wants to. It's a well-known fact that I think the town's one-and-only bridge troll is hot as hell. I'm pretty sure he knows it too, and while he's very flirtatious, he's never made a move.

And I am not the girl to put the moves on a man who's not interested. Plus, I've got bigger fish to fry. Like figuring out how to grow things in this garden with my magic, instead of burning them to the ground.

Thea sets the crystal back in the center of the table. I grab it and close my eyes, focusing on the garden itself. Like always, I sense the earthworms under the dirt and follow the myriad network of plant roots. I can do that part just fine, but then my focus changes, and the crystal zings my hand so hard, I drop it to the table with a yelp.

Catherine gestures to the crystal with an expectant look. She's always so encouraging and never makes me feel bad that I didn't pick up magic quickly like Thea.

Grimacing, I reach for the crystal once more.

CHAPTER TWO
OHKEN

Carefully lifting the flat top off my mead barrel, I dump in three cups of calais mushrooms. They'll give my mead a nice earthy but sweet flavor, which is what I'm going for with this batch. I lay my hand against the side of the ancient barrel and whisper a troll spell, urging the mushrooms to disintegrate quickly in the hoppy mix. This batch needs to be ready for the big tournament coming up.

Looking around, I smile at the dozens of barrels currently filling my mead-making room. I'm a home-brewer, so this isn't my job, but it's been a long-time passion.

The cave rumbles a little, sending a vibration across the floor.

I look down at the comm watch around my wrist. "Got to go, thanks for the reminder, love."

Black stone walls rumble and creak politely.

Heading out of the dark, cold room, I stride up the hall and into the main living area to grab my bag. I tuck a few things into it and wave goodbye to my cave. She cracks and groans a response as I leave.

When I duck out from under my bridge, the wonderfully clean scent of deep forest fills my senses. A tiny head breaks the surface of the glowing stream that runs underneath my bridge.

Delicate, pink-tipped ears flutter as the mermaid minnow smiles at me. She rises farther out of the water, pink hair swirling around her. Blue eyes crinkle at the corners, her lips parting as her smile grows wide enough to reveal a mouthful of sharp teeth.

I drop to a knee at the riverbank and hold my hand out. "Good morning, Cece. Off to school?"

With a flip of her tail, she darts toward me and takes my forefinger in both tiny hands, pumping it vigorously.

"Yes, Mister Ohken! We're learning about trolls and orcs this week and it made me think about you!" Blue eyes flick over to the bridge and her smile falls. She drops my finger and scowls, crossing her thin arms. "I really wanna see inside your bridge cave. Is it nice in there? Is there water? Miss Cross said most troll caves are actually really nice inside, but it seems to me like it would be damp and grody."

I laugh, rising to a stand as I cross my arms. "You'll learn to shift in a few years, Cece. Maybe I'll do a tour for the other minnows once you're all able to do that. What do you think?"

She nods in excitement, her pink hair dancing on the surface of the turquoise water. "I'd love that! Just a few more years until I get legs and then I totally need to see in there! I'm just so dang curious." She gestures at my body. "Especially like, how do you fit in there? You're so"—she waves one hand around in the air—"enormous."

My grin grows bigger. All trolls are big, but I tower over the tiny child. Even when she's full-grown, she'll be about the same size as an average human.

She lets out a cute little harrumph and waves goodbye,

joining three other mermaid minnows as they swim by. I watch them go, and then I turn to the stone path and head toward Sycamore Street. The weather is perfect like every other day, the forest around me calm. Birds chirp and animals scurry through the underbrush.

At the sign for my bridge I hook a right on Sycamore. A few minutes later, I hang a left on Main Street, admiring how beautiful it looks this early in the morning. Businesses line both sides of the street, cherry-red-and-white awnings fluttering on a soft breeze.

Across Main from me, a centaur reaches up to water a hanging basket filled with petunias. He waves with his free hand when our gazes meet.

To my right, Higher Grounds has a line out the door. Smiling, I cross Sycamore and sidestep the line, stalking toward the office in the back. Alessandro sits at a desk, sipping a cup that looks to be full of blood. Dark eyes flash up at me and he sets the cup down, sticky red liquid dripping down the side.

The dark-haired male shifts back in his seat and grins. "My delivery?"

I reach into my bag and withdraw a long, thin canister. "I simplified it this morning, so it's ready for whipping."

"Perfetto," he croons, taking the canister. "Thank you, my friend." He gestures to his computer. "I send the payment right now, okay? Many thanks as always."

I dip my head in acknowledgment and head back toward the front of the coffee shop. Like always, the scent of coffee and sugar assaults me. I'm not much of a coffee drinker, but I've been bartering with the vampire brothers for years—it's one of the many jobs I fulfill here in Ever, my chosen home haven.

I head up Main toward the General Store, one of my two stores. Birds chirp and a few elderly centaurs walk slowly up the street toward town hall. I love Main Street this early in the morning. In fact, I love Ever. I've lived here for almost fifty years—this is the perfect haven for me. But lately, I find myself wanting something more.

My friend Shepherd, one of the two gargoyle protectors of this town, recently mated a human woman. He looks blissfully happy, and his mate Thea constantly stares at him with stars in her eyes.

Something deep and primal in my gut yearns for that.

But I suspect that desire is rising because of a certain someone who's begun to regularly invade my thoughts.

I shove my key in the lock at the General Store. I've got some shipments to unpack for the skyball tournament next week. It hasn't been held in Ever for almost a century. Next week is an opportunity to capitalize on the thousands of extra monsters who will be in town for the skyball final.

Pushing into the General Store, I smile at the stack of boxes sitting just inside. They were delivered last night, but I didn't want to ask Taylor to stay late unpacking them. Almost as if I summoned him, the big centaur pushes through the door after me, grabbing two boxes and depositing them on the countertop.

He shoots me a quick wink, purple eyes flashing in the low morning light. "Thought you might want help opening them, and I'm dying to see how the tees came out."

I clap him on the shoulder and grab the remaining boxes, hoisting them onto the countertop. Taylor cuts the tape and opens the top, his angular features breaking into a big grin. "Hells yes! I've been waiting for these to arrive!"

Reaching in, I pull out a hunter-green T-shirt with a golden logo for the Ever Misfits, our hometown team.

Taylor boos when I pull out a second shirt with the black and blue of the Finrel Fevers. He makes a sound like he's puking and tosses the black shirt to the side. "I'm going to pretend you weren't a responsible business owner trying to capitalize on a special event, because that shirt makes me want to barf."

Laughing, I unpack the shirts and lay them out. Taylor's working the morning shift too, so he can put them away. I count each one, making sure my order is correct. Taylor grabs stacks of them and refolds them so they look nice, placing them on the table we cleared specifically for this order.

He glances at me while he folds, thin lips curling into a devious smile. "I know you're playing this year, but any chance you can convince the Keeper to? He told me he wasn't participating, but damn, it's a loss for our team."

Shrugging, I toss him the last shirt from the very last box. "He's more focused on security after the recent attack. I can't blame him. I don't think he'd be able to focus on a sporting event."

Taylor nods, folding the green shirt and placing it carefully on top of the pile. Brilliant amethyst eyes meet mine. "I don't feel unsafe here, no matter what happened. You, the Keeper, Alo, Shepherd... you protected us."

I give him a lukewarm smile. "The credit goes to Alo, Shepherd, and the Keeper. I was just there for the end of it."

Taylor clip-clops over to me, slapping my shoulder with his big hand. "Don't downplay your involvement, Ohken. You're a pillar of this community and I'm grateful you're here." He winks at me. "But if you could absolutely crush the Fevers, I'd really appreciate it. I've got a little money riding on the finals."

Classic.

∼

An hour later, I shuffle around the cash register in the General Store, looking for paper to refill the receipt printer. The store is always so quiet and peaceful before we open for the day. Peeking under the worn wooden countertop, I see there's no extra paper. Taylor is friendly as hells with our customers, but he's got absolutely no closing skills. The store is never quite ready for opening after he works the night shift.

It's fine, though, because I like coming in to get the store ready. It's a source of pride for me that my store is a hub for all Evertons. You can get just about anything here from toilet paper to divining crystals to potions.

Now Fleur, that's another story. My flower shop is purely for the garden nerd in me. Then again, most trolls are into practical, earthly hobbies—mead-making, construction, gardening, pixie dust-making, and the like. The flower shop doesn't make much money, but it's a sinful pleasure to walk in there and smell all those blooms.

Although, there's something far more sinful taking up most of my attention lately.

My thoughts jolt back to the present when the front bell dings, and a pixie glides in, touching down delicately as she stills the colorful wings at her back.

"Morning, Miriam." I smile at my petite friend.

She beams back at me before jerking her head toward my storeroom. "I'm here for the moonflower powder."

I nod and head for the back, gesturing for her to follow me.

"Just came from the garden," Miriam chirps. "Wren is looking particularly lovely today."

My dick goes hard at the mere mention of Wren Hector's name, but I will it to go down. I've got a lot of shit to do today before I can go flirt.

"That so?" I respond noncommittally.

Miriam is undeterred.

"Yep." She draws out the 'p' on a long pop, grinning at me as I pick through the shelves and hand her a large canister. Her smile falls a little. "That's all for today?"

I give her a curt nod. "That's all I could grind out of the moonflower blooms you gave me."

She shakes obvious frustration away, going right back to her cheerful self. Neither of us wants to give voice to the reason why we have less blooms than usual—a thrall ripped the moonflower vines from their hedge in the garden. It's going to set us back in making pixie dust, and we need the dust to bolster Ever's protective wards.

"It'll be fine," she murmurs, more to herself than anything. "As soon as Wren gets a handle on her magic, we'll catch back up."

That's something I don't love to hear. Wren and her sisters are Ever's newest residents, they've only been here a few weeks. It's not fair to put the pressure on any of them to protect our town. Protecting Ever is a team effort.

I bite my tongue, though, because Miriam's nervous expression has returned. It goes devious when the front bell dings again, and a throaty voice calls my name.

"Ohken? You in here?"

Miriam shoots me a thumbs-up and flits out of the store room. I follow her out, watching Wren's green eyes move from Miriam to me.

It's well-known that Miriam is head over heels for one of Ever's two gargoyle protectors, Alo, but still. I wonder what Wren thinks Miriam was doing so early in my store? If she thought we had something going on, would she be jealous?

I like the idea of her being jealous.

Miriam ruffles Wren's chocolate waves with her wing, then zips out the door with her canister in tow.

"Let me guess, pixie dust ingredients?" Wren's green eyes spark with something between curiosity and mischief, a heady combination for a troll male.

"Indeed," I rumble, reaching down to roll up the sleeve of my long shirt. I watch Wren's gaze drop to my fingers, following as I tug the sleeve up to reveal my forearms. I'm messing with her. Women love watching a man roll up his sleeves. I'm sure it's got something to do with how we look like we're about to take care of business, and that's attractive in a partner.

"The pixies gather dust ingredients and bring them here for me to grind. I return it to Miriam and they stir it for ages, adding their magic to it. Once it's ready, I deliver it to the Keeper for them. I'll show you sometime, if you like."

Wren smiles at me. "I'd love that, Ohken."

The way she says my name pulls me with an invisible tether. I take a step closer, smiling when her focus returns to my face. Her pink, bow lips part a little, giving me a peek at her tongue. Would it be as soft as the rest of her?

"You're staring, little witch," I murmur, locking my gaze with hers. A pink flush steals over her round cheeks. I am *mightily* enjoying this. I have no doubt I could toss her up onto the long, wooden countertop and have my way with her between the stacks of candles and the postcards. She'd welcome it, and that's precisely why I'm going to wait.

Trolls are huge fans of edging, and I've been edging Wren Hector since the day we met.

Her eyes crinkle at the corners, and she grins at me. "Apple green. That's it."

I snort and take a step closer. "That's the color, huh?"

She winks. "I could say chartreuse, but—" She waves her hands from side to side as if weighing her options.

This is a game we've been playing since the first time I met her, and she blurted out, "Oh my God, you're green!"

What shade of green am I?

Apparently today's answer is apple.

"You want to take a bite then?"

Wren gasps and throws one hand over her chest dramatically. "I would never hurt you like that." She winks.

But my eyes fall to the heavy breasts beneath her palm. Even the suggestion that she might bite me is enough to make my dick twitch in my pants.

I put a finger under Wren's chin and take yet another step closer to her, close enough for her body to brush against mine. She sucks in a hesitant breath, but looks up at me with those big, doe eyes.

"Your eyes are the color of freshly cut grass and your lips the shade of cherry blossoms. Now, can I help you with something, or are you using this visit to get out of lessons?"

Her chest heaves, her hardened nipples dragging against my upper stomach. There's a sizable height difference between us, almost two feet. Dark lashes flutter against her cheeks when she opens her mouth.

Her scent blooms, filling my senses. I resist the urge to bury my face in her neck and rake my tusks across her skin. I bet her smell would be so much stronger there, and I want to know.

I let out a soft growl, wondering how she'll respond to it. All trolls are natural Dominants, and we're slow to form attachments as a result. It takes most troll males months to identify good partners once there's initial attraction. We tease and test and sort out if a person might be sexually and emotionally compatible before we ever make a move.

But it's been weeks, and I am highly attracted to this witch. Early indicators are there that we'd be good together.

Wren gives me a saucy look. "I'm awfully new to town, are you sure you wanna growl at me? You might scare me away."

She bats her eyes—brat that she is—and I drop her chin, taking a step back.

Gods, I adore a brat. I've been pushing my sweet witch a little more every time I see her, and I think she's just about ready for me to start a formal pursuit. But part of that means teasing the shit out of her.

When I say nothing, Wren jerks her head toward the crystal display behind the cash register. "Catherine asked me to come grab an aragonite crystal if you've got one."

My pleasure at playing with her falls flat at the request, but I nod and stride around the countertop. Reaching up, I grab a peachy crystal, admiring the hundreds of tiny, sharp points as I hand it to her. "Did Catherine tell you why?"

Wren shakes her head, her expression morose.

I grab her hand and flip it over, placing the crystal in her palm. With my thumb, I stroke the inside of her wrist. "Aragonite is an earth element meant to center or ground you. It's often used to stabilize emotion and focus, so it's particularly useful for green witches. And new people," I tack on at the end, a gentle reminder that she only just discovered that she's a witch.

Wren's easy smile falls, her mahogany brows pulling together into an irritated vee. Her fingertips curl around the crystal. I resist an intense urge to haul her over the countertop and fuck her against the crystal display.

"If I never get it, will the Keeper kick me outta town?" There's a sarcastic, playful edge to her tone, but it's a mask. I know it hurts her that she hasn't picked up her magic as quickly as her sister, Thea. But Thea's magic is different. Hers is protective like her mate, Shepherd's. Plus, she's benefitting from living with him now. Their situations couldn't be any more different.

"Never," I state simply. *If for no other reason than I want you,* is the part I don't say aloud.

There's still a deflated look on her face though, so I jerk my head toward the front door. "You know what you need? Coffee with troll whip."

She laughs and brightens at that, nodding as she watches me come back around the counter.

I jerk my head toward the door. "I'll go with you to Higher Grounds, and then we can head to the garden together."

She nods her thanks as I open the front door. Taylor can finish getting ready for the day.

Wren sails through the door when I open it. She smells like the end of summer peaches with a hint of bourbon. I flare my nostrils as she passes, willing more of that heady scent to cling to me.

"Miriam said you were busy this morning. You don't have to come watch the fireworks. There will be plenty more, I'm sure." It's another deflection, her reference to the multiple fires she's sparked in our community garden with her magic. We stroll up Main toward the coffee shop slowly.

"Miriam's got what she needs for the dust," I remind her, stalking slightly ahead to open the door to Higher Grounds.

Wren goes through, the crystal still in her hand.

The scent of fresh coffee blasts my senses for a second time today. Trolls have exceedingly sharp senses, and Higher Grounds is always a little overwhelming for me, smells-wise.

The coffee shop is long and narrow with a bar running along the left-hand side. Monsters of all sorts sit and stand at tables to the right. The brick walls hint at the age of this building, constructed at the same time as the general store building, hundreds of Ever-years ago. Only the shiny onyx countertop and hissing, metallic machines make the coffee shop look modern.

Behind the register, Pietro, Alessandro's brother, smiles up at us. Pearly, white fangs glint in the overhead light. He grins at Wren, and I have to resist the urge to slap him, which is a good thing, really. It means my natural instincts are working right on time, identifying her as compatible with me, and me as wildly interested in her. If we couldn't be good together, I wouldn't be feeling possessive right now.

"I fucking love the coffee here," Wren murmurs to me as we wait in line. There's a big centaur male in front of us, his tail swishing lazily side to side as he scans a menu hung from the ceiling.

I don't miss the way Wren's eyes fall to the centaur's enormous sack, clearly visible between his thighs. His balls hang heavy and full-looking, and they sway when he takes a step forward and orders. Monsters don't care about nudity as a general rule, but I've been doing some research at the historical society—humans are very weird about bodies and sex, I've learned. I'm guessing she feels a little horrified to be staring at a big pair of balls.

Wren presses closer to me. I reach up and place a hand at the small of her back, just above her jeans. She's warm to the touch. I wish there wasn't a shirt between my fingers and her soft skin. If I licked my way up her spine, would she taste like bourbon and peaches too?

The centaur moves aside, giving us a polite smile as his eyes drop to her ample cleavage, and then to my hand. His expression falls and he clops away into the low light of the delivery end of the bar.

The Hector triplets are Ever's first new residents in a long time. That's generated a lot of interest from the town's unmated monsters. Thea took up with Shepherd almost immediately. The Keeper—our mayor, for all intents and purposes—declared Morgan his the day they arrived. Wren's the only one who might appear to be available.

My hand on her body makes it clear to the centaur that she's not.

Pietro clears his throat and raises one black brow at us. "Drinks today, friends?"

His nostrils flare, and I know he's scenting the blood in her veins the way vampires do all other beings. They can feed on just about anything as long as it's alive. He's single and probably interested.

I shoot him a discouraging look.

Wren stares up at the menu, then chuckles. "Whiskey latte with oat milk, please."

He nods and punches in her order before looking up at me expectantly.

I thrum my fingers against Wren's back. "You want troll whip?"

"Oh yeah!" she chirps. "I almost forgot. God, it's good."

The barista smirks at me, the tips of his smile twitching upward as he finishes her order and rings her up, putting her drink automatically on my account.

"Wait, I need to pay," Wren says, looking confused.

"Coffee was my idea," I remind her, guiding her to the side of the bar while we wait for her drink.

Steam and all the normal coffee shop noises are a soothing background with Wren tucked by my side. My hand is still on her back, but I slide it up between her shoulder blades to grip the base of her neck.

She looks up at me, something between curiosity and surprise in her expression.

"What are you doing?" Her voice is huskier than usual, her pupils dark spots against the brilliant green of her irises.

I squeeze her neck lightly. "Come to dinner with me tonight."

There's a momentary pause, and a pretty pink flush returns to her cheeks.

"Like a date?"

"Exactly like a date," I confirm. I slide my fingers a little higher up into the back of her hair, fisting some of it in my hand. Every possible shade of dark brown fades to pale peach at the tips. It's stunning, and gods, it's soft.

"Happy to," she says finally.

"Happy to?" I say straight-faced, tugging her head backward with my grip, which arcs her body into mine. "You're happy to? I didn't pop over to your house asking for a cup of sugar, sweet witch."

She doesn't miss a beat. "I think that's exactly what you just asked me for, my jolly green bridge troll."

I don't let go of my hold on her hair, even when she wriggles a little.

"Did you make that up? Or do humans believe trolls are all jolly and green?"

Wren laughs, a husky sound that strokes my cock as surely as a hand would. "It's a play on words for the Jolly Green Giant."

I scowl. "Giants are assholes; you don't want to ever meet one."

"Not this one." Wren sighs and brings both hands to my chest. "This one sells green beans."

I laugh and open my mouth to respond, but Pietro calls her name. I release my grip on her hair so she can take the drink. It's in a brown to-go cup, but pale green troll whip is piled high on top of it. Pietro hands her a lid for later, his dark eyes flashing to mine with a knowing look.

We thank him and leave Higher Grounds, heading back toward the community garden. Wren laps at the whipped topping and sighs. "Jesus, this is better than any whipped cream I've ever had."

"We do things a little differently in Ever." I laugh.

"Ya don't say." She gestures around us at the small town's Main Street filled with monsters of all shapes and sizes.

That pink tongue swipes at the troll whip again and I grin. I love that she loves the troll whip. Its main ingredient is something troll-related. And I want to feed that ingredient to her right from the godsdamned source.

CHAPTER THREE
WREN

I can't believe Ohken asked me out! I'm playing it cool as a cucumber, but I'd be a damned liar if I didn't adore how he halfway manhandled me in the coffee shop. The reality is that I love a man who's in charge. I think I have an in-charge kink, if that's a thing. And everything about Ohken screams dominance.

It's not just that he's physically huge and imposing, although he is that. He must be eight feet and four hundred pounds of beefcake, all broad shoulders and impossibly muscular thighs.

There's always a confident look on his face, like he doesn't give a shit what anyone else thinks. Plus, there's the fact that both of the town's gargoyle protectors and the Keeper rely on him. He's part of the town's leadership circle, and that's hot to me.

Sipping carefully at the troll whip, I glance up at him.

His dark green lips part into a gorgeous smile, lower tusks poking up at the edges of his grin.

"Let me guess, you're thinking of a color for the troll whip, too?" He seems amused at our little game.

"Mint," I decide, scrunching my nose as I examine it. "Maybe seafoam?"

Ohken laughs, and it's a deep rumble that sets fireworks off between my thighs. I've been wet since the moment he touched me, but it's getting sloppy downstairs. He points down at my shirt. "Explain this one to me."

Ah, here we go again. I swear, monsters just don't get it. Shaking my head, I laugh.

"For some reason it amazes me that this is so uniquely human. Um, there are a whole host of reasons for this, but people are really weird about plus-sized bodies. 'Fat' is considered a derogatory term, but there's nothing wrong with my size. So I'm reclaiming a formerly hurtful word to indicate I'm proud of who I am. People can fuck off if they don't agree with it."

Ohken cocks his head to the side. "So, human men would see your figure, and try to find some way to improve upon it?"

"Well…" I laugh, because this conversation is just so damn refreshing. "It would be hard to improve on perfection but yeah, plenty of men would say I should lose weight and be thinner like my sisters."

Ohken scoffs. "Imbeciles." He smiles down at me, more of a smirk, really. "I'll let you in on a little secret about trolls. All troll women are what you call plus-sized. They're big and strong and most definitely feral. And if my mother was still alive, she'd be warning me to feed you more. Trolls like a woman with substance."

Sounds perfect to me. "Oh, don't worry. Shepherd is feeding me plenty, so there's more of me to go around by the minute."

Ohken's eyes crinkle at the corners. "Good. The more of you the better."

We fall silent as I try not to visibly preen over his words. He's every plus-sized girl's dream—a man who doesn't try to define me by the size of my ass or thickness of my thighs. Or God forbid, run away when he sees a stretch mark. Which leads me to thinking about the date he just asked me on.

What does one even do on a date with a troll?

"So," I say. "About this date tonight…"

"Mmm?" Ohken murmurs, sliding both hands into his pockets as he walks slowly next to me. It draws my attention to his muscular, veiny forearms. God, I could lick every inch of this man.

Troll.

Bridge troll.

"What can I expect from tonight? Are there troll dating customs I need to be aware of so I don't accidentally insult your family line, or something horrible?"

That gravelly laughter rings out again, and he reaches up to pull half his auburn hair up into a bun at the back of his head.

Why is that so hot? All I want to do is climb on top of him, rip that bun out and run my fingers through his hair while I ravage those plump lips. Not sure how to work around the tusks, but I'm nothing if not an overachiever in the bedroom.

"What do humans do on first dates?" he counters.

"Oof. Well, dinner and a movie. Dancing or a walk are fair game, too."

"Alright," he says. That's it, just 'alright.'

"That's it?" I snort.

"I'll plan something along those lines for us, it'll be a fun surprise."

"Fun fact, I hate surprises," I counter. "What do trolls do on dates?"

He grins when we pass through the hedge opening that leads into the community garden. He stops just inside and leans down to my ear, his lips brushing against the lobe. A soft growl floods my panties with slickness, and then those lips are moving against my skin.

"We usually just fuck, Wren." His voice is impossibly low, so raspy it sounds like sandpaper.

"Goddamn," I groan, whining at the need that's building in my system for this man. He straightens, and there's pure deviant mirth in the way he looks at me. Dark red brows travel up as if he's daring me to say something. When I don't, he grins and turns from me, heading for the table where Morgan and Catherine still sit.

I blink my eyes a few times, trying to center myself and catch my breath. My heartbeat races, but I turn and follow Ohken, joining the group.

Catherine beams at us. "Thea left to meet the Keeper and Shepherd for a ward patrol."

That sobers me right up. My sister's a white witch, meaning she has protective power. I suppose it makes sense she ended up mating one of the town's two gargoyle protectors. Together they keep an eye out for the dangerous thralls who try to get in. We learned about that and Thea's power the hard way when they attacked us not long ago.

I set the peach-hued crystal I got from Ohken down in the middle of the table. Catherine's eyes light up, and she beams at Ohken.

"Oh, you still had one, good! I was going to send off to one of the other havens if you didn't."

Ohken nods.

"How many havens are there?" Morgan asks. "There wasn't much mention of them in the welcome packet you gave us."

Ah, the good ole welcome packet. What kind of town has an entire welcome packet for new residents? Secret monster towns, I suppose.

Catherine smiles and looks at Ohken for clarification. He clears his throat, and when he speaks I try not to wonder how he'd sound moaning my name, or grunting as he fucks me. Is that what we're doing tonight? Did I ruin that by telling him what humans do on dates? God, I'm a dummy. Because the reality is I would tap that troll ass so fast.

"Fifty-two, at last count," he offers. "Although new havens open every few years as monster numbers grow."

"Do more havens make the wards stronger, or how does that work?" Even more than Thea or I, Morgan's become obsessed with the monster world and how it all connects. Some days it seems all we do is ask questions. Catherine has never declined to answer one.

Like now. And just like every other time Morgan questions her, she smiles and it's genuine. "The havens' existence does provide a sort of strength in numbers against the thralls, but it also makes us a greater target for the monsters who seek to control us. The larger the number of monsters in one place, the easier it could be to bite and enthrall them in order to create an army."

It's a sobering fact we've recently learned. Most monsters live hidden from humans in "havens" like Ever, but not all monsters are content to do that. And the ones that aren't use thralls, and other methods, to try to infiltrate havens all the time. Those are the monsters who believe humans should be subjugated. It's a terrifying concept, but as it stands today, they'd need armies to take over, and it's something they don't have.

"There's certainly risk," Ohken continues in an even tone. "But there's always risk. Just being alive is a risk. Try not to let it consume your thoughts, Morgan." His tone is gentle, but when she looks up at him, her expression is sad.

"We knocked a hole right in Ever's wards when we arrived in town. Who's to say it won't happen again? Or some other weird freaky thing? I swear, I wake up at night worrying about it."

"Ah," I correct her. "Technically it was Thea's magic that knocked the hole in the wards, and she's got that sorted out now."

Morgan grunts noncommittally.

"Plus we have the Keeper," Catherine reminds her. "It's his job to monitor the wards and the town's safety."

"Yeah, what a gem," Morgan mutters. I reach under the table and put a hand on her leg to pat it.

We're all silent for a moment, and I think maybe Ohken or Catherine will try to reassure Morgan for the millionth time that the Keeper is a good man with a good heart, even if his personality is a little off-putting. They don't, though, and Catherine's focus turns to the aragonite instead.

She waves a perfectly manicured hand at it while looking at me.

"Okay, Wren. Let's do the same thing we did with the first crystal. Pick it up and think of the garden. Try to focus on identifying what you can see, that's it." She nods and smiles. God, I wish I had as much confidence in my green ability as she seems to. Next to her, Ohken's russet eyes are focused on mine.

We usually just fuck, Wren.

I don't know how I'm supposed to concentrate after that. When one corner of his lips turns up, I know he knows what I'm thinking about.

Sexy bastard.

I pick up the crystal and hold it carefully in both hands, closing my eyes. Like always, I can picture the garden and the dirt underneath it. This time, though, my vision expands up out of the dirt, and I see the moonflower vines. I try to focus there, on the beautiful white flowers that the pixies use to make the dust that powers the town's wards.

My focus blurs so I try to move elsewhere, and I seem to fly across the garden to the pixies' A-frame of gourds. My attention is drawn to one in particular, its green and orange jagged stripes are fascinating to me. Its domed top morphs smoothly into a rounded fat bottom.

I'm enthralled by its beauty when I realize the gourd itself has started expanding right in front of me, vibrating a little as it grows larger. Its surface swells and bulges, and then it explodes with a loud pop. Tiny furniture goes flying, landing somewhere in the grass. Slippery seeds drip out of the remains onto the gravel path below. A pit opens in the bottom of my stomach.

I shake my head in frustration. Groaning, I open my eyes only to realize there's actual shouting in the garden. Oh fuck. I didn't blow something up for real, did I?

Morgan and Catherine jog up the crushed gravel path toward a group of pixies, their small-form lights flashing back and forth in agitation.

My heart sinks, and my eyes meet Ohken's. His gaze is kind.

"Did I just blow up one of the pixie's houses?" My tone is bitter and sad to my own ears. I've scorched the table twice, but I've never done something like this in my training.

"You did," he admits, reaching across the table with one big palm facing up. He crooks two fingers at me, indicating I should put my hand in his. "Are you alright?"

He's worried about me?

Ignoring his proffered hand, I shrug my shoulders and stand.

"No," I admit. "I can't keep trying to learn this if it hurts people."

I jog away from him so he doesn't see the tears forming in my eyes, and I join Catherine and Morgan who are now surrounded by three full-sized pixies. Each one is slight like Miriam, but their hair and wings are all different jewel-toned shades.

I look past them inside the A-frame. Most of the gourds sway as if pushed by a soft breeze. But sure as shit, the gourd I pictured in my mind is blasted in half and dripping seeds onto the ground.

"We'll grow another," one of the pixies says kindly, but the other two scowl at me. They look so frustrated.

"I'm so, so sorry. I'll stop trying to learn here," I say. "Let me help you clean up, and then I'll find a place that's safer, okay?"

I expect them to reassure me, to tell me it's not that bad and there are plenty of gourds to go around. Instead, the first pixie who spoke nods.

"Okay," he says. "That would be good."

It's a gut punch for him to confirm that the way I feel is accurate, and they'd rather I not learn here.

Ohken joins us, peering inside the A-frame with a sigh. He looks at the purple-haired pixie who's the only one that's spoken so far. "Kiril, let me grab you a temporary box from the store until we can grow you a new gourd, alright?"

The pixie nods, and then all three disappear into a puff of smoke, their small forms buzzing back into the A-frame. They land on the top of the destroyed gourd and pause there.

My heart sinks.

Ohken's focus moves to Catherine. "I'm sorry, friend, but these methods aren't working."

Catherine gives me a sorrowful look. I feel like I'm in the damn principal's office, and someone's telling my mother that I need to shape up.

All I can do is look away from everyone and down at the dirt, kicking at it with my shoe.

Ohken reaches out and rubs my lower back. "I'll teach you at my place. There's space there."

"I'll come with you," Morgan offers, threading her fingers through mine.

"Not necessary, Morgan," Ohken counters. "My teaching methods are...nontraditional."

Fuck me. That sounded so, so sexual. I risk a glance at my sister, whose nostrils flare as she gives him a pointed look.

I don't know if Ohken is saying what I think he's saying, but I'm halfway terrified to find out.

CHAPTER FOUR

OHKEN

I leave Wren, Morgan, and Catherine to cleanup duty as I head for the store to grab a temporary box for Kiril. I've got plenty of extras at the moment because of the upcoming skyball tournament. There will be pixies visiting from nearly all the other havens, and I'm building an extra A-frame for these boxes in the garden later today. Between that and hanging lanterns in the tree for pixie royalty, there should be plenty of space for monsters who have a smaller secondary form.

I don't want to tell Wren how devastated Kiril likely is about his gourd. He's probably got family coming to stay with him for the tournament. It was clear Wren felt bad enough.

Reaching down to the small leather band around my wrist, I tap it once and speak into it. "Call the Keeper."

There's a moment of silence, and the Keeper's name hovers over the blue band like a hologram. Moments later, a deep voice echoes tinny out of his name.

"Ohken, what's wrong?"

I smile. "Nothing's wrong, Keeper. You asked me to check in after the Hectors' lesson this morning." He knows I join most of the triplets' lessons. I'm sure he'd prefer to do it himself, but things are tense between him and Morgan.

I suppose announcing that someone is your mate and then not following up on that pronouncement does make things a bit awkward. Then there's the fact that he took Thea outside the wards as bait to catch a thrall and it went sideways. To say Morgan steers clear of him is putting it lightly.

The Keeper's voice is stretched taut like a bowstring. "Ah yes. I need your help setting up Main Street tomorrow for the parade. I'd like to go over the security measures another time. Alo, Shepherd, and Richard are confident, but I could use a fourth pair of eyes for anything we might have missed."

"Of course," I murmur. While I'm not in charge of security, it's true that trolls are often involved in it in their respective havens. My interests lie elsewhere, but I'm happy to help when needed. "Are you really worried about security for the tournament?"

"The Hearth has a three-strikes policy for Keepers, Ohken. I can't risk trouble here if I want to continue protecting Ever."

That's news to me. Then again, the Hearth, our ruling faction, has never been forthcoming about why they do things the way they do.

"Surely they wouldn't remove you because of the attack. That was so far outside your sphere of control."

"Yes, well," he huffs. "Let's hope it doesn't come to that." He clicks off without saying anything else, but I find myself lost in thought as I head back to the garden.

When I arrive, Morgan's the only one left at the lesson table. She sits there, looking morose, picking at a splinter, but she looks up when I arrive.

"Catherine asked Wren to help prep the Annabelle for the tournament. I think she's just hoping to distract her from the gourd incident, but do you want me to grab her?

"Nah." I shake my head. "You look like you need a job, so why don't you come help me for a few minutes."

She hops up and dusts her hands off on her jeans.

I point to a pile of lumber just inside the garden gate. "I was supposed to spend this afternoon constructing A-frames for the visiting pixies, but I might as well do it now and hang a new box up for Kiril. You down to help?"

"Of course!" she offers. Her voice isn't high like Thea's, nor low and throaty like Wren's. She's somewhere in the middle. I'd wager she's the oldest, based on her bulldog personality. But I hate that I can almost see her receding into her own mind since the triplets decided to stick around. She's not happy here, and it seems to be getting worse.

I don't say anything as we walk up the crushed gravel path to the garden gate. I gesture at the pile of long, round timbers. "I've got to dig twelve holes and set the planks in them with a crisscross at the top. You can help me with that, if you don't mind. I'll dig and you set."

Morgan nods and grabs as many of the wide planks as she can, and then we get started. She doesn't say a word through the entire first side of the A-frame, setting the planks next to the holes as soon as I've got them dug. By the time we switch to the opposite side, I can see she's holding back.

"Cat's got your tongue, Morgan?"

She swipes dark auburn hair off her sweaty forehead, tucking it behind one delicate ear.

"I think the Annabelle is trying to kick me out. Is that a thing?"

A low chuckle leaves me. Morgan's proven to be highly perceptive to the ways of our haven. Shepherd told me she was the first sister to realize the Annabelle's noises were the inn talking. And her question now is incredibly astute.

"What makes you think she's kicking you out? She's an inn, hosting guests is her entire purpose."

Morgan sucks at her teeth, clearly thinking about how to answer the question. She looks back over her shoulder. The Annabelle's pink siding and white, gingerbread trim are just visible over the top of the garden hedge.

"She's tripped me a couple times this week. And she locked me out this morning. And"—Morgan throws one finger up, seeming to remember something important—"she slapped me in the face with a strip of wallpaper yesterday. It hurt like hell!"

Oh yeah, the Annabelle's trying to kick her out. And I suspect I know exactly why that might be.

"Have you spoken with Catherine about it?" I phrase the question gently.

Morgan shakes her head. "I don't want her to think I'm ungrateful or that I'm just being whiny because I'm not happy."

I pause from digging a hole. "It's okay not to immediately fall in love with this place." It's a soft reminder, but I hope she takes it to heart.

Her dark brows furrow, lips pulling down into an unhappy frown.

"Thea is so happy here, I could never take it away from her. And Wren will find her place too, but I—"

"You don't think there's a place for you here?"

She crosses her arms, making sure to hold up the last plank. Eventually, gray eyes come to mine. She looks deadly serious, even a little distraught.

"The Keeper called me here with a map, Ohken. He called all three of us here because he felt we belonged. And since then, he's made a point to connect with Thea and even Wren to a degree. Do you know he's never called me? Never stopped by to visit? Never asked how my training is going. It's not that I want his attention, fucking weirdo. But why bother to call me here just to treat me like dirt?"

She's not wrong about any of that.

"And what's more," she continues, now that the floodgates have opened. "Everyone seems to just chalk it up to 'that's how he is because he's the Keeper.' I'm tired of it."

I wait until she's done before saying anything. I could give her decades-worth of context about the Keeper and why his personality is what it is, but it sounds like she's tired of hearing about that.

I stand on my shovel and jump, inserting it deeper into the hole. "You want my take on him, or the Inn, or the excuse people keep giving you about why he is like he is?"

Morgan blows out a breath. "All of the above, I suppose."

I don't move my gaze from hers, I want her to know I'm giving her my full attention.

"The Inn's trying to kick you out to get things moving with the Keeper. And he's focusing anywhere else he can to avoid having to deal with you, because I suspect you're under his skin. And nothing has gotten under our Keeper's skin in the entire time I've known him. That's almost fifty Ever-years, Morgan. He's always calm and collected. Or he was, until he called you here."

She lets out an exasperated growl. "Then why even call me, if it was such a big deal?"

"That part you'll have to ask him," I say.

Morgan nods, but her focus moves away from me as she stares across the garden, lost in thought.

"Help me with this last beam." I gesture to the final wooden pole lying on the ground.

She grabs it, setting it in the hole and we angle it to meet the other. I tie them together at the top, and she helps me tie a beam that supports each triangle from underneath. The pixies will decorate the whole structure overnight.

Morgan helps me hang the box for Kiril and then all the

rest too. The special lanterns for pixie royalty go up in the garden's one-and-only tree, and then we're done.

I give Morgan a playful bump on the hip when she dusts her hands off.

"Listen, I know Ever hasn't been easy for you, but I firmly believe you have a place here. Your road just isn't as quick or easy as Thea's."

"Tell the Keeper that," she grumbles, crossing her arms.

"Oh pretty girl." I laugh. "When he gets out of his way and unleashes on you, you'll be in for the ride of your life, have no doubt."

She sputters, her cheeks flaming a brilliant red, and then she slaps me on the shoulder.

"Thanks for that awful vision. I think I'm gonna go find a bathroom and wash my eyeballs out with soap, ugh!"

"Whatever you say, Miss Hector." I chuckle. "Whatever you say."

CHAPTER FIVE
WREN

I stare out of the Annabelle's front windows. Across the street, pixies flutter around the garden. They must be fixing poor Kiril's gourd. I know Catherine was doing me a favor by asking me to come help her get the rooms ready for the tournament. She must have seen the devastated look on my face when Kiril and Morgan and the other pixies started picking up the pieces of his house.

That was his home, and I destroyed it with nothing more than the power of my mind. That's honestly terrifying. I mean, it would be cool if I had any fucking control at all. Normally I consider myself easygoing, but my power is a little scary. I'm trying not to be too hard on myself, but knowing I blew up Kiril's house is godawful.

My comm watch pings and Thea's name pops up. I answer my triplet quickly, I suspect I know exactly why she's calling.

"Mary, talk to me, girl. What happened? Are you okay?"

I snort. "I'm hardly Sanderson-sister worthy today. At least Mary had magic she could control."

Thea says nothing, and silence stretches between us until

black dots start to burst behind my eyelids. I feel sick, thinking about explaining what just happened.

"Did Morgan tell you?" My voice is horribly small and I hate that. I'm the sarcastic, confident sister, but I don't sound like me right now.

"Yeah," Thea hedges. "Just the highlights. But you accessed more of your power, and that's amazing!"

"Leave it to you to find the silver lining," I mutter, turning and heading up the Annabelle's curved wooden stairs to the second floor. I make it to my room and shut the door. Crossing the plush, purple carpet, I flop into the bed and sink into its depths, staring at the mermaids painted all across the vaulted ceiling.

"Listen," Thea says finally. "I punched a hole the size of a Buick in the wards and two thralls got in and attacked the fucking garden, Wren. If that's not a mistake, I don't know what is."

"Yeah," I bark back. "But you didn't do it on purpose and you didn't destroy anyone's home."

Thea sighs as if I'm entirely missing the point. But I get the point, I just don't agree. It's still too fresh and mortifying and terrible.

"Ohken offered to teach me at his place."

Thea snorts. "Mor told me he said his ways were nontraditional."

"Yeah," I mumble.

"I bet that means sex."

"Sexy teaching? Sounds a lot better than blowing up gourds." I don't mean to sound so bitter, but frustration is eating a hole in my stomach. I'd give anything to go back in time and fix Kiril's beautiful home.

"You're gonna get it, Wrennie." Thea's all calm confidence. "You're a naturalist, for God's sake. Once it comes to you, it'll come fast."

I hope she's right, but when a knock echoes at the door, I make an excuse and hang up. Sliding off the bed, I open the scale-painted door to find Catherine on the other side.

"Wren, my darling, are you still able to help me change the sheets in the remaining rooms?"

"Most definitely," I chirp. "I can probably do that without blowing anything up."

Catherine gives me a soft look that reminds me of the way my mother used to respond to my particular brand of sarcasm. My heart crumbles a little more in my chest, tears threatening to spill down my cheeks. I haven't cried since the funeral, and I don't want to start now. If those floodgates open, I'll be a snotty, bumbling mess for an hour.

Thankfully, if she notices the tears, she doesn't comment on them. Instead, she gestures toward the door across the hall from mine. When she reaches for the big ring of keys at her waist, I take the stack of sheets from her arms. She lifts a key, the ring dangling below it, and opens the door.

I follow her in and gasp. The front wall of this room faces Sycamore Street, so there's a perfect view of the community garden. The other three walls are painted floor to ceiling with dark, spooky forest scenes. The far-left wall has a snow-tipped, stony castle with round turrets and red flags. It could be something out of a fantasy novel.

"This is stunning," I breathe, spinning to check out the whole room.

Catherine preens. "Each room in the Annabelle is inspired by other havens. The Gargoyle room is for Vizelle in Switzerland. The Rose Room for a haven called Delight in the United Kingdom. This room represents a beautiful old haven in the French mountains called Pouyet. She follows my gaze around the room.

I'm gobsmacked. The mermaids in my room are stunning, but the scenes on all three walls here look incredibly real. I reach out and touch the wall, trailing my fingertips along the ridge of a snowy mountain.

"Who painted them?" I murmur, following a trail in the paint to a high mountain meadow filled with wildflowers.

"I did," Catherine says, pride evident in her tone. "When I was much younger, I was a prodigious traveler."

I turn to my hostess and scoff. "You could be exhibiting in any gallery in the human world with work like this, Catherine. Have you ever considered leaving?"

She shakes her head immediately, gesturing out the window. "My home is here, and the human world simply holds no interest for me. I'd miss magic, and my friends. And of course, I could never leave the Annabelle." She reaches out and pats the wall next to my hand, her smile growing broad and mischievous. "We've been through a lot together, this old girl and I. Who could ever leave such a beautiful, magical place? Not me."

I sense an undercurrent of suggestion there. Thea's happy here, but it's no secret that Morgan isn't. Catherine has told us many times that she believes we belong here. I thought maybe we did too, but blowing up Kiril's gourd has me second-guessing that sentiment.

She must sense she's lost my focus, because she grabs the sheets from my arm and sets them in a blood-red velvet chair. I jump to help her change the sheets and we get lost in hours of cleaning and remaking beds. I get to see every bedroom in the Annabelle. They're all so gorgeous.

By lunchtime, I'm a sweaty mess but I feel accomplished. At the very least, I've got a future as a very useful maid. So, there's that. Catherine leaves me to go make lunch.

My comm watch pings a second time and I groan. Here comes Thea to needle me again, I bet. But when I look down, Ohken's name flashes above the blue band. I fluff my waves and toss them over one shoulder before directing the watch to answer him.

"Wren, how are you?" His already deep voice sounds impossibly low through the comm's connection.

"I'm okay," I admit. I don't have the energy to be chipper after a morning of hard labor.

"Mmm," he says. But without expanding on the thoughtful noise he just made, he moves right past it. "Meet me at my place at six, if you would."

God, I love how he doesn't ask me if tonight's still good or if our date is still on. He just knows it is, and that makes me hot.

"I'll admit, I'm not sure where a troll might live," I deadpan. "Perhaps under the nearest bridge, or…"

Throaty laughter rings out of the watch. "That's precisely right, Miss Hector. Take Sycamore past Main a couple hundred yards, and you'll see a sign for my bridge on the left."

"Wait," I bark out. "I was fucking around about the bridge. Are you serious?"

"Six, then," he croons.

Oh my God.

~

At five, I'm in my room getting ready. Thea and Morgan lie on the bed, scarfing down donuts she brought from Shepherd while I try on outfits.

I emerge from my closet in an ankle-length black dress, but Morgan shakes her head. "Too funeralish." Then she winces. Funerals are too recent of a topic. My heart drops in my chest.

"Okay," I chirp, returning to the closet. "Funeral isn't a good date vibe."

"Go for ruffles," offers Thea around a mouthful of donut. "Dudes love ruffles."

Morgan groans. "Please don't start telling us about a time Shepherd ripped ruffles off you, I can't hear another thing about his sexual prowess!"

The sounds of a scuffle reach me and I poke my head out of the room to scowl at my sisters. Morgan's slapping Thea and Thea's growling and shoving at Morgan's chest. Their legs tangle together until I clear my throat. "I need you two to make sure I look hot, so get it together."

Thea slaps Morgan's boob before sliding forward off the bed like an inchworm. She tumbles less-than-gracefully to the ground, then jumps to her feet and joins me in the closet. Morgan grins at us both.

"You're a goofy bitch, you know that?" I say.

She slaps the side of *my* boob before shoving my clothes around on the hangers. She scowls at them until she finds what she's looking for, handing me a black tank top and black high-waisted ruffly skirt.

"Here. I've got some gorgeous earrings you can wear. This and your combat boots and you'll look like a goth princess."

"Love it," I whisper, grabbing the clothes from my sister. "Will you curl my hair?"

"Duh," Thea snarks, shoving me toward the bathroom. "Get changed and I'll give you beachy waves that would make Jennifer Aniston jelly."

Morgan grins at me around a mouthful of donut. She's covered in powdered sugar.

Forty-five minutes later, I check out my reflection in the mirror. Thea and Morgan crowd into the small, ocean-themed bathroom and stare at me.

"You're stunning," Morgan says, laying her head on my shoulder.

"I hope you get fucked six ways from Sunday," Thea adds,

handing me my French perfume. I don't mean for tears to well up in my eyes, but my mother bought the perfume for me on a girls' trip to Paris a few years ago. I think of her every time I wear it.

"I know today was hard," Morgan says, "but you look beautiful and you're going to have a wonderful night, okay? I'm manifesting it for you."

I pull my triplets in for a hug, blinking the tears away.

"You're right," I whisper when the hug goes long. "As long as I can find the bridge he lives under, it'll be just fine."

Thea jerks out of my arms, looking incredulous. "Wait, he lives under a fucking bridge?!"

CHAPTER SIX
WREN

After the girls question me regarding the bridge, I leave the inn and head up Sycamore Street. Alo, Shepherd's older brother, is playing with his son Iggy in the front yard next to the Annabelle. Much like Shepherd, he's built like a tank with miles of purple-gray skin. His black hair is longer than Shepherd's, giving him a more rakish look. His features are a little more classically elegant. It's easy to see what Miriam finds attractive about him.

He whistles when I stride by.

"Let me guess." He stalks to the edge of the sidewalk and casts a quick glance over me. "Off to see a certain bridge troll?"

My cheeks flush. Alo was a grumpy fucker when we first met him, but since his brother and Thea officially mated, he's been a whole lot friendlier. Well, he's been less grumpalicious, at least.

I nod and do a little twirl. Iggy flies over to join us. He heads right for my shoulder to perch, but Alo grabs his tail and pulls his son up onto his own shoulder instead. He points at me, giving Iggy a stern look.

"Miss Wren is going on a date. We don't want to get dirt on her nice outfit."

Iggy turns bright blue eyes on me, squinting as he gives me the same once-over his father did. He looks back at Alo. "What's a date?"

"Hoboy," I snort. "You opened a can of worms there, Alo. I'm gonna leave you to explain that one."

Iggy looks over at me, wings fluttering as he tries to lift off his father's shoulder. Alo wraps his son's tail around his fist to hold him in place.

"Can you take me with you, Wren? We can hold hands and maybe we can go see Miriam at the candy store? I want to do the date with you!"

I step up onto the grass and open my arms for the adorable five-year-old. He hops off Alo's shoulder and throws himself into my arms, burying his face in my hair.

"You smell really nice Miss Wren."

I look up at Alo, but he's staring at his son like he can't believe how lucky he is.

Iggy nuzzles my ear. "Tell me what a date is. Dad doesn't wanna say, I can tell."

I cast Alo a help-me glance, but he just groans and hoists Iggy out of my arms. He tosses his son up into the air, and I marvel when Iggy's tiny purple wings fan out wide. He hovers and then dives down toward his father, shouting about cannonballs.

"He's distracted, better git," Alo offers helpfully. I wave goodbye as he tries to redirect their conversation, but Iggy relentlessly pesters him.

I walk the few blocks to Main Street and cross over, continuing straight. Sure as shit, ten minutes later there's a big white sign that says "Troll Bridge" with an arrow pointing to the left.

"Okay, Wren." I give myself a little pep talk. "It's not weird to meet a man under a bridge. It's not like every serial killer movie or every Grimm fairytale gone bad. It's gonna be fine."

A wide dirt-and-stone path leads into the darkening forest. I pause and put both hands on my hips, staring at how ominous the path looks. I've met all sorts of monsters in Ever, and they've all been friendly. But this walkway looks creepy as fuck. I can just imagine some weird snake-like monster slithering across the stones or popping out from a tree branch above my head.

Am I really doing this? Nerves jangle in my stomach, but I think it's half from anticipation. I straighten my leather jacket as I walk slowly up the path and into the forest.

"He's probably excited to show you his bridge, so don't be rude," I remind myself. "You could say something like, what a nice bridge, Ohken. The stones look so..." I wave my hands around, trying to summon up an appropriate compliment for rocks.

"Perfectly aged," a voice rings up the walkway. "Stunning in the complexity of their construction."

I leap in place, my heart racing. There's nobody on the path in front of me, but I know I heard a voice. That voice. The voice that visits me sometimes when I'm asleep.

Ohken comes around a bend in the path, both hands in the pockets of tight-ass jeans. He's wearing a white collared shirt with the sleeves rolled up and a fitted navy vest. Gorgeous auburn hair is pulled into a loose, messy bun on top of his head.

He could be walking off the monster edition of GQ magazine cover. Russet eyes travel quickly down to my boots and back up. Dark green lips curl into the barest hint of a smile.

Heat floods my cheeks as I straighten. "I was just..."

"Trying to figure out how to compliment my bridge?" He stalks quietly up the path toward me until he's close enough to touch. He slides one big hand out of his pocket and reaches for the fingers of one of my hands, twirling me in place. When I'm facing him again, he lets out an appreciative growl.

"Breathtaking."

"Oh, I'm sure it's a lovely bridge," I snark, "but I was hoping to summon up a better compliment than that."

Ohken chuckles. For one long moment, his gaze locks to mine and I'm sure he'll kiss me. His eye contact game is hella strong. He might as well be ripping my clothes off my very willing body right now.

But after a tense beat, he pulls my hand into the crook of his elbow and guides us back the way he came, pointing at the path ahead.

"While it's true that I live under a bridge, I think you'll be surprised with my home."

I look up at his chiseled jawline and the dark shadow that graces it. He's somehow elegant and manly and rustic all wrapped into one gigantic package. I'm not as tall as Morgan, but Ohken towers over me.

"Do all trolls live under bridges? I mean, would it be the same for trolls in other havens?"

Ohken smiles and nods. "Without exception, bridge trolls live under bridges, it's the way of my people primarily because our magic is tied to our homes. I'll tell you more about that when we go inside. Mountain trolls live in mountain caves. River trolls live in underwater caves. Trolls as a species aren't creative in terms of naming conventions, but then again, those are the English versions of our words."

I look up as we walk. "Trolls speak another language?"

He smiles as we round a corner. "We do, and in our language, "bridge," "river," and "mountain" have words that tie into our magic. In general, most monsters have a mother tongue, but English is the common tongue for havens in America. If we went to Europe, you'd find those havens to function much like the human world in terms of language.

They speak the local language but also English, in many cases."

"I haven't thought much about other havens," I admit. "I'm still sort of wrapping my mind around Ever."

Ohken pulls me around a bend in the pathway. Up ahead, there's a faint blue glow. He stops just behind me, my back pressed to his front. Gargantuan hands slide up my arms to rest just above the elbow. Warm lips come to my ear and brush softly against it.

"Good," he croons. "There's a lot I want to help you discover about this one, Miss Hector."

"Fuck," I mutter, not bothering to hide what a turn-on it is for him to talk to me in that tone.

"Indeed." The back of his hand comes to the underneath of my breast and strokes gently along the swell. I hiss in a breath. Ohken says nothing, but removes his hand and slips past me up the pathway. I reel from the loss of that contact, my nipples pressed firmly to the front of my dress. My breasts feel huge and swollen. I'm achy and desperate for more of what he just hinted at.

He gives me a superior, knowing look and jerks his head toward the glow behind him. "Come, Miss Hector. Let me show you how beautifully constructed my bridge is."

Usually, I'm the sister with the snappy comebacks, but I don't have one right now.

Ohken holds a hand out for me. I marvel for the millionth time at how big and strong that hand looks. And now I know what a tease he can be with it, because my body is throbbing from his barely there touch.

The bridge is about twenty feet ahead of us. And sure as shit—it's, well, it's just a damn bridge. It spans a glowing crystal-blue creek, stretching maybe twenty feet long. It's made of ancient-looking stones with green moss peeking out from between them.

I give Ohken a sage nod. "Very fairytale. Quite picturesque."

The purse of his lips tells me he's barely holding back a comment, but he guides me carefully down the riverbank and along a stone path I didn't initially see. We duck under the bridge where it's nearly pitch-dark.

The only sound is Ohken's soft breathing. I can't see my hand in front of my face, but I hear a footstep, then another. And then his big body is pressing me to cool stones at my back. I let my head fall back against them. I'm desperate to know what he'll do next. But warm lips don't come to my neck. He doesn't trail his lips from my shoulder to my ear.

No.

He presses hard on a stone to my left. There's a rocky scraping sound and the stone lights up blue enough to highlight his face in the dark. His eyes are hooded with lust, his gaze on my mouth. His lips curve into a devious grin.

The stones at my back disappear and I shriek as I fall into darkness.

One of Ohken's big arms comes around me, bracing me before I land on my ass. He pulls me upright with a mischievous snicker, then presses his hand to another stone inside… wherever the hell we are. Oh God, what if he lives in the troll equivalent of Harry Potter's broom closet?

As I think that, blue glyphs in an unknown language light up along the wall, illuminating a path to another door. A faint overhead light flickers on, then grows bright. The glyphs flash brighter in a pattern from one end of the long hall to the other.

"Is this your language?" I breathe in wonder, reaching out to touch the intricate, blocky symbols.

"It is," he confirms, stroking the stones next to my hand. "The bridge is welcoming you by flashing them in this pattern. She's thrilled you're here."

I stare around at the small space, in awe of how beautiful it is.

"I wasn't expecting this," I murmur. "I swear to God I thought you might live in a hole."

Ohken shakes his head. "When a troll bridge is constructed, every stone is carved to ensure the magic makes the bridge strong. This bridge has been in Ever for centuries. I took it over and remodeled it after the first owner passed."

There's a creaky sound at the end of the hall that sounds like a door opening and shutting.

"Coming!" Ohken calls out, grabbing my jacket. "Should we leave this here? Or would you like to keep it…"

"Here's fine," I murmur, staring toward the faintly lit hallway. I shrug my coat off just as a hook pops out from the wall. "Thank you," I tell his home. At this point, I've read the entire Welcome Packet. I know each home has a personality, and if his is handing me a coat hook, well I know better than to be rude.

He hangs the jacket for me then leads us up the hallway. I didn't initially notice stocky wooden doors lining it, but when we pass they glow from within.

Ohken raps his knuckles on one of the doors. "Troll bridges are quite large, and mine doubles as Ever's emergency center. There's enough space and extra bedrooms here for all 835 or so residents if we need it."

I gasp. "You've got 835 bedrooms?"

He shakes his head. "Not at the moment. Right now there's one extra behind each of these doors. But the bridge, or rather this space underneath it, grows depending on the community's needs."

"Is that normal?" I mutter as we reach the door at the end of the hall. A pale blue glow peeks out around all four edges. It's stunning.

Ohken turns and leans against the carved wooden door, its surface smooth as butter. "Define normal."

I return the laugh. Really, what is normal when you live in a hidden monster town?

He grins while I ponder it, pressing against the door. It opens and he steps gracefully through, gesturing for me to follow.

And holy shit. I've stepped into a huge, cavernous room. Ohken and I stand on an entryway stoop, but four steps to my left lead us down into the room.

Oversized vintage-style chandeliers hang from the ceiling, casting muted rays of light in every direction. There are two different sitting areas with plush, oversized sofas that give off a Moroccan vibe. Ohken strides down the stairs, pulling me with him.

A cottage-style kitchen is built into the wall below the door we just came through. There's an ancient-looking oven with metal burners just like a human might have. A long, wide island sticks out from the back wall, its black countertop laced with white streaks.

Something smells delicious. A pot of red sauce on the stove bubbles happily. Clasping my hands together, I follow Ohken into the kitchen. He grips my waist and lifts me easily onto the island across from the stove. Big hands run down my back, bypassing my ass, sadly, and making their way to the tops of my thighs.

"I need to feed you." He smirks. "And then I'll give you the full tour. Talk to me while I cook?"

"I feel shitty about earlier," I blurt out. Goddamnit, I meant to keep that to myself, but now it's out there. I didn't even really mean to start by saying that, but here we are. I search his gaze, wishing I could crumple in on myself, away from the big troll standing in front of me.

Ohken lifts my chin so I'm forced to look into those

shocking rust-colored eyes. "Kiril is happily rehomed in a temporary box until a new gourd is grown. Whenever your mind runs wild like it is now, come to me. I'll quiet it for you. Let me be your refuge, Wren, your safe haven."

Guilt constricts my throat, but I nod.

He takes a step closer. "I want to be that for you, sweet witch."

I nod again, willing unwanted tears to go the fuck away.

Ohken bends down and brushes his lips over mine. They're soft and plump, and his short tusks rake against my mouth. It's the barest hint of a kiss, but goosebumps cover my arms and exposed thighs. He lets out a pleased noise, squeezing just above my knee. "I have something for you."

I'm too overwhelmed by his entire presence to be witty, but I *am* intrigued. A present on the first date?

"Is this a troll thing?"

"Nope. It's a me thing. I love giving gifts."

Part of me preens about that.

He reaches into his pocket, and my traitorous brain goes right to a vision of him down on one knee in front of me, pulling out an engagement ring. I mentally bitch-slap myself. I've been on this date for all of ten seconds. Ohken's just the coolest person I've ever gone out with.

He does pull out a small box, though, and when he opens it, tiny, peach-hued stone earrings sit there. He holds the box higher.

"Aragonite studs. I made them for you this afternoon."

My skin goes hot and cold at the same time. They're gorgeous, glinting from the blue velvet confines of the tiny box. But this is about my power, then, or lack of it.

"They're beautiful," I whisper, reaching down to touch the small peach studs. It's true that they're gorgeous, but I struggle not to let disappointment into my tone. I just brought up what happened earlier, but I don't even know why I did. I definitely don't want to talk about it anymore.

The look Ohken gives me is understanding, which makes me feel worse.

"Hey." He sets the box down next to my thigh. "I feel compelled to clarify that trolls tend to be big gift-givers, but we're very into beautiful yet practical gifts. It's part of how we express our interest. This isn't really about your power."

I grab the box and look at the studs, glinting in the low light of his cave. "Isn't it?"

"No." His voice is soft as he parts my thighs and steps between them, forcing me to look up. His body is warm against my core. There's an obvious bulge at the front of his pants. "This is about how fucking beautiful these will be in your delicate, tiny ears. It's about how proud it'll make me to see you wear something I gave you. They'll help you, but I made them because I wanted you to have something as lovely as you are."

CHAPTER SEVEN
OHKEN

I'm almost certain Wren isn't aware how rare it is to find a green witch. I wanted the earrings to feel special for her, but I didn't foresee that she might see it as a reminder of what happened earlier today. I'm not sure I can backtrack out of the hole I dug myself into, and in any case, tonight isn't about her power, it's about us.

More specifically, it's about my desire to see how she responds to my interest in her. To see if what I think is there, truly is. When I pressed her to the wall underneath the bridge earlier, she sank easily into position for me—head back, lips parted, body arched toward mine. And that hint of a kiss? I'm sure she'd have let me take it further than I did. My cock throbs in my pants with the need to do more.

Grabbing the earrings from her a second time, I set them aside. "Let's forget about these for now." I turn and grab a stirring spoon while I add pepper to my tomato sauce. "Are you excited for the skyball tournament?"

She laughs, and that, at least, sounds joyous. "To be honest, I'm not really sure what to expect. Does Ever have a team? Or are there professional monster teams? Or what?"

I stir the sauce and turn the heat up. "The tournament is at a different haven every other year. It hasn't been here in a very long time. The Keeper and I have been building the stadium for the last six months or so."

"Building a stadium? By hand?" Both dark brows are high. She looks skeptical.

I gesture around at my home. "Troll magic. Most trolls are builders by nature. In fact, most haven buildings are built by trolls because of the magic we carry that helps them to come alive."

"So, you're a magical construction worker. But also the town's Welcome Master. And you own two businesses on Main Street. Damn, Ohken, is there anything you don't do?"

I dip my spoon into the sauce and cross from my ancient stove. Blowing softly on it, I lift it for her to try. She leans forward and sips delicately at the sauce, smiling at the flavor.

"That's delicious. Is it spaghetti sauce?"

"Chicken parm. Thea told me that was your favorite."

Wren purses her lips together and tries to look peeved, but it only serves to heighten the dimple on one side of her plump cheeks. I want to bite it. And then I want to take her into my greenhouse and fuck her against the wall. But I rein in all of those urges, because trolls move slowly when it comes to relationships. We won't be fucking for a while, if we get that far.

"She snitched." I grin at her and set the spoon down. Crossing back to the stove, I put a lid on my sauce and take her hand. "That needs to cook another half hour. How about I give you the full tour."

She brightens and grips my fingers, allowing me to help her off the countertop. Her soft body slides down my much bigger, harder one, and I hold back a groan of pleasure. She's all soft curves and sugary-sweet scent. I've never met a woman so enticingly feminine. I've been hard since getting ready for this date, and having her in my cave is intoxicating.

Pulling her close to me, I bend down enough to brush my mouth against her ear. "To answer your question, Miss Hector, there's not a lot I don't do. I'm a man of many talents, and I have a lot of interests."

She cocks her head to the side to look at me, which brings her lips close to mine. "Ya don't say?"

I smile but straighten, not missing the way a flash of disappointment flickers in those pretty emerald eyes. Oh yes, she's feeling the same desire I am.

I guide her through the living room and toward the back of the cavernous space. Two separate hallways lead to more bedrooms. A third leads to my mead-making room and greenhouse. I show her that last, because I'm curious to see what she makes of the space.

When I pull her through the arched stone doorway into the greenhouse, her eyes go wide, her pouty pink lips parting.

"Oh my God, Ohken, this is incredible!" She claps her hands together and strides to the nearest wall, which grows a variety of vegetables. I try to see this room as she might. One entire side is a hydroponic garden, lit from above with the same magical light that lights the rest of my cave. Toward the back of the long, rectangular room, plants coil and fall from the ceiling. There's a bubbling pool of water at the back, too, but she seems not to have noticed that yet. Or the hooks in the walls opposite it.

I smile, following as she makes her way toward the back.

She looks up from a long, purple eggplant. "I honestly expected these to be green too, or something. Just regular eggplants? How do you get them so big?"

I'm about to launch into a primer on hydroponics, but she digs behind the plants and examines my system. The entire upper half of her body is buried behind the leaves, which gives me a perfect view of the back of her thick thighs. They tease me when her skirt snakes up, showing me miles of luscious, pale skin. The sudden urge to drop to my knees and feast nearly overtakes me, but I shake it off and smile. My instincts about her were right. We could be an excellent match. It's the only reason why such sharp urges would hit me this hard.

She leans farther into the plants and asks a question, but her voice is muffled by the foliage. Still, I want her to come to me. I *always* want her to come to me—on hands and knees would be preferable. I grin and pace away, toward the back of the long room, admiring the plants as I go.

"Oh, where'd you—there you are."

I look back over my shoulder with a smile. The soft tread of combat boots echoes faintly.

"I thought you left m—oh my God is that a hot spring? Right here? Does it come up from an aquifer? Or..." She leaves me and drops to one knee next to the hot spring, reaching out to touch the softly bubbling surface.

"Yes it does, and there are a number of hot springs throughout the haven. I believe I'm the only one with a location in my house though. Perks of building the interior like I wanted to. Another troll built the actual bridge about five hundred Ever-years ago. But when I bought it, I redid the inside how I wanted."

She looks up at me and smiles, and it's so radiant, I forget to keep talking.

"We can swim after dinner, if you like."

"Hell yeah!" she almost shouts. "And then I'll pepper you with questions about your system and how you accomplish this level of growth with no natural light. And then you'll really regret bringing me in here, because our entire date will be you answering questions about hydroponics." She snorts.

I wave my hand at the plants that surround us. "Aside from being builders, all trolls are naturalists of a sort, just like you in your role. Or similar, maybe."

She's spoken a few times about the naturalist job she left behind in the human world. But just like her sister Thea, I sense she's not in a hurry to return to it.

Wren draws one arm in front of her torso, rubbing at her elbow. "My job was supposed to help ensure that city parks are built with the environment in mind so they could truly be tiny havens in the midst of New York. Unfortunately, bureaucracy made it nearly impossible to get anything done. I miss it, but I was already thinking about leaving, before things happened." Her voice trails off. I suspect I know what she's referencing. The untimely death of her parents and then the discovery of Ever.

"Do you want to talk about them?" I keep my tone open. I'm a safe space for her. But I know she'll tell me more about their deaths if and when she wants to.

Wren scrunches up her nose, and I sense I won't get those answers today. "Let's not. It'll bring the mood down, and this place is amazing. But when my Aunt Lou gets here, you'll love her. She's probably a green witch too, but I bet she'll pick up on it faster than I have."

There's that insecurity about her power again. I hate that for her. She's expecting too much from herself given she's known she was a witch for such a short time. I don't say that, though, but focus on her family reference. "You've mentioned Lou many times. You're close with her?"

"Yeah," Wren says. "She's my mother's sister, but only a few years older than us, so she was always more like *our* sister growing up. After Mom and Dad died, Lou was our lifeline. I'm so glad we were able to invite her here. I don't think she'll even be surprised to find a hidden world of monsters. You'll see what I mean when she arrives."

I cast a glance down her body. Combat boots are laced up her ankle, but her legs are bare. I stare at beautifully curved calf muscles and plump thighs. The ruffles accentuate them, teasing me, making me wonder what would happen if I slipped my hand up her leg and pushed that skirt up.

Wren laughs. "Have I seen everything? Minus the 835 rooms that don't exist, but would exist if you suddenly needed them to?"

I shake my head and take her hand, pulling her out of the greenhouse and up the hall toward the main living area.

"You haven't seen my bedroom." I grin as I push against the door and drag her inside with me. I'm curious what she notices about my room, so I lean against the wall to watch her.

Wren enters the room with a shocked look. "This is incredible, Ohken." She turns to me, all wide-eyed enthusiasm. Then she stalks past me with a gasp. "Is that a reading nook in the corner with a little library? My God, it is!" She jogs past me in the other direction. "And a row of chamomile right here, growing inside." She scoffs and glances up at the ceiling.

I can almost see the wheels of her mind turning, wondering how plants are growing in a dark cave with no sunlight. She either hasn't noticed or hasn't commented on the enormous bed taking up the middle of my room. Or the hooks in the headboard and footboard. Or the hooks and supports built into the ceiling.

We'll cover that another day, then.

A faint ringing noise echoes from up the hall, and I twitch an ear to better hear it. There it is, a little louder—my kitchen timer.

"Sauce is ready. Let me feed you, and then you can poke around in here a little more if you want, or we can go for a swim."

"Deal," she chirps, crossing the room to reach for me. For a long moment, green eyes scan my face. She presses herself to me, her heavy breasts soft against my stomach. My mouth waters as I look at her. She's giving off all the right signals—nipping her lower lip, touching me, coming to me rather than me chasing. Not that I mind chasing.

The timer pings again, breaking the moment.

Wren laughs and grabs my hand, pulling me out of the room and back into the kitchen. She hops up onto the island, telling me stories about her sisters and Lou while I finish the chicken parm and stick it in the broiler. Ten minutes later, we're both in hysterics at her retellings while I toss extra cheese on the tray of chicken.

I grab both plates and head toward the table, which I set earlier with my mother's china. Green vines trail along the outer edge of the plates; it's one of the few items I have of hers. Tapered green candles burn at the center of the table.

"Green, huh?" Wren laughs as she takes a seat. "Let me guess, it's your favorite color?"

I set the chicken down and plate hers first. "Tell me when you've had enough sauce. And no, green isn't my favorite color." Pausing, I reach over to trail my fingers down her cheek. Her skin is so soft, so smooth. A pink tinge follows the stroke of my hand.

"Looking into your beautiful eyes, though, I think it could be." My voice pitches low, going rough. And there's that instinct again, telling me to swipe everything off the table with one hand and have her on top of it. I can't do that though, for a variety of reasons including our size difference. Still, it's a delicious burn, the way my natural instincts edge me.

Wren sucks in a breath. "You keep sweet-talking me like that, sir, and you might just get another date." She winks playfully, but a blush covers both cheeks and crawls down her chest.

I don't respond to the date comment. We're going on another date, and another and another. That's a foregone conclusion to me at this point. Now, my only job is making sure she wants to. So, I change the subject.

"Back to your earlier questions, Ever does have a skyball team. I'm on it, so I'll be playing. Nobody's a professional, it's just fun, although the entire monster world gets pretty nutty about it. Players can use their natural power, so it requires a great deal of forethought as to who your opponents are." I sit in my chair and cross an ankle over my thigh.

For the next three hours, we talk about every topic under the sun. We chat more about her parents. She was closer to her mother, although it sounds like she adored her father too. I hear more stories about Lou and a wide variety of shenanigans—one involving a group of girlfriends and a bathtub full of something called Jesus Juice.

Wren tells me all about her sisters and how much they love Shepherd. She's a vivacious storyteller. There are just enough theatrics and embellishments to make the stories great, and I find myself easily lost in her words.

We switch over and talk about my childhood in Arcadia in northwestern Canada. It's a beautiful haven, but mostly full of orcs and trolls. Once my parents passed, I was ready to leave. I still have family there, although Ever is home to me now.

She asks a million questions about Fleur and The General Store, I know she's fascinated by Fleur in particular. I make a mental note to plan a date for us there. A room full of flowers is a room full of sexy opportunities.

Eventually, Wren starts to shift in her seat. Dinner's done and we've polished off a bottle of wine. There's a happy flush to her cheeks. She wants to be kissed. I can tell in the way she keeps nibbling at one lip, her eyes focused on my mouth. I teased her earlier under the bridge and again when she came in. I'm a troll, we're natural Dominants. Teasing is in my DNA.

Not that I've told her quite that much detail yet.

I pull her legs between both of mine and lean forward. I'm so much taller than her that like this, I still tower over her. She leans closer to meet me.

Bringing both hands to the outsides of her thighs, I squeeze and touch them.

"Soft," I murmur, my gaze dropping from her beautiful pink lips to the way her ruffled black skirt rides up, showing me a tantalizing hint of plump inner thighs. A hot flash of need crackles down my spine as my sack draws up tight against my body. I'm teasing her, but in doing so, I'm torturing myself.

"Are you gonna kiss me or not?" Wren finally crosses her arms and pouts, and it's the cutest thing I've ever seen.

Laughing, I shift a little farther forward, brushing the tip of her nose with mine. My lips are close enough that I could take her mouth. I could bypass the typical troll pace and pull her into my lap right here. I bet I could even rip that skirt off her body and do delicious things to her.

But I want her feral by the time we touch, so when she leans forward even farther, I collar her throat with one hand and growl.

"I'm not kissing you tonight, Miss Hector. But I love the way you're looking at me like you can't wait for me to do it."

Wren scoffs but doesn't pull away. "Is that so?"

"Mhm."

"Maybe you should consider that teasing a witch who doesn't even know how powerful she might be could be a poor choice."

The suggestion that she might be able to dominate me with her power makes my own rise. With my grip on her neck, I pull her out of her chair to stand between my thighs. I notice the heat in her eyes, dropping my focus to her lips. Still parted, still begging to be kissed. Casting a glance down her body, I revel in how good she looks between my legs. Big, tight nipples are pressed against the fabric of her dress. I'm half desperate to know what color they are and how they taste.

"Delectable." My voice is an appreciative rumble. I slide my free hand up the back of her left thigh, reveling in the smooth silkiness of her skin. She shudders and lets out a desperate little strangled sound.

When my hand reaches the apex of her thigh and travels toward the crack of her ass, she does whine. And that needy noise ends in a demanding growl.

I trail my fingers along the crack of her luscious ass. She's wearing a barely there thong. I'd love to flip her onto her stomach and remove it with my teeth, but this date is just the beginning, just a testing of the chemistry and connection between us. And godsdamn, the chemistry between us is fucking spectacular.

I slip my fingers between her ass cheeks and trail them back down until I meet her core. Then it's just the softest hint of a stroke. She's soaking wet, and when I push my fingers farther, gently rubbing them along the outer edges of her folds, she presses closer to me, eyes closed.

She purses her lips like she's about to say something. I watch the pink tinge on her cheeks turn to red, and then her head falls back. Pressing the tip of my finger inside her slit, I watch for her reaction. She steps her legs farther apart, inviting me in. I stroke gently at her core before making my way to that little nubbin at the front Shepherd told me about —the clit. The moment I circle it with my fingers, she gasps and jerks in my arms.

"Powerful magic indeed," I murmur, leaning forward to press my nose into her neck and breathe her in. She smells like coffee and wine and my house, and that fills me with satisfaction. "What would this little button do if I licked it, Miss Hector?"

A breathy sigh tumbles from her soft throat. "Try it and find out."

I drag my tusks along the side of her neck, never relenting. Arousal spills onto my fingers. I thrust one farther in, nearly halfway. When Wren gasps, it takes everything in me not to follow her suggestion.

"Time for me to take you home, my sweet," I say instead.

Wren turns furious eyes on me, but quickly schools the look into something neutral and innocent. "Alright, Ohken."

Two can play this game, she seems to say.

Good, I want her to play this game with me. This is the troll way, and I'm curious how a human will respond to it.

So far, so good.

CHAPTER EIGHT
WREN

True to his word, Ohken doesn't kiss me. Not when our eyes meet and his hand slides out from between my wet thighs. Not when there's a tense moment up against the door to the bridge. Not even on the Annabelle's front steps when the perfect opportunity arises.

"Good night, Miss Hector," he rumbles. I don't miss the absolutely enormous hard-on pressed to the front of his pants. The fabric does nothing to hide it. And he lets me look my fill. He's not trying to hide it in the slightest. He wants me to stare at him and admire what he's packing.

With some effort, I manage to drag my eyes away from it, putting my hands on my hips. "It's a real shame you're going to go home so unsatisfied, Mister Stonesmith. I could have done something about that." I gesture at his humongous dick.

He smirks and shakes his head, slipping his hands into his pockets. "I'm going to go home and do something about it, Miss Hector. What do you think about that?"

God, I cannot get one over on this man.

Clearing my throat, I cross my arms. "Sounds lonely."

Ohken steps forward and leans down until his lips are

almost touching mine. "I'll think of you when I do it, Wren. Think of me when you get yourself off tonight. I want to hear about it tomorrow."

I bite my lip to avoid begging him to take me to the nearest bed, and wish him good night instead. Dark green lips are set in a seemingly permanent smirk as he inclines his head, turns, and walks away.

Lord help me, he looks just as good from the back. Impossibly beefy, broad shoulders taper down to a thick waist. His ass fills out the pants, the fabric clinging to the muscles of his thighs. I hate the idea of him going back to his bridge alone with that gorgeous dick and nobody to tend to it.

So he's going to go back and masturbate? I would desperately love to watch that.

Sighing, I watch him disappear into the night. When I can't see him anymore I go inside. The inn is silent, although several of the windows open and close quietly. The Annabelle is welcoming me home.

"Hey girl," I whisper. Everybody must be asleep, except that when I get to the top of the stairs, Shepherd and Thea stand there wearing matching Ever Misfits tees.

Jesus, they're two dorks in a pod.

Shepherd holds out a small bag and winks at me. "Come on, sis. Morgan's already waiting for you. Tell us everything."

I groan but follow my triplet and her mate up the long hallway to Morgan's room, the rose room. When I enter, she looks up from where she's reading in the window seat. Shepherd flops down on the other end of it and pulls Thea into his lap, nuzzling her cheek playfully. Near-black eyes flick up to me, then down to the bag.

"Chocolate-covered almonds. Morgan said you loved those."

"You're the best," I huff.

Thea claps her hands together. "Tell us everything!" Her

blue eyes flash with mischief. "You're all flushed, did you get laid?"

A tiny light zips through the bedroom door and Miriam pops into large form. "You got laid? Really?!"

Shepherd snorts. "'Course she didn't." He reaches into a bag like the one he gave me and pulls out a chocolate, tossing it in the air and catching it easily in his mouth.

"'Course I didn't?" I echo his words, surprised he could know. An icky thought worms its way through my mind. "Can you like, smell his jizz or something?"

Shepherd scrunches his nose. "Yuck. If I thought about it I probably could. Most monsters have excellent senses. But no. Trolls move very slowly in relationships. Sort of the opposite of gargoyles." He winks at Thea. "You're not getting laid for a while, sis."

I groan and flop on the window seat next to Morgan. We both scream when a shadow descends out of the sky, darkening the window. The Annabelle slides the window frame up and Alo leans into the open frame, looking around until his eyes land on Miriam. He seems surprised to find us all in this room.

"Mir? You asked me to come over?"

She flops down on the window seat next to where he leans. "Thought you might enjoy a little adult chit-chat. Wren didn't get laid on her date tonight, but she was just about to tell us everything else."

Alo nods sagely, his lips curving into a soft smile. "Of course she didn't get laid. He's a bridge troll."

When Morgan, Thea, and I all scoff at the same time, he shifts farther into the room, grabbing the bag of chocolates from me. "Didn't you ladies read the welcome packet? There's a whole section about the mating habits of different monster species."

My nostrils flare. "I read the welcome packet and I can't say I remember that."

Morgan shakes her head. "I finally read the whole thing too and there's nothing about mating rituals."

Alo shoots Shepherd a look, and Shepherd lifts his wrist. "Comm Catherine, please."

"She could be sleeping," I hiss.

He rolls his eyes. "She's not sleepi—hey, Catherine. Sounds like the Hector triplets didn't get the mating rituals part of the Welcome Packet. Do you have extras?"

Catherine's voice rings out that she'll be right down.

"Dang." Morgan shoots him an exasperated look. "What else might we be missing?"

Moments later, we hear Catherine's footsteps from the stairs at the end of the hall. She knocks twice and lets herself in the room with three welcome packets in hand. "Girls, I'm terribly sorry. I gave you the new monster welcome packet, but you needed the human one. My apologies."

I take a manila envelope. "This is shockingly thicker than the other packet, Catherine."

Gray eyes flash with mirth. "There's a lot you need to know if you didn't grow up in a haven."

"Like how trolls mate," Shepherd offers helpfully.

I reach out and slap his wing, something he tells me I can only do because we're family. He sticks his tongue out. Catherine laughs at our antics.

"I'd love to hear the story, I'm in the middle of something so I'll head back upstairs. Wren, dear, if you'd like to talk about Ohken, please find me. I'm happy to shed light where I can."

When she leaves, I turn to Shepherd with the saltiest scowl I can muster. "Much as I love for everyone in town to know all about my date, a lady never tells all her secrets."

"Oh I bet I can take a wild guess at how things went."

Shepherd crosses his big arms over Thea's chest, pulling her tightly back to him. "You found the bridge, he showed you the bridge, he fed you and gave you a tour, maybe plied you with a few drinks, and it was all heated looks and barely there touches until he announced it was time to go home."

My mouth falls open. "Is this guy for real?" I point at him. Thea shrugs but smirks.

The whole story spills out of me. Shepherd nods sagely, because apparently he knew exactly how this would go.

When I get to the part about the earrings, I gasp aloud, my hand flying to cover my mouth. "Oh, shit! I left the damn earrings at his place!"

"Ouch," Shepherd helpfully supplies. "Rejecting a gift on the first date. No good."

"Wait, is that for real?" Morgan gives him a skeptical look. "Or are you just stirring the pot?"

Thea elbows her mate in the ribs and rolls her eyes. "Stirring the pot. But it might be nice to comm Ohken about the earrings. Do you want them? Or…"

"Yeah." I think I do. They were beautiful and he took the time to make them. And they could help. Now that I'm not feeling quite so tender about this morning, I recognize that.

I'm lost in thought when Shepherd shifts Thea up into his arms and stands. She yawns and gives me two thumbs-up. "Don't forget we're going bowling tomorrow. It's girls' night so no hanky-panky with hot trolls, 'kay?"

I laugh. "Sounds like there's not a lot of that in my near future, according to everyone in town."

Miriam hugs me and then disappears into her small form, zipping out the window. Shepherd snorts and shoves his brother out and into the dark sky. The Annabelle opens the window wider for him. Morgan and I marvel at the way he tucks out of it and bullets up into the sky with our triplet held to his chest.

Morgan watches them disappear into the night before turning to me. "Still so weird. Our sister mated a gargoyle. And now you're dating a troll? Lou is gonna have a field day once she arrives."

That pulls a smile to my face. I can't wait to talk to Lou about Ohken.

I open the bag Shepherd gave me and pull out a chocolate ball that's coated in a fine powder. Plopping one in my mouth, I groan at how fucking good it is. There's a hint of cinnamon and something else a little tangy.

Morgan laughs. "I keep telling him he doesn't have to continue feeding us now that he's got Thea hooked, but he swears it's a gargoyle thing and he'll never stop." She shrugs.

Biting into the crunchy almond center, I savor it for a moment. "I'm not complaining." I look over at my sister. "You wanna talk about anything, Mor? I'm here, if you do."

She bites her lip and seems to think about it, but eventually shakes her head.

"I'm working things through. Truthfully, I think I'll feel better once Lou gets here. I'm sort of lost without her, and I don't think I realized how much I rely on her constant presence until we came here."

I've felt the same way. "We had a new groove after we moved back into mom and dad's house. Sister hugs every night and commuting together into the city. It's different, now that we're here." I gesture around.

"Exactly." Morgan nods. "So, I need Lou."

With time passing faster inside the wards than in the human world, it's not like we can just text our aunt at any old time. I've got to do math to figure out what time it is, and I hate math. Lou's on her way, but it'll be a few Ever-weeks before she arrives.

"She's gonna love it here," I whisper, handing Morgan an almond. "Don't you think?"

My sister snorts. "Of course. She'll probably find a mate on day one and then I'll be alone again."

I don't think she even meant to say the words that way, but it tells me what I need to know about how Morgan's feeling—alone, left behind, bypassed. I'm sure the Keeper's behavior doesn't help.

"Have you thought about talking to the Keeper about all of this?" I pat her leg, but she's lost in thought, staring out the window, and she doesn't answer the question. Eventually, when she yawns, I take the hint and head back to my own room.

I fall asleep thinking about a certain big troll and all the things that have changed about my life in the last six months. But for the first time in a hot minute, I feel hopeful.

∽

The following day passes horribly slowly. The Keeper pulls Ohken into some issue with the stadium, so he isn't able to join our witch lessons with Catherine. When he comms me to let me know, I make a point to thank him for the earrings. When I leave the Annabelle for lessons, the navy velvet box sits on the front porch for me.

Today, the gift makes me smile. Thea and Morgan make a big fuss over how gorgeous the earrings are, and I put them in right away. If he swings by, I want him to know I appreciate his thoughtfulness.

"Hot," Thea deadpans. "They bring out the warm undertones in your skin. He picked well."

"He picked it to help center my power," I correct.

Thea shrugs. "Potato tomato. Let's see if they work."

"Ugh." I slap a hand to my forehead. "I promised Kiril I wouldn't practice in the garden anymore because of yesterday. I totally forgot."

Thea purses her lips. "Ooh, that's right. Daddy Ohken is doing the teaching now, right? Are you supposed to like, go wait seductively under the bridge or what?"

"He didn't mention that," I deadpan. Ultimately, I elect to join my sisters and watch their lessons. I don't try to call my power, although today I feel it simmering under my skin. But watching the pixies zip around the new A-frame where the temporary housing is sobers me right up. Thea crushes it as always, and even Morgan seems to make progress.

By lunchtime, they're both beat so I suggest the Galloping Green Bean. Alba, the centaur owner of our favorite retro diner, is my third-favorite monster in town. Ohken is obviously first. Shepherd and Miriam tie for second. But Alba is so bitingly sarcastic that I feel like I've found my people when we see her.

Lunch is as tasty as ever. Alba's nephew Taylor makes the best burgers on the planet. I've wondered if there's magic imbued in them somehow, but he refuses to spill Alba's secrets.

By the time girls' night is rolling around, I'm anxious and sweaty. I didn't get a lesson today, and I don't want to bug Ohken. But now I won't get a chance to because of goddamn bowling.

Still, girl's night is important. When my sisters and I decided to stay in Ever, we swore we wouldn't let time together fall by the wayside, no matter how *cough cough* involved we might otherwise become.

When we leave the Annabelle, she waves her pretty pink shutters at us. Sycamore Street is abuzz with pixies working in the garden.

Morgan points at the tiny lights zipping around, just visible over the hedge. "Catherine told me the pixies are expecting a bunch of royalty for the tournament, so that's why the extra gourds. I guess the king and queen will be here for the games."

Thea wraps an arm around my waist. "Know what that means? You two should come stay with me so she can rent out your rooms! Imagine it, nightly sleepovers!"

"Yeah." I draw the word out long. "I'm sure Shepherd would love having us in the nest."

"Hell no," Thea chirps. "You're not allowed in there. There's a guest nest, duh."

I marvel at the change in my sister since we arrived in Ever. She was always confident and strong, but there's a lightness to her that I haven't seen since our folks passed. I like it, and I'm grateful to Shepherd for putting the twinkle back in her eyes.

We hook a right on Main and walk a few blocks to the movie theater. We haven't been there yet, or the bowling alley. Apparently it takes up the backside of the theater building. A blinking sign directs us down a cheerful, light-filled alleyway that opens into a big parking lot.

I gasp when we round the corner to the lot. There's a band on one side comprised of half a dozen monsters of varying species. They're playing a raucous song that reminds me vaguely of country music, but with a little more flair to it. I recognize all the instruments, and even that feels weird.

Dozens of couples swirl and sway across the concrete, dancing to the lively beat.

It seems like half the town is here.

"Shit, I had no idea there was a place to dance." I'm stunned, staring at all the couples and even a few solo people jiving on their own.

Two centaurs sway past us, wrapped in each other's arms. They're a tangle of legs and limbs and I can't look away, but somehow they're incredibly graceful. It seems like they should go down in a heap on the slick concrete, but they fly past, seemingly entranced by the upbeat song.

"I met them at the General Store this week," Morgan leans into both of us. "Apparently they're competitive dancers. That's a thing in the monster world. They teach lessons here! I forgot to tell you."

Just when I thought I was finally getting the hang of this place. This town is like peeling an onion, I swear. As soon as I get the lowdown on one layer, another appears!

We watch for a moment, admiring their incredible rhythm, but Thea drags us toward the bowling alley. There's a competitive look in her eye.

"Oh you two aren't going to get crazy, are you?" I try to cross my arms and look stern, but she just laughs.

"Me? Competitive? Morgan, competitive? What gave you that idea?" She yanks the front door open, ushering us through.

Inside the bowling alley, everything is just as retro as the Galloping Green Bean. Monsters seem to have a thing for retro stuff, I'm learning. The walls are covered in red, turquoise, and white bowling ball and pin cutouts. There are probably twenty or so lanes, and despite the old-school feel, it's clean and shiny.

"This place looks too nice, I hope there's standard bowling alley fare." I stick my tongue out at Thea as she drags us to the check-in counter. We turn our shoes in and pay for a lane. No sooner do we sit down than I hear a loud whoop.

Thea slips her foot into a bowling shoe but jerks her head up. "No freaking way."

Mor and I follow her gaze. Sure as shit, Shepherd, Alo, Ohken, and the Keeper are bowling at the far end. Shepherd apparently just did something awesome, because he's shimmying victoriously from side to side, shaking his ass.

Thea crosses her arms and scowls over at me. "I didn't say

a peep about where we were going. I just knew he planned boys' night since we had girls' night. I figured, what are the odds of us ending up at the same place?"

"Pretty damn good, I suppose." I slip my shoes on and give my triplets a devilish look. "We can keep to ourselves, or we could go talk a little shit. How are you two feeling?"

At the end of the room, Shepherd jeers at the Keeper. Moments later, there's the whoosh of a ball and a tinny loudspeaker announces the Keeper got a strike.

Morgan's eyes drift over my shoulder. "Talk shit, obviously." She stands and grabs her coat. I grab my purse and Thea trots ahead of us toward the guys, both arms open wide.

I smirk at Morgan. "She wasted no time talking smack, I see."

"Has she ever?" Morgan complains, but she doesn't mean it in a negative way. Thea's the most outgoing of the three of us. It didn't even really surprise me when she was the first to start dating a monster.

By the time we reach the boys' lane, Thea's heckling Shepherd but he's just grappling with her hands, dragging them behind her back and angling for a kiss.

My eyes are drawn elsewhere. Ohken stands next to the Keeper, studiously ignoring my triplet and her shenanigans. Shocking, rust-hued eyes are locked onto the studs in my ears. His hands are slung easily into the front pockets of his jeans. Like most days, he's wearing a beautifully tailored vest, his hair half up in a messy bun that compliments his rough-hewn features.

"Beautiful," he mouths. His eyes fall to my tee, which has the word "Fatbulous" written across it in big scrolly rainbow letters. The corners of his mouth turn up, tusks peeking out from behind his plump lips.

The Keeper rolls his eyes and looks down at his comm watch, scowling. "Your turn, Aloitious."

Morgan's always reserved around him, so it surprises me when she speaks up. "Actually, Thea thought we might challenge you boys to a competition."

The Keeper's eyes flash as he purses his thin lips. The scar that runs down over his left eye makes his upper lip curl in what looks terribly like disdain. But next to me, Morgan doesn't waver.

"Done," the Keeper snaps. He strides to the control panel and jams a few buttons to restart the game.

Ohken comes closer to us. "You don't know what you've unleashed, girls. The Keeper holds a bowling record not just here in Ever, but in the international league as well."

Morgan huffs. "I'll have you know I was a state champion bowler in high school. Bring it on, ding-dongs."

God, I love Morgan in competition mode. Between her and Thea, there was plenty of that to go around. Mom and I used to sit in the stands and cheer them on while they played sports. She and I would sit there crocheting and talk about life. Some of my most amazing heart-to-hearts happened in soccer stadiums and at track meets.

My heart clenches. I miss her so damn much.

Ohken reaches out and strokes a stray wave back behind my ear. "Lost you for a moment, Miss Hector. Everything alright?"

"Mmm," I agree. "Just thinking about how I'm going to kick your ass."

His smirk turns almost feral, his auburn brows rising until he looks like a big green devil. He says nothing, though.

The Keeper rejoins us and points at Morgan. "You talk a lot of shit, so go first. Let's see if you can back it up."

My sister scoffs and flips him the bird.

"Crush 'em, Mor!" I whoop as Thea takes up the snark, shouting for Morgan right along with me.

There's a slight flutter of breeze, and Miriam pops up in

large form. Fuchsia eyes flick from me to Alo and back again. "*Girls'* night, huh?"

I shrug and shout for Morgan, who smirks at the Keeper and turns to face the lane.

"Girls' night has turned into fuck-up-the-boys night. You down?"

Miriam snorts. "Hells yes, soulfriend. Much like Thea, I'm very competitive."

I groan. "That makes three of you, and little old me who will happily cheerlead for you."

Morgan examines the balls then turns around. "There's nothing magical about this, right? The balls don't turn into fucking birds and fly away or have an opinion about the lanes or some shit?"

"They're just balls, Morgan," the Keeper snaps. Shepherd coughs something lewd out under his breath. A red tinge crosses the Keeper's cheeks, and I resist the urge to comment on it. Just like Thea, I've seen a softer side under his brusque exterior. Morgan can't see it yet, but I hope she will eventually. Of course, he's got some groveling to do for her to even bother trying.

Two hours later, we've played four games and we're tied but just about to lose the fifth to the boys. Miriam's up, but when she hits a spare instead of a strike, the dudes cheer and clap each other on the back.

Morgan flops down next to me, the picture of irritation with her arms crossed and a big ole scowl on her face.

The Keeper dips his head at her. "Better luck next time."

She turns apoplectically red with rage but he strides off without another word.

"Jesus, that was fun," Thea laughs. She's sitting on Shepherd's big thigh, and he's already nuzzling the side of her neck. That's my first clue that girls' night is over. The second is when Morgan scowls after the Keeper and then stomps after him, presumably to rip him a new asshole.

"Do you need to follow her?" Ohken's deep voice breaks through my focus.

"Nah." Thea answers for me. "Shepherd and I will handle that. Why don't you two go get ice cream or hang out or just, you know, whatever."

I slap the side of her tit, hissing under my breath. "Could you be more obvious?"

"Ouch!" Thea complains loudly. "Yeah I could be more obvious. Hey, Ohken, since you didn't give it to Wren last night, how about you try ag—" I muffle Thea's ridiculousness with a hand over her mouth and shoot him an apologetic look.

Like always, he simply looks amused. I think he must always be smiling, or maybe it's just what I see when I look at him.

"Noted, Thea," he rumbles, his focus turning to me. "Nightcap, Wren?" He says nothing else.

Nodding, I turn to my dumb sister. "Get the hell out of here and don't let Morgan stab the Keeper, we need him."

Thea gives me a mock salute, then hops in Shepherd's arms. He squeezes my shoulder and gives me a quick peck on the cheek, then hauls Thea away from us. Alo trails after them with Miriam by his side.

I open my arms wide and smile at Ohken. "Well, your bridge or mine?"

CHAPTER NINE
OHKEN

It was a lovely surprise to see Wren at the bowling alley. I spent most of the day finalizing the stadium with the Keeper, so she and I never got a chance to get together for a lesson.

A quarter-hour after we leave the bowling alley, I've offered to take Wren to Miriam's Sweets, Scoops. and Higher Grounds, but she's not interested in dessert. I suspect there's some truth to what Thea mentioned at the bowling alley—Wren didn't get more than a taste of heat last night, but she wants to.

Good. I held back from taking what I wanted, and I've been deliciously on edge since. Even now, walking up Main with my hand on her lower back, I itch to slide it lower. She's wearing a tight pink shirt and jeans, but all the outfit does is enhance the swell and curve of her breasts, her stomach, her thighs. She's plump everywhere, and it's an incredible turn-on for me.

"You're not what I expected," Wren says when we turn the corner onto Sycamore and head for the bridge.

"In what way?" I'm curious what she thought a troll would be like.

Wren steps a little closer, which puts my hand at the top of her left ass cheek. I give it a squeeze, and she smiles. "Well, for one, I imagined trolls to be grouchy bridge guardians like human legends make them out to be."

That pulls a laugh from me. "I suppose some are, in the same way some humans are more introverted. But because trolls have builder magic, they nearly always live close to haven downtown areas. Most trolls don't care to live deep in the woods alone. It's not our way. In fact, most havens have troll clans that all live together in close proximity."

"Oh," Wren says, looking up at me. "But you're alone here. That doesn't bother you?"

"No." I smile and tuck my thumb through a loop on her jeans. "I'm happy in Ever, and I go home to visit my extended family a few times a year. That's enough for me. Trolls have a habit of making any other troll part of their family. So I've got about a million aunts and uncles who aren't related to me by blood. Then again, the trollish words for aunt and uncle are more about the sentiment of familial connection than anything."

We chat about builder magic the whole way to the bridge, and this time, she's less surprised when the doorway opens. She watches me press my hand to the cool stones, marveling at how they light up and sink to the side for us to step through.

"Can anyone open this door?"

"In the case of true emergency, yes. Otherwise, no."

"So you never have to worry about anyone surprising you by showing up at your place?"

I laugh as I guide Wren down the hall and into the cavernous living space. I hold her hand as she descends the stairs behind me. "Trolls don't just show up at other troll's bridges. We always comm first."

"God, that's nice. Being a triplet means your door is permanently open to two other people. Once, in college, I was hanging out with a guy and the door was locked. Thea needed something so she broke in through my window. No big deal."

"And the male?" I ask. I don't miss how my tone dips low and possessive. The idea of another male touching her stout thighs makes me see red.

Wren blushes and fiddles with her hair. "Oh, he hated that she came right in. He grumbled for about five minutes then left."

I grin at that. Good. I want to be the one to give her pleasure, and I don't want anyone else near her.

Grabbing two glasses, I set them on the countertop. She hops up just like last time she was here. Turning, I root around my aged-wood cupboards for a good wine to offer.

Wren crosses her legs and leans back on both palms. "We didn't do a lesson today, were you busy?"

I pour her a glass and hand it to her. When she takes it, I lean against the opposite counter. Sniffing at the wine, I enjoy its fragrant bouquet. I take a sip and watch her do the same.

"We're doing lessons, just not in the way you might think, Miss Hector."

She rolls her eyes playfully. "You're being obtuse."

"I like it that way," I admit. "You trying to pry information out of me. I don't have to give it, and I love that. You're learning, whether you think you are or not."

"Alright." She sighs, taking a sip of the wine. "I don't know how I'm supposed to ace this ambiguous lesson, but I suppose you're planning to tell me."

I set my cup down and cross the kitchen, taking hers from her hand.

"There's a conversation I'd like to have with you, Wren. We've been on a singular date, so now seems a good time."

The pink blush on her cheeks goes deep red, but she nods and spreads her thighs, inviting me between them.

I lean forward and slide my hands up her legs, squeezing as I go. So soft, so lovely. "Some of this is in the welcome guide, but in case you haven't seen it, I feel I should tell you a little more about how a troll pursues his partner."

I focus on the throb of her heartbeat, visible in the soft skin of her neck. I notice the way the pink blush has spread all the way down to the neckline of her sweater. Would she be pink all the way down her chest too? What does she smell like between those thick legs? I want to part them and taste her. My body goes tense when her heartbeat speeds up.

I glance down at her pretty legs, squeezing them before running my hands around to her luscious ass. It gets the same firm treatment as her thighs.

"Trolls don't form attachments quickly, not like gargoyles. We typically get to know someone over weeks or months before we express formal interest. But even once we do, it's not uncommon for trolls to go on many dates before deciding if they like each other or not. The Keeper tells me that's not common for humans."

"Not so much," Wren agrees. "Some people do start as friends first, but…"

"This isn't really like that," I correct. "We're not friends, necessarily, we just move very slowly."

"We've known each other for a few weeks," she murmurs. "How are you expecting to proceed?" She picks up her wine glass and takes a sip.

I can't help but stare when she swallows and her throat bobs.

"Well," I continue. "Once a troll decides he wants to pursue a female, things pick up a little faster. They'll usually begin a physical relationship, and that builds to a crescendo called a rut. Do humans have such a thing?"

Wren chokes on her wine, clapping herself on the chest as she sets it aside. "Nope, not really. I mean, I've read about that in omegaverse romance novels, but is it what it sounds like?"

I cross the small kitchen and grip her thighs, spreading them wide to position myself between them. "I don't know, Miss Hector. What do you think a rut sounds like?"

Green eyes lift to mine. They're full of so much heat and interest. Her pale pink tongue pokes out, wetting her plump lower lip.

"Lots of sex," she whispers.

"No," I correct, bringing my lips to brush against hers. "A troll's rut is a wild frenzy of sexual tension. It's days' worth of unhinged fucking." I pull back. "What do you think about that?"

She lifts her glass to her lips and takes another sip of wine. "Again, not what I expected from you…"

I laugh. "Trolls tend to get a bad rap, particularly bridge trolls. I'm told the outside world tends to think of trolls as hunched-over, wart-covered drunks with walking sticks. That's a rumor started by our orc cousins because trolls are generally far handsomer. That's why we have a very famous saying. The best for your hole is always a troll. A bit crass but we're not all poets."

Wren chokes on the wine, spitting it all over my shirt. The laugh that rings out after that has me joining her until we're both doubled over. She apologizes and wipes at the wine, but there's nothing to do about it.

"Stop." I laugh and swat her hand away. "I'll just take it off."

She falls silent, and the air between us heats. "Let me help." Her voice goes throaty and deep. I can just imagine what she'd sound like after hours of screaming in my bed. Of course, it'll be a while until we get to that, but I want it. I'm certain of it. Wren Hector will be mine.

I undo my vest and toss it aside.

Quivering fingers come to my shirt and undo the top button, then the next one. My chest hair pokes out, and I don't miss the way she nips at her lip when she sees it.

"Is it alright for me to undress you?" She looks worried halfway down the shirt.

"Don't hold back," I demand. "Just because I said trolls move slowly doesn't mean I don't want your hands all over me. I just meant we're slow starters."

Wren smiles and undoes the rest of my buttons before shoving the shirt off my shoulders. I'm big and broad, though, and she can't get it off without help. Reaching behind my back, I yank on the sleeves. Her eyes are locked onto my chest, her hands reaching up. At the last moment, she puts them back down on her thighs.

"Touch me," I command. "Don't hold back, Wren."

Her green gaze flicks upward, and her hands come up. She places them on my chest. I shudder under her soft touch. Delicate fingers trail along both my pecs, stroking over both nipples and down the rough cut of my abs. I'm not like some monsters. I'm big and muscular, but I'm not cut in the way gargoyles are.

"Incredible," she murmurs. "You're as gorgeous shirtless as I imagined."

It fills me with delight to know she's imagined me without clothes.

"Come with me," I demand, pulling her off the counter. I toss my stained shirt on the island behind her and lead her across the living area and down the hall toward my greenhouse.

"Let's go swimming," I suggest, pointing to the pool. "We can work on your magic for a few minutes."

"Ugh," Wren groans. "I was feeling so sexy but if we work on magic I'll ruin it."

"Listen." I turn to her with a stern look. "I'm going to reward you with a kiss, so let's try, alright?"

She gives me a prim look. "Maybe you shouldn't be withholding them at all, but giving them freely because they're totally unrelated to my shitty witch abilities."

Laughing, I reach for the hem of her shirt. "May I?"

She takes a moment, but nods. When I pull it over her head, I let out a groan. Underneath, she's wearing a burgundy lace bra. It accents how big and luscious her breasts are. I drop the sweater to the ground. Without really thinking about it, I cup both breasts in my hands and knead them gently.

Wren lets out a muttered curse but cants her neck to the side, her eyes closed. The movement presses her breasts to my chest. We're almost skin to skin for the first time, and I'm becoming desperate for it. I reach around behind her and unclip her bra. She goes tense in my arms, so I check in.

"Too much too quickly? Tell me to stop if so—"

"Don't you dare stop," she growls. "You've been teasing me for weeks and I'm about to combust."

A possessive snarl does leave me then. Yanking on the bra I toss it away, and then I see her breasts for the first time, naked and unveiled in perfect glory. Puffy red areolas surround swollen nipples. Her breasts hang large and heavy unsupported by the undergarments. I try and fail to resist the urge to suckle one of them. Dropping to both knees, I press my lips to one nipple and pull it between my teeth.

Wren jolts in my arms, her hands coming to the tops of my shoulders. In this position, I still have to dip my head to reach her, she's so much shorter than I am.

I suck for a long moment, relishing her sweet, smoky flavor. And then I lave my tongue flat over the raised, pebbled surface. I move my attention to her other nipple, sucking and biting to test what seems to feel good for her.

Wren's back bows, her body arched close to me.

Heat draws my sack up tight to my body, my cock a rigid length in my pants. Reaching down with one hand, I unzip my jeans and shove them down my thighs.

I ignore Wren's breasts just long enough to shove her pants over her thick thighs and down to the floor. Then she's in nothing but lingerie in front of me. And I'm in nothing but tight boxers that barely restrain me.

Green eyes drop to my crotch before coming back up. "Let me see." There's demand in her tone, and it causes the Dominant side of my nature to rear its head.

"After," I command. "Lesson first. You've had a few drinks, your guard is down. I'll tease you while we practice, it'll be fun."

Wren's pink lips curl into a dismayed sneer, but when I pull her toward the hot spring, she relents. I carved this one to have steps all the way around, so when I sink into the warm water, I know where to go. She follows gracefully in, her breasts bobbing in the water.

I pull her across the pool and turn her to face the wall of plants across from us. I press her up onto the first step on her knees and I take my place behind her. My hands come to her stomach, my lips to her ear.

"Grow my plants, sweet witch."

She shudders once in my arms, but I sense her determination. Wren's not the extroverted, loud energy of Thea. And she's not the seething, quiet fury of Morgan. She's sunlight in a dappled glade. She's the quiet growth of my favorite herb in a window box. She's perfect.

I reach up and pinch her nipple hard.

She squeals and reaches around to slap my side. "If that's supposed to help me concentrate, it's not working!"

"Grow them," I murmur again, rubbing my tusks gently along her shoulder. Tusk play is a troll favorite. I can't wait to rub them all over her luscious figure.

I fall silent while she concentrates. Across from us, the plants begin to shift and move. Her green magic strokes across my skin like a caress. "I feel your magic, Wren. It's as beautiful as you are."

She grits her teeth. Tendrils snake over the side of pots and begin to trail across the ground. I say nothing as she focuses, but her muscles start to quiver.

When I slide my hand down under the curve of her belly and toward her core, she yips. A moment later, several of the pots explode, sending shards of terra-cotta across the room. Wren yowls angrily and turns in my arms, green eyes glinting with fury.

"See! I fucking kne—"

I pinch her cheeks, forcing her lips into a pucker. Then I silence her with the slant of my lips over hers. She freezes, then relaxes into my arms. When she opens for me I delve deeper, a teasing swipe of the tongue. My first taste of her is perfect. Her lips are as smoky sweet as she smells, sultry heat flooding my senses. She's the crackle of a warm fire mixed with burning caramel. The barest hint of my own scent breaks through from where I touched her last night.

Groaning, I reach down to cradle the back of her head, my kiss growing hungrier, more demanding. Between us, my cock throbs in my boxers, pressing against her stomach. I ache with the need to pull her onto my length, to seat myself deep between her thighs. My usually impeccable control slips when she rolls her body against mine.

I let out a growl and run my other hand over the swell of her ass, gripping her tight as I press her to the pool's edge. She's soft everywhere, pliable and willing in my arms. Stroking the back of her neck, I focus on the silky smoothness of her lips and the pillowy press of her breasts against me. I'm balancing on the knife's edge of sanity. Everything about this woman feels made to tantalize me.

I want to fucking unleash on her.

Wren moans into the kiss and deepens it, her tongue sliding against mine until we're a frenzied clash of tusks and teeth and need. Her arms come around my neck, and I kiss her until we're breathless. When we part, the black of her pupil has eaten away the green of her iris. My little witch needs to be sated. I've teased her for weeks. Enough is enough.

I want her on her hands and knees in front of me while I feast, but I don't want her staring at the destroyed plants. Instead, I slide both hands up the backs of her legs and lift her onto the pool's edge.

"That was some kiss, Mister Stonesmith," she purrs. She reaches out to tuck a stray lock of my hair behind my ear.

I press her thighs open, pulling her slick undergarment to the side. Dark hair barely hides swollen pink folds. She's not so different from a troll female, but so much more enticing, because this is *Wren*. And I've wanted her since we met.

Grinning up at her from between her thighs, I slide my hands down her legs. Just a little tease.

"I plan to kiss you in other places tonight, Miss Hector."

Her pink lips pull into a sexy smile. Then she shifts backward onto her elbows and opens her legs wide.

"Be my guest, Ohken."

Chuckling with pleasure, I reach down to stroke along her swollen folds. She lets out a happy sigh, but when my fingers arrive at a tiny nub nestled at the top, her back arches. Ah, the magical clit Shepherd told me about. I rub and touch gently, watching as pink steals across her cheeks and chest. Her lips fall open, eyes closed the more I play with it.

I want her ecstasy, and I want her screams to ring off my

cave walls until they fill my head. And I need it to be my name falling from her lips like a prayer. The very idea of it has me dripping precum like a damn waterfall.

Leaning forward, I slick my tongue flat over her clit. Wren jerks, moaning my name. Under my hands, her thighs tremble and shake. I wonder how many times I can make her come with just my mouth?

I aim to find out.

Heat streaks between my shoulder blades and up my thighs, settling in my balls. They're full and heavy, almost painful with the need to unload deep into her womb.

I slowly explore every inch of her with my lips and teeth and tusks, sucking and nipping and licking. Gods, that's good. Every quiver of her thighs and belly sends a hurricane of possessive need building and building inside me.

"I need more, Ohken," she manages. "Stop fucking teasing me." A little growl must be meant to show me she's serious.

I laugh and rise from between her legs. Her answering scowl might be the most adorable expression she's ever directed at me. Gently, I slip my fingers up her inner thigh. Pressing my thumb to her clit, I slide my forefinger into her pussy. Even I can't help the moan of pleasure at feeling her wet heat tighten around me. Even here she's so soft, so hot.

I curl my finger and rub against a rough spot inside her channel.

"Is this what you need, Miss Hector?"

Wren rocks back and forth, fucking herself on my finger, too lost to even answer.

Thank gods for the historical society and their research books on humans. I've read quite a few of those leading up to this evening.

Soft cries grow more insistent, her beautiful breasts heaving in my cave's low light.

"Come for me," I whisper. Leaning forward, I lick a soft

circle around her clit. Wren detonates beneath me, sweet cream flooding my fingers and mouth. Her legs clamp tight around my head, one of her hands tangling in my hair to hold me in place. Her screams echo beautifully around us, bouncing off the walls and filling my mind with ideas for all the other ways I want to take her.

And just like that, I know I want to keep her for a really fucking long time. Forever, if I can.

～

The following day, Alo comms me early for help putting up tents on Main. They'll serve a variety of purposes during the skyball tournament. Not only will vendors sell their wares, but there'll be a first aid tent, a volunteer tent, and a few other things.

Alo shoves half a tent up while I press the other half, clicking it into place.

He grunts as he clicks his side, then tosses me the white tent cover before we put the tent all the way into position.

"Did the Keeper tell you that the Hearth reps are threatening to move the tournament because of the thrall attacks?"

I scoff. "As if they could do it this close to the game. It's simply a scare tactic."

"Agreed," Alo murmurs. "But still. Two attacks since the Hectors arrived. It's…a lot."

I glance under the tent at my friend. "You're not suggesting they should leave, I hope?"

He scoffs. "Gods, no. Shepherd would shrivel into a pebble if Thea left him. I just…the Keeper told me the Hearth has a three-strikes rule for Keepers. He's got two now. Imagine, for a minute, if they stripped him of his title and we had to deal with some other bozo."

"I just heard about that rule myself." I pull the white canvas over my side of the tent and clip it into place, watching Alo do the same on the other side. "I don't believe they'd strip him of his title. He's successfully defended Ever for almost forty years. They didn't blame him for Wesley."

"Wesley wasn't his fault," Alo agrees. "I want to support him the best we can so it's never an issue. We know Wesley's behind the prior attacks, so it might be better to go on the offensive, ya know?"

He's not wrong, but the Hearth has its own branch of hunters who track down wayward monsters. They're supposed to be doing that, not us. Our job is simply to keep our haven safe from the outside world.

We fall silent, both lost in thought. When Miriam and Thea walk up the street to set up Miriam's tent, my thoughts head straight into the gutter. Which is where they've been since I got my first taste of Wren last night. I teased her for an hour before she finally yawned. Then I walked her home and licked her pussy again on the front porch of the Annabelle, off in the corner where nobody could see. Now that I've tasted her, that needful fury is starting to build between my thighs.

It's fucking delicious.

I want to take things further with her, but preparations have to be made.

Alo grunts as the tent in front of us collapses and folds in on itself.

"You're distracted, Ohken. What gives?" When I scowl and lift the tent back up, he groans. "Gods, you too? First Shepherd and now you. Boys' night is going to get slimmer and slimmer. Whatever happened to pals before gals?"

Laughing, I click the next tent support into place. "There's no reason we can't have both." I glance under the tent to shoot him a pointed look.

"Don't start," he snaps. Miriam walks by us, carrying a

stack of boxes for her tent. She glances over at Alo and smiles, but it falls when he doesn't return it.

His gaze goes angsty and irritated as she leaves us. I'd say something, but everybody else in town is already telling him to make a move. He doesn't need me to reiterate it. So my thoughts turn to Wren again. There's a huge troll holiday next week, the night before the final skyball tournament. I want Wren to come as my date, and I want to ask her tonight after we practice.

CHAPTER TEN
WREN

I hum while I dress in my room. I've got a lesson slash date tonight with Ohken and I'm buzzing after last night. To say that man is a genius with his tongue is understating it. His tongue was so big and thick and he learned crazy fast what I like. I'm starting to understand a little better how Thea said she could never go back to a human man after experiencing Shepherd.

Almost as if my thoughts conjured her, Thea lets herself into my room with a box in her hands. She offers it to me with a wink. I take it with a laugh. I can already smell my favorite double chocolate chip cookies.

"You've got to hand it to him," she chirps. "He is fairly obsessed with taking care of you two. And me, of course." She shrugs good-naturedly and flops down on the bed. "So," she draws the 'o' out long. "How'd it go with Ohken last night?"

A door slams and Morgan jogs in, sweaty with her hair up in a bun. She must have been working out.

"Are we dishing about Ohken? Do tell!" She flops in my window seat but leaps right up. A small piece of wood pokes up from the cushion. "Damnit, third time today!" She raises both arms up in the air. "I get it! You want me out! But there's literally nowhere for me to go right this minute, and especially not this week with skyball. Can we agree to give it a rest until the tournament is over?"

The window sash shrugs up and down a few times.

I cast Morgan a deadpan look. "I do believe Annabelle is telling you to fuck off."

"Ugh." She crosses the room and examines the edge of my bed before gingerly sitting down next to Thea. Thea hands her a second box of cookies, her expression sympathetic.

I cross to my nightstand and grab the sheet of paper I was looking at earlier, waving it at my sisters. "This is the human's guide to troll mating rituals." I hand them the page. "Ohken's told me most of this already, but I guess it's essentially the opposite of gargoyles."

Thea sighs, putting her chin in her hands. "I guess I won't expect daily snack boxes from daddy Ohken then, huh?"

"Looks like not," Morgan intones, her dark eyes raising from the paper. "A rut? For real?'

"Yeah." I nod. "He explained that to me too. I guess the tension builds over a few dates until he's feral, more or less."

Morgan gives me an incredulous look. "Imagine a dude that big going feral. What would that even look like?" She snorts. "Are you gonna survive that?"

I run a comb through my hair as I consider her question. "To be honest, I've seen the outline of what he's packing, and I don't know if it'll fit."

Morgan shoves a cookie in her mouth but still manages to get out a question. "What are we talkin'? Baby arm?"

I nod. "We're talkin' several stacked soda cans. I mean freaking enormous. Which tracks, really. He's got to be almost eight feet tall, because I'm almost six and he towers over me."

Morgan chokes on her cookie. "My God, Wren. What if

you're like, the first person ever who just can't ride the monster because his dick is too big."

I sigh. "I'll die of sadness, then, because he gives head like nobody's business."

Morgan chokes anew, but Thea just grins. "I get it, girl. I am team monsters over men, for sure."

Morgan groans. "Some monsters. Not all monsters are created equal."

Thea leans back. "Speaking of unsatisfactory monsters, Shepherd told me that the Keeper usually plays skyball because he's a kickass athlete. He's not playing this time because he's focused on security, but apparently it's a huge deal."

"And?" Morgan's tone goes tight.

Thea shrugs. "Just saying. The two of you have a lot in common."

Mor rolls her eyes. "Not enough to make a difference. Plus he's betrothed, remember Moira the harpy?"

Thea lets out an unhappy noise. "How could I forget Moira the bird lady? Do you think their betrothal is for real, or what? I mean, why would he announce to everyone that you're his mate? There's more to that story."

"I'm sure there is," Morgan says, "but I don't know because he hasn't bothered to take two seconds to enlighten me."

My sisters fall silent, and I can't think of anything to say either. I'm not the one to give anybody false hope, and I truly don't know what'll happen with Mor and the Keeper. So far, it's been a whole lot of nothin'.

She stays quiet, and Thea and I take the hint—she doesn't want to talk about him.

We switch topics and chat about everything and nothing while I finish getting ready. An hour later, I'm dressed and headed to Ohken's bridge for a lesson. To my surprise, when I arrive, he's standing in the walkway. Russet eyes flash as he takes in my outfit, then leans down for a tender kiss.

"We're going somewhere else for our lesson. You up for an adventure?"

"I'm always up for an adventure." I laugh. "Unless this is like the adventure the Keeper took Thea on where he dragged her outside the wards and thralls attacked. I'm not up for that sort of shenanigans."

Ohken gives me a concerned look. "I will never put you at risk like that, and the Keeper shouldn't have done it, either. If I was Shepherd, I'd have ripped his head off."

"Oh, I think he wanted to," I agree. "But Thea wouldn't let him."

Ohken strokes a stray wave of hair back over my shoulder, sending fireworks sparkling across my skin.

"You're in no danger of that sort of nonsense from me, Miss Hector." There's a serious tone to his voice despite the sparkle in his eyes.

"Noted, Mister Stonesmith." I reach for his hand. "In that case, I still hate surprises, so where are we going?"

He grips my fingers and pulls me out from under the bridge to walk along the wooded pathway.

"Deep into the woods where nobody will see you," he murmurs. "You're definitely in danger of getting teased by a big troll out there, but that's about it."

I hold his hand a little tighter and grin. Teased by a troll has a nice ring to it, if I'm being honest.

Half an hour later, we've walked way far into the woods to a clearing of pine trees. Their soft needles cover the ground. In front of us there's a huge boulder, rising so high I can barely see the top of it. It's covered in flowery vines. Even from twenty feet away, I can smell their scent. They remind me of moonflowers, which the pixies use to create the dust that powers the wards. They're the wrong color, though. Moonflowers are white, and these are a pale peach.

Ohken jerks his head toward the vine-covered boulder. "Sunrise flowers are a distant cousin of moonflowers, although they can't be used for the same purposes. They're important to trolls, though. Sunrise flowers are often a main ingredient in troll mead. I use this particular garden for my own stores. I want you to grow them, but know this—if you raze this whole boulder full to the ground, they'll be back in a day." He shrugs. "They're basically a weed, you can't kill them permanently."

I blow out a breath. "Okay, so you're telling me there's zero pressure."

He smirks. "Zero, unless you'd like another kiss, and then I suppose there's the pressure of performing to a certain degree to—"

I silence him by swatting his big chest hard. He doesn't move at all, but he does laugh and catch my hand, bringing it up to his lips, which pulls me up onto my tiptoes.

He rubs one tusk and then the other across the back of my hand, his russet lashes fluttering against the pale green skin of his cheeks. When his eyes open again, he presses a gentle kiss to the back of my hand. Chestnut eyes are focused on mine.

"There's an event the night before the skyball tournament happens. It's an annual troll celebration. It'll be huge this year because the tournament is at the same time. I'd love for you to come as my date."

My breath hitches. "Are you sure? Is this the troll equivalent of meeting the parents? It's not too fast?"

He licks at the tips of my fingers before sucking one into his mouth for a moment. He lets the tip go. "Remember what I told you, Wren? Once we get going, things happen more quickly? Well, I'm going, my sweet. I'm halfway to a rut and I'm not sad about it."

"What does a rut really mean?" I thought about this on the way over. "Would we be mated? Or is it just lots of fuckery?"

Ohken's devilish expression falls into something more neutral, his eyes hooded. "Troll ruts often end that way. But I recognize humans might be different. If we enjoy ourselves but decide to part ways, I'd struggle to accept that. I want to keep you, Wren."

His big green tongue swirls around my fingertips. I gasp and press closer to him. But then, true to goddamn form, he drops my hand, steps back and crosses both beefy arms.

"Grow my garden, sweet witch."

Goddamn his teasing and insinuations. I'm already sweating with anticipation.

I straighten up and crook my neck. I can do this. I've been practicing with Catherine's aragonite crystal, and I swear the earrings really have helped. I've been able to focus on her rose garden a little bit without blowing anything up.

Turning to the boulder, I focus on sensing the flowers themselves. I do that easily and move on to the vines and the roots. I'm surprised when I realize the roots trail under the ground for nearly a hundred yards in every direction—a weed indeed. The naturalist in me wonders what other purpose they serve to the surrounding forest, or if they have one.

A warm body presses to my back, an enormous hand coming around to my stomach. Ohken pulls me hard to his body. "Grow them, Miss Hector," he growls into my ear.

"Stop being bossy," I snark.

Rough lips come to my neck and nip hard. "You have no idea how bossy I can be." His voice is broken gravel. He grabs my right hand and pulls it between us, planting it on his hard cock and wrapping my fingers around it.

We're pressed so tightly together, I can't stroke or move, but I'm overwhelmed by the feel of him.

"Focus," he rumbles, stroking my hand slowly up his length.

"You're fucking huge," I snap.

There's a knowing laugh, and Ohken's lips come to my shoulder. He rubs his tusks along my skin, something I wouldn't have thought was so hot, but it's clearly a display of desire.

My chest heaves, my body tightening with tension. I fight to center my focus on the sunrise flowers. Power bristles under my skin, anxious to get out. One of the flowers explodes with a pop, but the one next to it quivers before expanding to double its size. I expel the breath I was holding and try to turn toward Ohken, but he spins me back around.

"I said grow my garden, Wren, not a flower. Do it quickly, witch. I'm losing my sanity behind you like this. Here's a fact the Ever mating guide on trolls won't have told you—you on all fours in front of me is going to be my favorite position." The growl he emits in my ear has me nearly crying with need.

My arms shake as I lift them toward the giant boulder. Everything in front of me goes blurry, until I can only see one flower, glowing in my mind's eye. I push my power to it and watch it grow. Sound blots out, dark stars dance behind my eyes. I grit my teeth so hard my jaw hurts.

The sunrise flower in my mind bursts and expands into a dozen of the same size. Ohken thrums his fingers along my stomach. "Well done, Miss Hector. Absolutely stunning. Do you see what you've done?"

What?

I hadn't realized I shut my eyes. Blinking them open, I'm shocked as shit to see the entire boulder is now covered in dinner-plate-sized blooms. Their color is even more vibrant than before, starting as a deep red inside the flower and fading to orange and peach along the elegant, square-shaped petals.

Ohken strides to the boulder and strokes one of the flowers. When he turns to me with a grin and a slow clap, I can't help but preen.

"Absolutely magnificent," he murmurs.

I cross my arms and shoot him a sassy look. "Me or the flowers."

His proud smile drops, his expression more heated. "Both. Most especially you, but the flowers are lovely in their own right." He crooks two fingers at me, his gaze fierce. "Come here."

My body moves before my mind can even react to his command. I've never been dominated by a man the way Ohken does. But it's not overbearing or off-putting. He looks at me like I'm the pot of gold at the end of his personal rainbow. I'm getting really fucking used to that.

The moment I'm within arm's reach, he snatches me by the waist. Before I even register his movements, he's hauled me up into his arms and guided my legs around his broad stomach.

"Better," he growls. "Everything is better with you in my arms."

He holds me easily, like I weigh nothing. I'm not used to that. I'm always the triplet people love to call "curvy", but I like to call it what it is—I'm fat and proud. I've always had rolls and thicker thighs. I've always had soft arms. I'm strong and healthy, but I'll never be athletic-looking like Morgan or a stick like Thea. It's not me and I don't even care.

But something about the way Ohken holds me so easily still makes me feel special. He doesn't care about human body standard bullshit any more than I do.

I press my lips to his, taking what I want. With a rumbly groan, he attacks them, swiping his tongue inside my mouth to taste me. I moan and clench his neck tighter, running my hands up into his glorious hair. It's rough to the touch, coarse and rugged just like everything else about him.

"I need to see you," I pant the moment we part. "All of you, please."

"Deal," he agrees, setting me carefully down. His hands move to his shirt, releasing the buttons before he shrugs it over his enormous shoulders. Just like before, I'm fucking entranced by the sight of his muscular body. He's a beefcake in every sense of the word. Every ounce of him denotes incredible power, but he's not cut in the way Shepherd and Alo are. I can see eight abs, but they're not outlined perfectly. I love it.

I undo his jeans and carefully unzip them, helping him to shimmy out of them. I haven't seen him fully naked yet, but I need to examine every inch of this man. Now that we've kissed and…other things, I need it all. I'm hooked.

When I reach for his boxers, he laughs. "Wait a moment, Wren."

I look up into those gorgeous eyes. I realize now they're not just rusty brown, they're flecked with caramel and gold and dark ochre. They're every gorgeous shade of gold and brown. They're striking like everything about him.

He hesitates, his beautiful gaze focused on me. Like always, one side of his dark lips is tipped into a half smile. "I'm big, Wren."

I snort and reach for him again. "Complained no woman ever."

He laughs but allows me to grab the waistband of his boxers.

"I'm serious," he mutters, frowning. "Don't run for the hills, please."

I'm far too busy staring at the chunky vee guiding me to heaven, but when I pull his boxers down, I am not ready.

Because the thing that falls out of them is enormous. I knew it was; I saw it outlined in his pants. I was still unprepared.

It stands proudly between us, as big as a damn baseball bat.

I blow out a breath and flick my gaze up to his. "Okay I'm not running, but good lord."

He glances back down with a frown. He's hard, and without the confines of the boxers holding him up, his cock juts toward me. Green precum drips steadily from the tip, so steadily that if he were a human man I'd assume he was coming right now. The whole thing is a darker green than his torso, the head swollen and flushed, almost the color of the pine needles that surround us. But it's not just a regular dick. Oh no. Layers of ruffled skin surround the bulbous head, forming a line on the underside.

Oh my God he's got a petticoat. A dick petticoat.

When I reach out to touch it, it bobs up into my waiting fingers, coating them with stickiness. I rub his head, stroking my way along the ruffles and down to his slit. My hand is covered in slick precum.

Ohken reaches for my hair, pulling it gently through his fingers.

"Taste it, witch."

His command sends a wave of heat through me, obliterating my humorous thoughts. I bring my fingers to my lips and suck. Sweetness bursts across my tastebuds. Jesus, it's like licking a giant green cinnamon roll. I thought I'd died and gone to heaven with this man, but it gets better and better.

I gaze back down at his cock. When I touch the frilled skin around his cockhead it flutters against my fingertips.

"Wren." Ohken sounds ready to snap like a taut bow string. "Look at me."

I can barely take my eyes off his dick, though. It's as big as my fucking arm, no lie. I rip my gaze up to his. "There's no way in hell this thing is fitting inside me. You know that, right?"

"Of course," he agrees. "That's to be expected."

Disappointment settles hard and painfully in my gut. Expected? No, I didn't expect a future where this perfect man wouldn't be able to fuck me. What about the rut? What about—

"I have a plan," Ohken growls. "There are ways around this. Every troll who ever mated a nontroll had this to deal with. We aren't the first."

"That's not enough of an explanation for me to be relieved," I admit. "How could I ever satisfy you during a rut if we can't even—"

"We will." His voice is confident and reassuring, even if I still have my doubts. "All nontroll pairs take a one-time potion. I'll brew it and then we'll both take it for a few days. But after that, we'll fit."

I raise my brows. "Without splitting in half?"

"Mhm." He grins. "It'll even feel good. I want that with you, Wren. Do you?"

At every turn this man surprises me. He's utterly confident, always in charge, incredibly thoughtful. He checks in with me about everything.

I point to the boulder behind him. "Sit down against that. I'm going to show you how much I want it."

Auburn eyes flash, but he backs up until his back hits the boulder, then slides down it. I nearly come in my panties at how good it looks when he steps his thighs out so I can get a good look at what he's packing.

His balls are as big as swollen oranges under the shaft itself. His length pokes out of a thick patch of dark green pubic hair. I don't think I've ever seen anything this masculine in my life. He never pulls his eyes from mine, not even when one big hand reaches down to stroke the monster between his thighs. Green precum drips in a stream from the tip, traveling down the length and coating his fingers.

I shrug my shirt over my head and unclip my bra. I unbutton my jeans but don't take them off. Two can play his teasing game, and I'm wearing sexy-as-fuck lingerie.

Ohken growls, an animalistic noise that lifts the hair on my nape.

I smirk at him. "Do you like to play chase, Ohken?"

His lips curl around his tusks. "I adore that game, Miss Hector."

"Good." I drop to my knees between his thighs, placing a hand on each one. "I'd like you to chase me sometime."

He groans, his head falling back against the boulder. His throat bobs, and I can't resist myself. Shifting forward, I tilt my head to the side and bite him hard. He jerks against the stone, a heavy whine falling from his lips.

"Do you ever let yourself go wild, Ohken?" I tease my lips down his neck until I reach his shoulder, and I bite that too. "Could I push you far enough to see you out of your mind with lust?"

"Careful, woman," he snaps, bringing his triumphant gaze back to me. "You don't want me in a rut in the middle of skyball or we'll miss the entire tournament."

Winking, I shift backward but lean down, swiping my tongue up the underneath of his cockhead. I swirl it around the tip, that silky sweetness coating my tongue.

"Gods, fuckkk," Ohken bellows. "Your tongue, Wren."

I lift my head long enough to wink. "We're past 'Miss Hector' are we?"

His brows form a vee, his eyes squinting shut when I suck on the huge tip. I can't wrap my whole mouth around his dick, not with the size of it, but I try to make up for that by licking and nibbling and sucking every inch I can reach.

Ohken's hips rock up to meet me, one hand coming to the

back of my hair. "I can't wait for you to be able to take me all the way, my witch. I want to watch you swallow down every drop of me."

"Will your magical potion help me do this too?" I'm teasing and horny, but I'm curious. How the hell is that gonna work?

He growls. "It will. The magic makes it so my size and shape are ideal for your body—the perfect fit. For you, it'll allow your inner muscles to be more pliable and flex to meet my size. It'll work with your throat too, making those muscles more flexible. You won't have a gag reflex Wren. And your ass, gods, it'll take me too."

"Sounds like I'm doing a lot of changing, Mister Stonesmith."

He grins, but it's slow and devious. "We both will, Miss Hector. Until our fit couldn't possibly be any more perfect. And then when I take you for the first time, it'll be pure bliss."

I'm ready to cream my panties from how sexy this all is. Surging forward, I press my tongue into his slit, gathering up that deliciousness before lapping at him.

"You taste so fucking good." I'm ready to slide a hand between my thighs. Actually, come to think of it, sixty-nine would work really well for us.

A growl pulls me out of my thoughts. Ohken gives me a triumphant look. "Now you know why you like the troll whip so much."

Time stops, and all I hear is my heartbeat pounding in my ears.

I shoot straight upright.

"Wait, what?"

CHAPTER ELEVEN
OHKEN

Wren's gorgeous eyes have widened in shock. Shit. I assumed someone would have told her about the troll whip by now—it's common knowledge in the monster community—but it seems that's a poor assumption.

She rocks back on her heels, eyes narrowing.

I struggle to keep my eyes from dropping to her magnificently swaying breasts.

Her chest rises and falls with rapid, shallow breaths. "The what now? What did you mean about the troll whip?"

I want to pull her to me, to stroke her hair and take her obvious worry away. But I sense if I reach for her now, she'll pull away. I shift forward, propping my elbow on my left leg. I focus on her face so she can see the truth of what I'm saying.

"The main ingredient in troll whip is troll cum. I thought you knew, Wren. I'm the only troll in Ever, so..." My voice trails off. It's clear this isn't a human custom, because her eyes go even wider. Possessive fire burns in them. Normally I'd relish it, but right now she's upset. Knowing that makes me feel fucking awful. I want nothing more than to tuck her to my chest and make this better.

She scoffs and crosses her arms. "You're telling me you provide cum to Higher Grounds and they turn it into troll whip, *the* troll whip that everybody in town is absolutely nuts for?" Her voice rises in shrillness. "The troll whip I get every goddamn day on my latte?"

I nod slowly, watching her go from shocked to almost crestfallen.

The desperate need to make her understand consumes me. "Troll cum has a variety of healing properties. Because of that, it's used as currency in many havens. This practice isn't abnormal for monsters, although I'm guessing it is for humans? You seem surprised, Wren."

Her nose scrunches up and she rolls back far enough to push to a stand. She looks down at me. "You could say that."

"Don't shut down on me, Wren. Talk to me, sweetheart."

She turns and reaches for her sweater, pulling it over her head. I groan when the soft fabric hides her lush body from my hungry gaze.

I stand and take a step toward her. "Wren, talk to me."

It's easy to see she's about to hike it back to downtown. That's the last thing I want. This is obviously a big deal to her. I want to understand why so I can fix it and return the happy smile to her face.

She buttons her jeans and begins to walk away.

I let the boom enter my voice. "Wren Hector, do not walk away from me. Talk. To. Me." I stand my ground as my full command hits her.

Her shoulders jolt up and she screeches to a halt. She whips around with a ferocious look on her face, pointing one finger at me.

Throwing both my hands up, I implore her. "I'm missing

something here, Wren," I continue in a more contrite tone. "Please help me understand."

She glowers at me, and she's stunning in her fury. "No, it's not a common practice for human males. No, women don't swizzle dudes' jizz into whipped cream and no, goddamnit, I hate everything about this!" Her foot taps on the ground and she crosses her arms, then uncrosses them and plants both hands on her hips.

"Wren," I encourage her. "I'm so sorry. Truly, I thought you knew. We've made so many jokes about the color..." My voice trails off as her head jerks back up. She still looks ferociously pissed. "This is obviously an unpleasant shock. Tell me how I can make this better." I take a step toward her, but she wraps her arms around her body protectively.

Closing the distance between us, I put a finger under her chin and guide her gaze to mine. "Tell me what part about this makes you so upset, sweet witch. Help me understand how I can fix this."

The anger drains from her face, but in its place she looks heartbroken, her dark eyes filling with tears.

"Wren," I murmur. "I can't change what happened in the past, but I can stop providing it to Higher Grounds. Would that help?" With my free hand, I tuck her beautiful chocolate waves behind her ear, stroking her neck.

She scoffs. "You said it has healing properties. Is that why people drink it? I mean...I just thought it was like whipped cream." She slaps one hand over her face. "It is whipped cream, it's just not the cream I thought. God, I don't know whether to be grossed out or pissed or what. But no, you can't stop providing it if people are expecting it. They'll blame me."

Ah. I press my body to hers, not letting her rip her gaze from mine. "You are my priority, Wren. The decisions I make have you at the center. I'm sorry that I assumed you knew. I wouldn't have been so flippant about it."

She slumps into me, pressing her forehead to my chest.

I stroke my way down her spine, holding her against me. "Do you want to talk through this now? Or would you rather have some time to think about it? We can discuss it later if you need a minute." I wrap her hair around my fist and guide her head back so I can look right in those glittering emerald eyes. "Just promise me we will talk about this, Wren. Don't let it fester. This is a cultural difference between us, and we should explore how to handle it together."

"I know," she grumbles, "but I'm kinda mad about it. My sisters have been drinking it, Ohken. They're gonna freak out when they learn what it is." She puts both hands over her eyes and rubs at them as if she can scrub the last five minutes from her brain. When she drops her hands, I sense she's come to a determination. "I need to process for a little bit. Can we talk about this later? I'm sure I'll have questions, but right now I'm running on pure adrenaline."

"Of course." I tug gently at her long hair. "May I distract you, sweet witch?"

She glances up, a resigned look on her face. "What did you have in mind, Mister Stonesmith?" The words are playful but her tone isn't. She's slipped a mask over her emotions.

I lean down and kiss my way up the side of her neck. "I was thinking I'd bury my tongue between your gorgeous thighs and eat until you've come a few times. Then I'd like to take you home, feed you, and finish this conversation."

"I'm mad."

"Would you prefer to be alone?"

She hesitates. "No."

I take a step back. "Then take your anger out on me, Wren."

One chocolate brow travels upward. "I don't want to accidentally hurt you."

I scoff. "I'm not in the least bit worried about that."

Her eyes grow hooded as she stalks closer to me. Before I know it, vines rip off the boulder behind me and wrap around my arms and legs, dragging me back against the cool surface.

I bellow as I struggle against them, marveling at the warm sensation of her green power snaking across my skin. "Your power," I choke out. "Gods, Wren." My eyes roll back in my head as the vines tighten around my core. Phantom hands move down my stomach, touching and stroking until they get to my dick, running the length of my cock and teasing my balls.

"Your control is exemplary, Miss Hector," I purr, groaning around the ghostly sensation.

She stands in front of me looking gleeful. Ah, my witch likes a little bit of control. I can work with that, especially if it gives her time to process the conversation we need to finish.

"Would you like to explode today?" Her voice is sing-song sweet as she trails her fingers down my stomach. She's teasing me.

"Yes," I admit. "With you, all over you, inside of you. Yes, Wren."

Normally I'd find it unnatural to be dominated by a partner. That's never been my preference. But watching Wren so casually wield her immense power turns me on more than anything she's done yet.

I growl as I stare at her, wanting to rip out of the vines and fuck her into the ground.

Her power rakes claws down my skin, pulling a yowl from my chest. I push against the boulder, my lip curling from the pleasure. "You're so fucking strong. Now let me out of here so I can tease you against the side of this rock. I need to taste you."

"Oh this is far too much fun," she says with a laugh. "Think you can get out of there without help?"

Magic snakes behind my sack, trailing a warm path to my

ass. It nudges my thighs wider apart, and I laugh. "Do you want me to attempt an escape, Miss Hector? And if so, what do you expect me to do once I'm free?"

She falters for a moment, eyelashes fluttering. "Try to get out, Mister Stonesmith. If you're able to, you may have me."

Gods, that's hot. My need for dominance screams under my skin, battering against my bones and demanding her submission. I shove that instinct further down, because dominating her during a disagreement is the opposite of what I should be doing.

I press forward, jerking my arms, but the vines wrap tighter.

Wren grins and crosses her arms, and her magic dips inside my ass the slightest bit. It's just a tease, but I've never had a partner put something there. Groaning, I sink against the rock and let her magic taunt me. It's not enough to get me off, although I'm still hard and dripping everywhere.

Her eyes flash down to my bobbing cock, to the precum that leaks from me like a faucet. Is she thinking about how it could be on top of a coffee right now?

"Wren." I growl. "This is all yours, sweetheart. Every fucking drop."

She wraps her arms around herself and looks up at me, eyes pleading for something. "Make me forget for a little while? I know we need to talk about it, I just—"

With a choked roar, I strain against the vines, pulling until they snap under the force of my heavy weight. I shake them off and stalk to my woman, pulling her up into my arms. Dropping to my knees, I lay her on the ground and draw her jeans down her thighs.

I toss them aside and haul her ass up to my chest, hooking her legs over my shoulders. And then I slick my tongue up her soaked core, groaning as her sultry, smoky flavor bursts on my tongue.

She cries out, and a fresh wave of cream coats my lips. I focus my attention on her clit, bringing one hand up her ass crack so I can slide a finger into her pussy. She clenches around me and wails.

"Ohken!" she shouts. "God, yes! That's it!" Her praise morphs into a shriek as her thighs clamp around my head. Honey floods my face as I shake my head from side to side, lapping every last drop. I groan at the sweet, musky flavor that coats my lips and chin.

"So good," I gasp out, thrusting my tongue into her channel as it pulses.

She shouts my name, her hands coming to my hair. She grips it hard, and that pain has me throbbing and leaking like a faucet.

I lick and suck at her until she's too sensitive, and then I lay her gently on the ground.

Wren groans. "You're too damn good at that. I think I just came in ten seconds flat."

Leaning forward, I stroke the backs of my fingers up her thigh to her stomach, marveling at her beauty. "Sex can be a good way to work out emotion, sweet witch. I still sense your worry, Wren. Need me to make it better another time or two? Or are you ready for dinner?"

"Dinner," she mutters, scoffing under her breath. "You're definitely cooking." She shoots me a grumpy look.

I pull her to a stand. Pine needles are stuck in her hair and there's a smudge of dirt on one cheek. Reaching out, I brush it away, trailing my thumb over her lower lip.

"I'm sorry I joked about the troll whip. Let's go home and we'll talk about it over dinner. Unless you need more time to process, in which case we'll talk when you're ready."

She mumbles something, but leans forward and plants a tender kiss on my pec.

I stroke her hair. "You've never looked more beautiful to

me than right now, like this in the forest. I'm crazy about you, Wren. You make me feel good, and all I want is to do the same for you." I pause and scan her face before tacking on the last bit. "And of course I'm cooking. I love filling your belly."

She nips at her lower lip, considering what I've said. Finally, she reaches for my hand. "Let's get your clothes and go home. I need more details, like, all the details. Okay?"

Grinning, I stalk back to my clothes, and dress.

Details are good.

Details I can do.

CHAPTER TWELVE
WREN

I shove a cheeseburger in my face, sitting in a booth across from Morgan at the Galloping Green Bean. It's busy today. Monsters began arriving from other havens early this morning, and it's fascinating. I didn't realize that Ever doesn't have every species of monster, but it makes sense. This morning I saw a gryphon, a snake-man Thea said is called a naga, and a herd of something I can only liken to giant rats wearing three-piece suits.

Morgan sucks at her soda, then sets it down. "Tell me again how the jizz gets turned into troll whip. Not gonna lie, I've had the troll whip like a hundred times and now I'm sort of grossed out."

I make a horrible face. Ohken and I talked through the troll whip issue for a solid hour last night. He answered every question, and despite my worry about it, when I went to Higher Grounds this morning, only I could get it. Alessandro, the owner, told me it was no longer available for anyone else.

Guilt sits like a ball in the pit of my stomach. I sigh as I chew on the burger. Morgan's nose is scrunched up as she swirls her mint chocolate chip milkshake. I swear it's the same damn color as—

Morgan's face pales. "You don't think…surely it's not green because…"

"No." I shake my head. "Ohken was clear—it's just the coffee shop that uses it. His jizz has some kind of healing properties. I mean, what am I supposed to do with that information? If he's healing people, then I shouldn't deny it to them, right? Even if it's weird for us?"

"I dunno." Morgan shakes her head, raking long fingers through her auburn ponytail before twisting the end around her pointer finger.

I set my burger down and give her a serious look. "And…I touched his dick with my magic."

Morgan's face goes incredulous. "You what?!"

"Yeah." I nod in agreement, pursing my lips together before blowing a breath out. I didn't mean to, it just sort of happened. "I tickled his balls with my magic and he almost came all over the damn—"

"That does sound like an interesting use of green magic."

Morgan and I both whip around at the intrusive voice. The Keeper stands next to our booth, long arms crossed over his broad chest. Like always, he's wearing black jeans and a black turtleneck. In the vibrant lights of the Green Bean, the scar that slices down his face is even more obvious.

"Err," I sputter. "How much of that did you hear?"

He waves his hand for Morgan to slide over, and to my surprise, she does. He drops gracefully onto the pleather bench seat next to her, but crosses his legs in the opposite direction.

Oof.

He gives her a stiff smile, then glances at me.

"Ohken told me you were making incredible progress with

your power. He said you made the sunrise blossoms as big as dinner plates. Is that right?"

Morgan crosses her arms and glares at him, shoving herself right up against the window. "What's it to you? And why does it sound like you want something?"

The Keeper rolls his eyes at her and gestures to me with an open palm.

"Of course I want something. Wren is a green witch. We've got a garden under duress and thousands of visitors arriving in Ever as we speak." He turns back to me. "Wren, this is a week where Ever will shine in front of not only our fellow Evertons, but monsters from every other haven. Not to mention representatives from the Hearth always attend as well."

Exhaustion settles in my bones. I can almost feel what he's going to say next.

Dark ruby eyes narrow on me as he shifts back in the booth.

"I'd like you to try fixing the moonflower vines again. We're behind on pixie dust production, and without pixie dust—"

"You can't power the wards that protect this place. We know," Morgan grouses. "I don't know what the hell you did before we Hectors came along, if all of a sudden you need us to keep the lights on around here. Jesus."

The Keeper grins, but it's not friendly. If anything, he looks like a spider about to rip the head off a fly.

I'm certain he's about to remind her that it's Thea's white magic that ripped a hole in the wards when we arrived. Of course, she was able to fix it. But still.

He looks away from my triplet and back at me. "It's not a well-known fact, but I understand I'm asking you to do something that's uncomfortable. The Hearth has a three-strikes rule for Keepers. If three major incidents happen on a Keeper's watch, he's immediately dismissed from duty and can no longer serve his community. I've had two strikes since you arrived. I'm doing my level best to keep Ever safe for all my residents, including the both of you." He gives me the first earnest, open look I've seen from him. "I want you to thrive here, Wren. Please, help me?"

"Well Jesus," I snap. "How can I say no after that impassioned speech?"

"Good," the Keeper purrs, rising to a stand. He never looks back at Morgan.

I cross my arms, so now we're all standing here looking like middle-aged dads at a barbecue.

"You'll check if Kiril's okay with it, right? Because he wasn't too pleased when I blew up his gourd."

The Keeper nods. "Absolutely. If he says no, I'll tell you straight away."

"I won't hold my breath." I'm grumbling, but my appetite has gone. What a waste of a damn cheeseburger.

He leaves without saying another word.

When I finally manage to look up at Morgan, her red lips are pursed together. "You've got this, bitch. You said you did amazing things with Ohken in the forest. Let's do that again in the garden. I'll go with you, okay?"

I nod.

Fuck.

~

Half an hour later, Miriam, Morgan and I stand in front of the destroyed wall of pale moonflowers in the garden.

Miriam stares at the wall with a frown on her elegant face.

"We keep tying the vines gently back to the hedge, but

they're just not taking like they should. The thrall ripped them off so forcefully. I think it'll be hard to recover."

I look over at her. "Some plant types are accustomed to rough treatment and it helps them propagate. How do moonflowers spur new growth?"

Miriam smiles at the naturalist in me that comes out whenever I'm in the garden—but this is my element. Talking about the natural world and how all the pieces fit together is literally my favorite thing to do. I've gone to house parties and gotten embroiled in hours-long conversations about someone's house plants or patio garden.

Miriam points at the far end of the hedge.

"All the moonflower vines spring from that root. We're lucky the thralls didn't attack that, but they must not have known to do that. It's odd they were attracted to a moonflower vine anyway. I assume Wesley must have directed them here, since he controlled them."

I shudder when I think back to the one thrall I saw. Its powerful, catlike torso but scarred humanoid face was enough to fill dozens of nightmares.

That's in the past, though. Shepherd and Alo protected us, and thanks to Thea's magic combining with the pixie dust, the wards are stronger than ever. Together, they form layer upon layer of protection.

Miriam places a delicate hand on my back.

"You can do this, soulfriend. Morgan and I believe in you."

Her words sink in deep. I think about my sister and my new friend. I think about Ohken and how much he believes in me. I think about the Keeper showing up at lunch and asking me to do something *because he believes I can*.

I purposely don't look over at the A-frame which buzzes with new arrivals. I don't mean to think about the pixie royalty that'll show up sometime today to inhabit the gorgeous paper lanterns hanging from the garden's solitary tree.

Shoving all that side, I think about this portion of the moonflower vine and I focus. I can sense the plant, and there's a well of hurt there. The moonflowers are cautious, and when my magic approaches, they shy away.

Something in me snaps, and my first instinct is to push my magic to them. But somehow, I know doing that will chase them away. They're skittish after the thrall's rough handling. So instead, I push my magic into itself, coaxing the moonflowers out by burning my magic bright and green in front of them.

As I watch, a snaky tendril of moonflower crosses my mind's eye and touches my magic. The moment it does, an overwhelming sensation of motherliness hits me. The moonflower drinks greedily from my magic, but all it does is make the magic stronger. Another vine slinks up and does the same. I faintly hear a sound, Miriam, maybe, but I try not to break concentration.

Another vine approaches my ball of magic, and another, and another. But then the ball begins to diminish in size. My magic slips away, and no matter how furiously I call it, the ball sinks until it's nothing but a speck. The moonflower vines sink out of view.

Moments pass. I can't hear a sound, it's all muffled. Or maybe it's just that my own internal screeching is drowning out everything else. Goddamnit, why can't I fucking do this? Do I need to throw myself in harm's way like Thea to get a handle on this shit?

Blinking my eyes open, I find Miriam standing at the vines. Except where the moonflowers were hanging onto the hedge, they're now hanging in bunches off the hedges because the flowers are larger. I managed to grow those, but without cementing the vine to the hedge, they have no support.

I could scream, I'm so mad.

Miriam turns, her expression carefully neutral.

"This is still amazing, soulfriend. Look at these blooms." She lifts a flower, but I can't bear to look at it.

Morgan rubs my back. "We're doing what we can, Wren. You're the one that always reminds Thea and I how it's okay to not be okay. I feel compelled to remind you of that now. We can't expect to find out we're witches and take to it snappy quick."

"Thea did," I remind her. I don't mean to sound so bitter—I'm usually not so hard on myself. But this is important. Thea and Morgan were always the competitive ones. I was happy with my plants and my damn knitting.

Miriam sighs. "Had you arrived in Ever a year ago, you'd have learned magic at a slow and easy pace. It's only because of recent events that you're being pushed so hard. Give yourself grace, my friend. Our neighbors might ask for your help, but it is only because they are in awe of your abilities. They don't mean to toss you into a corner you feel you need to fight your way out of."

Her words make sense. All of those things make sense. It's just the maelstrom of emotion in my brain that doesn't line up. Even plants make sense. The right mix of sunlight, fertilizer and great weather conditions will produce the right results ninety-nine times out of a hundred.

But me? I can't seem to get this right quickly. And quickly is what Ever needs.

CHAPTER THIRTEEN
OHKEN

Wren and I talked for a long while last night. I gave her all the details on troll whip, but this morning I let Alessandro and his brother know I'd only be able to supply it for her. I'm not human so I don't understand her discomfort, but I'm trying to. I knew a relationship with a human would result in surprises, but I didn't see this one coming.

I wonder what else we might uncover? I'm anxious to find out. There's a fiery heat coiling deep in my belly. Every day it burns hotter and stronger. Every day I find myself more on edge, more ready to dominate the sweet witch who so easily enraptured me. My senses are growing sharper, my patience a little thinner. Focus for tasks eludes me because it's all redirecting to her.

Wren Hector is my mate. I'm certain of it now. Which is why telling Alessandro no more troll whip was an easy decision. If Wren continues to accept my advances, she comes first. No questions asked.

I've got plans for us this evening, plans that involve naked torture and a discussion about our sexual preferences. I've chosen Fleur as the spot to have those conversations. I want to do dirty, dirty things to her, surrounded by beautiful blooms. I want to watch ecstasy burst from her while I torture her with soft petals.

My cock throbs against the front of my pants. It's nearly painful at this point. My body knows what's coming—a rut that'll have us fucking for days with no stop. I need to be ready. *She* needs to be ready.

To that end, I spent most of the morning brewing the potion we need to take to get our bodies ready for each other. The rest of the morning was spent putting the finishing touches on the skyball stadium. It's ready, but I knew it would be, despite the Keeper's worries. Finding Wren has my magic on high alert, wanting to bind her and build with her. Finishing the stadium was a snap.

I head to Higher Grounds and order a bourbon latte for Wren. *With* troll whip, because if she wants it, I won't deny her a damn thing. Alessandro gives me an irritated look, but I leave the shop feeling good despite it. Wren Hector is firmly wrapped around my soul, and I can't wait to keep discovering every layer of her.

Striding up Main Street, I check in at the General Store, but everything's good there. It's busy with all the extra monsters in town. Most of my extended family will be arriving tomorrow for Trolliday. I'm excited to introduce Wren to them. It's a point of pride, identifying one's mate and presenting them to your family. They'll love her, of that I have no doubt.

With the General Store in order, I leave and head up a bustling Main Street to Fleur. I had my assistant close it about half an hour ago. Normally, we'd do crazy business during skyball week, but my date with Wren is more important.

I unlock the front door and step inside, the scent of thousands of flowers washing over me. Gardenias, ginger, and columbines fill my nostrils, competing for first place in their beauty. Moments later, there's a soft knock at the door. Turning, I open for Wren.

Her long brown hair is twisted up into a loose bun with a pick through it. She's wearing a black sweater, black jeans and her combat boots.

"You look badass." My voice goes deep as I pull her inside and press her to the front door. "Absolutely mouthwatering."

Wren smiles at me, but there's a forced tension to her smile. It's fake, put on like a mask she's wearing.

I won't have it. Not between us. I could never stand for the miscommunication that happens between some couples. That shit is for the birds. I'm a fan of talking things through and being on the same page. As a rule, trolls aren't disagreeable. We're big fans of talking.

I tilt Wren's chin farther up so I can gaze into those beautiful green eyes.

"Tell me what's wrong, Miss Hector."

Clouds dance across the emerald of her irises.

"The Keeper asked for help in the garden, and I made the moonflower blossoms bigger, but it just pulled them farther off the hedge. The pixies are scrambling to keep them attached. I just...he told me about the three-strikes thing, and—"

"Don't let him pressure you," I say. "He's looking out for Ever, but sometimes that means he pushes harder than he should."

Wren presses off the door and plants a palm on my chest.

"He *should* push, Ohken. He should be able to count on someone to help him do his job well. I want to be one of those people. Just like you and Alo and Shepherd."

"Okayyy." I give her a serious look. "You grew the blooms and didn't blow up Kiril's home a second time. Can we call that a win? Because it is, you realize."

Wren's lips tip up. She's resisting the urge to smile.

"I suppose it is," she finally concedes. "Thanks for reminding me."

And here it is, the opening I've been waiting for.

Stroking her hair away from her round cheeks, I tuck it behind a delicate ear. My aragonite studs shine from her earlobes, which sends a stab of possessive pride through me.

"I think your issue relates to control, sweetheart. I want you to learn to let go, to ride the flow of power instead of fighting it."

Wren smirks. "I'm plenty aware of letting go. Naturalists know better than to control the world around us. That just results in lots of insanity. I'm perfectly capable of giving up control."

Her saying that has my balls pulling tight against my body. My cock throbs against the front of my slacks. My chest puffs until I feel like it'll burst the buttons on my vest. I'm heading toward a rut faster than I meant to, and it's making every Dominant ounce of me rush to the surface.

Shaking my head, I force those feelings down.

"There's a difference between what you can't control and what you shouldn't control."

Wren's grin broadens. She looks so devious, so mouthy. She's a brat if I ever met one, and if there's one thing I'm really fucking good at, it's taming mouthy brats.

"I suppose you're always in control then?"

Reaching down, I stroke at the neckline of her sweater, pulling it down so I can touch her gorgeous skin. "I strive for that, yes."

"And you want to dominate me?" Her voice takes on a sarcastic edge.

"Yeah, sweetheart." Her sweater is stretchy enough for me to tug it down, exposing one breast to the cool air inside the shop. I nip at her swollen nipple before bringing my lips to her ear. "I've already had time to learn my power, Wren. I'm at peace with who I am."

She lets out an adorable growl. "What if I'd like to see you out of control?"

I laugh at that. "Oh, we're headed there fast, sweet witch. Trolls during a rut are feral and untamed. There won't be anything rational about me once we're there. And sweetheart, I'm headed there fast." I bite at her neck before raking my tusks across her skin. "You're pushing me there, Miss Hector."

Wren grips my vest and hauls me closer. "What are you saying, Ohken? Be clear with me."

I bring my gaze back to hers. "I'm telling you not to mistake what's between us for anything less than a raging, soul-deep obsession. I'm telling you the bridge has been grumpy as shit since you left last night. I'm telling you that I want you, Wren. I want to show you my Dominant side. I want to see what it's like when you and I collide in the bedroom." I can't look away from the verdant shades of green that glitter like emeralds in her eyes. "What do you think?"

Wren's arms come around my torso and she smiles. "If being dominated means you're going to give me detention and make me suck you off under your desk like a naughty schoolgirl, then I like the sound of that."

I release a groan at the picture she's painting. Without taking the potion I brewed today, she won't be able to do much more than lick my cock. But once she's taken it, she'll be able to deep throat it, sit on it, shatter around it. I can't wait.

Reaching around her to lock the front door, I pull the shade down over the glass before spinning her to face the room. I gesture at the crammed shop. Every surface is covered in flowers, every bucket spilling with multicolored blooms.

"Fleur is my passion project. This place makes no money at all, but I could never shut it down. It's just a place to celebrate natural beauty. I wanted you to see it."

Wren claps her hands together and walks to the center display, stroking cut hydrangea blooms that fill a vase there. The center display is truly striking—dozens of clear glass vases with just as many types of flowers. It's meant for a build-it-yourself bouquet. We do a steady business in that, although I can't see it ever turning a profit despite this busy week.

She admires the flowers before heading to the far-left wall. The entire space is floor-to-ceiling shelves with every manner of vase and wrapping you could need. Hundreds of air plants dangle like green spiders from the ceiling. They're beautiful. I watch her admire them before moving back across the space.

"That far-right wall holds the more rare stems, but also two dozen or so premade bouquets to take home."

I know I sound proud, and I'm fine with that. Wren stares in what looks like complete adoration at the flowers in front of her.

I give her the space and quiet to examine everything in the shop. It's not until she reaches the checkout counter that I join her, guiding her toward the back room. It's cluttered and dark back here. Twine and ribbon hang in giant spools along the back wall along with a dozen colors of wax paper to wrap delicate stems in. In the center of the back room, there's a wide wooden prep table. I've already connected silky ropes to all four corners.

Tonight's not about Wren's power. It's not about dinner and conversation. It's about the physical and emotional connection between us. It's a strengthening of that part of our relationship.

Wren glances at the table and ropes and looks back at me with a knowing grin. "I know we have a reservation at Herschel's, but it's not for a couple hours and you asked me to come here first. What did you have in mind?" A barely contained smile curves her pouty pink lips.

I let my lips curl, tusks poking into my upper lip.

I pat the wooden surface of the prep table. "Up on the table, Miss Hector."

She feigns indignation. "For what possible reason, you brute?"

I press her chest, backing her to the table's edge before encasing her inside my arms.

"Pleasure, Miss Hector," I rumble. "Filthy pleasure."

"Well then," she says, hopping up onto the table's ledge and leaning back onto her palms. "By all means, Mister Stonesmith."

CHAPTER FOURTEEN
WREN

Ohken looms over me, his woodsy scent filling my nostrils. Tendrils of auburn hair hang down over his shoulders, his russet eyes focused on mine. Goddamn, this man is good at eye contact. His eyes trail down my chest to my thighs and slowly back up. The look on his face is pure appreciation. He grins at me until I can't take it, dropping my eyes to his chest just to get that intense focus off me.

"Good." He keeps his praise short and sweet, but I preen under it nonetheless. "I'm going to undress you, Miss Hector. Then I'm going to tie you down, blindfold you, and have my way with you. What do you think about that?"

Heat flushes my skin until my sweater feels like it's constricting my ability to even breathe.

When I give him a thumbs-up, he laughs. It's a deep sound that comes from his belly and echoes around us. It's the only sound in this tiny dark room save for the thunderous gallop of my heart. Tied down? Blindfolded? It's been ages since I trusted a man to do that to me. Like, probably a decade.

The anxious need to move slaps me, and I curl in on myself. "You're not gonna tickle me, right?"

One auburn brow angles sharply upward, full lips pulling down into a frown. He takes a step back and cocks his head to one side. "Tickle you? While you're tied up? Is that something you want?"

"Hell no!" I shout, letting my legs drop back to the surface of the table. I thrum my fingers on my knees, trying to tamp down a desperate need to flee. "I let a boyfriend tie me up once and he tickled me. I hated it, and nobody's ever tied me up since then."

Ohken reaches out and parts my thighs, sliding his big hands up them. He brings a forefinger under my chin and forces me to look deep into those gorgeous amber eyes.

"Most trolls are Doms, Wren. There are a lot of reasons for that, but the concepts of trust, safety, and consent are deeply ingrained in our culture. I will never do something that you don't allow and enjoy. You have my word."

He says nothing else, but those bright eyes don't leave mine. And somehow I know he's telling the truth. If he did something and I asked him to stop, I have no doubt he'd listen.

The silence stretches long, and I shuffle on the table, trying to get closer to him. Ohken's big hands come to the hem of my sweater and he pulls it effortlessly over my head. My bra is removed and tossed to the floor. He presses me to my back and pulls my pants and undies off. They get deposited on the ground as well, and I'm lying naked on the table in front of him.

He's still fully fucking clothed of course. Ohken smiles, and like always, I marvel at the twin tusks that poke out from his square lower jaw. His teeth are perfectly straight behind forest-green lips. God, he's beautiful. He's a statue come to life, absolute alpha male perfection.

He reaches into his vest pocket and produces a small glass vial, handing it to me.

I sit up and take the vial. Inside is a bright purple liquid. It bubbles, but the bubbles are hot pink. It looks like something Miriam might create in her candy shop to cure baldness or make you horny.

His hand comes to my stomach, where he gently strokes the dips and valleys of my skin. Ohken raises his other hand and thunks the glass with the back of his pointer finger.

"I brewed this today, and I've taken my dose. You'll need to take this in order for us to couple. You'll take it daily for a few days, but never again after that. I won't pressure you, and if you decide you don't want to take it, I'll understand." Dark eyes glitter in the low light. He looks absolutely monstrous the way he's staring at me. "But know this, Miss Hector. I'm dying for you to take it because I want to fuck you so badly."

I swallow to avoid my mouth dropping open.

"What would you do to me if I'd already taken this?" The question is out of my mouth before I realize it, but now that it's out there, I have to know.

Ohken's smile grows more fierce as he cages me between his beefy arms. He's so close, so warm, so overwhelmingly masculine. Amber eyes drop to my body and he lets out an appreciative rumble. When his gaze travels back up to my face, there's so much heat there, so much need.

"I'd flip you facedown and take you from behind first." The words sound like a promise to me. "I'd take that sweet pussy first to get you off and loose. And then I'd take your ass, because I can't wait to watch my cock slide inside you."

My chest heaves. Air isn't filling my lungs and my mouth is dry as the Sahara.

"I want that." I unstopper the liquid and bring the vial to my lips. Throwing my head back, I swallow the contents down. It leaves a sharp, acrid taste in my throat and I scrunch my nose.

Ohken takes the vial from me and levels a scowl in my direction.

"I was going to warn you that the taste isn't entirely pleasant, but it seems you're anxious to move forward."

"Yep," I pop. "I am on board, sir." I reach for him, running my hands up the front of his vest. "Please take some clothes off. I want to touch you, to look at you. It seems so unfair that I'm completely naked."

Ohken growls and swats my hands away, rounding the table until he's behind me.

"Lie down, Miss Hector."

My breasts grow heavy under his command, but I lie back, propping myself up on my elbows.

He unbuttons his vest and folds it, tossing it over the cash register. Whiskey-brown eyes fall to my arms.

"Is there some part of lie down that humans do differently?"

Oh God, I'm going to enjoy the shit out of this.

I shrug as much as I can, swinging one leg playfully off the table. "Well, you weren't altogether clear, so there was room for interpretation."

Ohken laughs and shakes his head like he can't believe how saucy I am. His big hands move to his shirt, but he rolls up the sleeves, exposing muscular, veiny forearms.

I whine, because it's obvious he doesn't plan to get undressed.

"What's wrong Miss Hector?" he teases. "Are you a little frustrated?"

I roll onto my side on the table, watching him as I prop my head in one palm. "I want to see all of you. Every green inch."

He smirks and leans back against the cash register, sliding both hands into his pockets and crossing his legs at the ankle.

This man is not about to get undressed. The thought occurs to me to leap off the table and just start tearing at his clothing, but somehow I don't see him allowing it.

"You ready to lie down yet?"

"No."

"I'll wait."

I smile, sliding one hand down my cleavage to circle one nipple. It's hard and aching. Everything feels hot and heavy. I'd pay good money to get his mouth on me, but he's playing hard to get.

Ohken's gaze follows my hand, but his expression remains the same. I play with my nipple, rubbing and tugging lightly until a moan slips from my lips.

"Lie down, Wren."

"No."

He clears his throat and crosses his arms, but the smile he levels on me is fierce and firm. "In a battle to see who has the most patience, which one of us do you think will win, my sweet witch?"

I cut him a glare and flop onto my back, crossing my arms over my chest to hide my bounty from his gaze.

He chuckles and steps toward me, grabbing one arm and lifting it above my head.

"Well done, Miss Hector." His big lips close over my achy nipple and he twists it, sucking hard. Heat streaks to the juncture of my thighs and I cry out. His warm tongue softly circles the hard bud once, twice, and then he bites. I jerk on the table, but Ohken stands. Reaching above me, he loops a silky rope around my wrist and pulls it tight.

My chest heaves. I need more than this slow-ass tease.

Ohken steps to the head of the table and pulls my other wrist above my head, securing it the same way as the first.

I try to arch backward to see him, but I hear him move away from the table. Gritting my teeth, I close my eyes, resolved to stop fighting. He's going to tease me within an inch of my life whether I like it or not.

There's a rustling sound, like leaves rubbing against each other, and then soft footfalls. Ohken comes into view at my side, but I can't see his hands. He stalks to the bottom of the table and grabs one of my ankles, propping it on his shoulder. Turning his head, he kisses my instep, his lips rough and hungry. He peppers harsh kisses up my ankle all the way to my knee, bringing his other hand to cover my pussy.

I squirm on the table. "I need more, Ohken. So much more than this."

"Surrender," he demands. "Stop trying to wrest control from me, Wren."

Growling, I close my eyes and will myself to focus on what I feel.

Ohken's fingertips stroke a path along my outer thigh, but then I hear him move and soft warmth licks up my pussy. His tongue traces a circle around my clit before he tugs gently. There's a soft rustling sound, and then something long and prickly rolls over my lower belly.

A rose stem covered in thorns. It must be.

The tiny stabs against my stomach combined with the soft swirl of his tongue overwhelm me. I don't know whether to squirm away or let my legs fall wide and beg for me.

I do whine when he moves away, my chest heaving. I'd do almost anything at this point for more pleasure.

He presses my thighs together and pushes them back against my stomach, exposing my ass to him. I keep my eyes closed, just waiting to see what he does. I'm unprepared for him to drag velvety petals down the seam of my pussy. Their soft coolness is a fluttery tickle that sends tiny zings of heat to my clit.

Ohken growls, and then it's his tongue replacing the flowers. He slips it inside my channel and groans, the vibrations tickling the petals as they rub against my clit.

"Oh God!" I cry out, grabbing the ropes as I struggle to position my clit closer to that magical tongue.

He shifts backward, and then it's the flowers again, dragging and stroking along the backs of my thighs and over my clit. It's not enough to get me off, not nearly. But it's enough to drive me fucking wild. My whole body is overheated, my cheeks flushed. I'm past the point of demanding anything.

My thighs fall open when he lets go.

Warm hands slide up the front of my legs, up the swell of my stomach to my breasts. He cups them and then pinches both nipples, tugging them to attention. He rolls the rose stem over my breast, the thorns poking my skin. They press against my nipple and roll past, and honey drips out of me down my ass.

Ohken sucks in a deep, appreciative breath. "Look at this bounty, Miss Hector. I love these. They're big enough to spill out of even my huge hands. Perfection."

Normally I'd have a comment here, something funny and sarcastic, but my whole body vibrates with need. I'm desperate to explode, and nowhere near close enough to.

Ohken's mouth closes over one nipple, and he lets out a needy groan as he sucks on it.

"You're doing beautifully, my sweet."

God, yes, just let me get off, please.

Without warning, he stalks to the end of the table and flips me onto my stomach. Big hands grip my hips and he yanks me to the edge of the table, burying his face between my thighs. He goes wild, plunging his tongue deep inside me as a finger plays with my ass. I rock backward for more, more, more when I feel him roll flower petals over my nipple, pinching it. My body's so confused at the dichotomy of sensations, and I explode with a choked roar.

Behind me, Ohken snarls and sucks at my clit. Stars burst behind my eyelids as I coat his face with release. It fades slowly, and he pushes me forward, flat on my stomach. I'm panting too hard to try to look back at him. I hear the rustle of fabric, and then a shirt drops to the floor next to me.

Warmth covers me from behind as Ohken climbs on top of me, bringing his lips to my ear.

"Beautiful, Miss Hector, but we're just getting started, witch."

Oh. My. God.

∼

The following evening, I'm helping Catherine and my sisters at the Annabelle. Catherine's zipping from room to room—most of which are filled at this point.

"Goodness." Catherine bites at her lip. "We are full, ladies. Thank you so much for your help!"

I open my mouth to tell her we're happy to, that she's been such a good friend to all three of us since we arrived, but her comm watching pinging interrupts me.

When a name pops up on the screen, she pales and answers quickly.

"Hello Bertram, how may I help you?"

A voice so deep I can barely understand it reverberates out of the watch.

"We require two rooms for His Majesties Van and Lorna Lief."

Catherine's eyes go wide, and she throws one hand up in the air, although she's polite when she responds.

"Bertram that won't be possible. The inn has been full for ages. I'm so sorry I won't be able to—"

Morgan elbows me in the side. When I look over, she gives me a 'you know what to do look.'

I tap Catherine on the shoulder and mouth "we'll go stay with Thea."

It's a testament to how frazzled she is over this request that she doesn't question us or tell us no. Instead she mouths back a quick "are you sure?"

Morgan and I both nod, and Thea gives her a thumbs-up. She makes the arrangements with whoever Bertram is and then clicks off, turning to us with evident relief.

"Girls, I would never ask you to vacate your rooms like this. Van and Lorna Lief are vampire royalty. They don't often make public appearances, so this is a big deal."

Thea snorts.

"You're just making it easier for Shepherd and me. Now we can deliver snacks right to the guest nest instead of trekking over here. It's no biggie, really."

Catherine pulls us all in for a hug, and it reminds me so much of the way Mom used to do that with all three of us. I miss those nightly hugs with her, although we still do them together when we're around each other. Less and less now that Thea lives with Shepherd.

We hold it a beat longer than is polite, but Catherine doesn't let go.

For the next half hour, Morgan and I pack up our stuff. Thea comms Shepherd, and he shows up to grab our bags. As it turns out, he's way stronger than I thought, because he holds our bags with his tail, Thea pressed to his front, and Morgan and I on his back. He flies us the entire way to his cottage like that. It should be awkward riding around on my sister's husband, but somehow, very few things seem weird to me anymore.

We get settled and then I start getting ready for Trolliday —it's tonight, and I don't know what to expect. Thea and

Morgan are lying in the guest nest, which is basically a gigantic cushy round dog bed on a platform. It's meant for a whole family, but they're pretzeled together in the center, poring over a stack of romance novels.

Wait. Romance novels?

I turn around from doing my eyeliner.

"Where'd you get romance novels?"

Thea scoffs and holds up *Her Bear Mountain Daddy: A Second Chance Stepbrother Romance.*

"Apparently, the historical society on Main keeps a section of books on humans. It's a mix of books people have brought from outside Ever, and donations from monsters. Someone donated these twenty or thirty years ago. There's a whole romance section! The historian told me monsters who mate humans will often come in for"—she tosses her fingers up in air quotes—"research."

Laughing, I turn back to the mirror. I can see Morgan's reflection in it. She smiles at me.

"You excited for tonight?"

I set my makeup down and turn, leaning against the mirror as I ponder my feelings about tonight.

"I'm nervous."

Morgan's brows slump down into a vee.

"Nervous isn't your MO, Mary."

Ah, here we go with our Sanderson sister nicknames.

"I know, Winifred," I counter. "But I really like this man. I mean, this night is a big deal to him and that makes it a big deal to me. What if I fuck something up? Or if the other trolls don't like me? What if they—"

"Breathe, honey." Morgan drops our nicknames, sensing how distressed I truly am. I don't lack confidence, not usually, but Ever has us all out of our element a little bit. We're living in an alternate reality, and that changes things a bit. I'm more worried about what I don't know than anything else.

TANGLING WITH TROLLS

Both sisters smile at me, but it's Morgan who speaks first. "Tonight's gonna be great. Just have fun, right? You get along great with Ohken, maybe all trolls are chill like him."

"That's true," I muse. Ohken's so easygoing, so perfect. Ugh. I want to be a good partner to him tonight. Because the reality is, I'm falling in love.

CHAPTER FIFTEEN
OHKEN

I stride up Main Street, past Miriam's Sweets and Scoops, hooking a left into the General Store. My assistant, Neil, appears harrowed behind the counter, but backup is on the way. The skyball finals haven't been held in Ever in decades—this is a big deal. The tournament itself is still two days away, but monsters have been arriving since yesterday. Our usual town of eight-hundred-and-some beings is in the tens of thousands now.

Pop-up restaurants line Main all the way up to the historical society and town hall, which has been repurposed as a hostel of sorts for those willing to rough it a little bit. Hel Motel is full too, although I know they tacked on quite a bit of space in preparation for this event.

I check in with Neil and make sure he's got enough supplies to last him the evening. Tonight is the Trolliday celebration, and I'm anxious to meet up with Wren.

"I haven't seen you smile this much in ages." Neil's high-pitched voice cuts through my thoughts, his pixie wings fluttering gently behind his back. Purple eyes are crinkled at the corners. He keeps his eyes on the group of centaurs at the end of the counter, eyeing the postcards.

"I suppose we have Wren Hector to thank for this? The pixies have had a lot to say about her."

A retort bubbles up in my throat, because I'm certain he means the mishap with Kiril's gourd, but—

"Miriam adores her," Neil continues. "Literally can't say enough good things about their friendship. It sounds like you've got yourself a keeper." Amethyst eyes flick to me and his smile grows broader. "Well, not a Keeper keeper. Just… hang on to that one."

One of the centaurs raises his hand to call Neil over, but I close my eyes and smile. There's a deep sense of knowing in my mind, a sense that my soul calls to Wren's and always will. Trolls believe that our magic grows stronger when we find our person, and mine's been stronger than ever since Wren and I started dating.

I wave goodbye to Neil and the customers and head out of the store. It's true that trolls are slow to build relationships, but what Wren and I are building is rock solid. We fit together in all the important ways, and tonight, after the ceremony? I'm going to tell her that I'm falling for her.

Main Street bustles with hundreds of beings visiting the dozens of tents that line either side of the road, which is shut down this week. I move through the crowd, greeting at least ten beings I know from other havens. But all they're doing is slowing me down from getting to Wren. I breathe a sigh of relief when I cross Sycamore Street and head toward my bridge.

When I make it to my sign, Wren stands there looking like an angel. She's wearing a pale peach corseted top that hugs her body and accentuates the fullness of her figure. A matching sweater hangs over one forearm. I had told her to wear jeans because we have to hike a little way, but I'd forgotten how luscious she looks in them. Her hair is a little curlier than usual, like she did something to make it that way.

I stop in the middle of the street and slip my hands into my pockets, resisting the urge to rub at my cock. I'm hard and throbbing at the sight of her, and it's getting worse by the day. That need to throw her over the nearest surface and have her is building and building. I'll be in a rut within days.

I've waited my entire life for this, for her—I don't want to wait a minute longer.

Wren's pink lips break into a smile as I approach. The moment I'm close enough, I pull her to me and dip low enough to take her mouth. It's not like our tender first kiss, and it's nothing like the teasing kisses I gave her last night. This is a wild frenzy of covetous desire. It burns under my skin like fire, calling me to bond her in the old ways of my people.

I want her tattooed and bound to me.

She groans and grips my wrists, pushing harder into the kiss. Standing like this we're too unevenly matched in height. She pulls away just long enough to gasp. "God, we need a bed!"

When I pull her hips tighter to me, she pulls an empty potion vial out of her jean pocket. "Second dose down. One to go. And then you're all mine."

I slick my mouth over hers again, sucking at her tongue. I pull away to rub my tusks carefully along her cheekbones.

"Yours," I murmur. "That sounds perfect to me."

Her eyes glint in the fading light. She slides both hands up my chest and thrums her fingers. "We're gonna be late, troll daddy. Come on."

I grin at the new nickname, wrapping my hand around her waist and guiding her up the street into the forest.

She playfully pinches my side. "Tell me more about what happens at this event."

I lean into her teasing touch. "Trolliday is our annual coming-of-age ceremony. All trolls who came of age this year, which is sixteen for trolls, will exhibit their power. The older trolls share their power too, and it's basically a big party."

Wren laughs. "Big party sounds nice. Will I need to do anything?"

"Not unless you want to. My kin will ask about your power, but they're just being friendly. There's no expectation for you to share, alright?"

Trolliday is low-key. I don't want her to feel pressured into anything, although it's true that once the trolls get a few barrels of mead in, they'll probably ask about her magic. Wren nods and tucks in closer to me, wrapping her arm around my waist.

We walk for a half hour until we're deep in the woods in the clearing troll elders picked for this year's celebration. She looks around, eyes wide as she takes in the bustling scene.

"There must be a hundred trolls here." Her voice is full of wonder.

I feel nothing but pride. I'm proud to show her off in all her perfect glory. She's mine and I'm excited to introduce her to everyone.

"Ohken Stonesmith! Good to see you!" Hern, a big troll from my home haven of Arcadia comes over and claps me on the shoulder. He stands almost a head taller than me.

Wren looks up, her eyes as big as saucers.

Hern grins and peers down at her. "You're a pretty young thing. What are you doing with old Ohken here? There are far better trolls to be had, and you know what we say, the best for your ho—"

"No thanks," Wren chirps, giving him a teasing look. "My hole's well taken care of."

Hern laughs and claps me on the shoulder again. "Just teasing, little one." He winks. "But of course, if you see tonight's show of power and decide old Ohken isn't looking so good anymore, well, I'll be around."

I roll my eyes and pull Wren tighter. Hern jogs off when someone calls his name. I look down at Wren, who's barely stifling a laugh. "I may have forgotten to mention that most trolls do love a good joke, and the majority of the trolls here have known me for almost seventy years. They've been waiting a long time to see me with a woman."

Wren sputters and whips around in my arms, slapping my chest playfully. "You're seventy years old? Oh my God, it's the biggest age gap in the history of age gaps. No wonder you're so confident—you've had a shitload of practice." She shakes her head, tsking at me. "What other secrets do I need to know before we get dirty in your bed?"

Laughing, I pull her up into my arms and back her into the nearest tree. Trolls are openly affectionate, nobody will think twice about what I'm doing. Still, Wren glances quickly around before returning her attention to me.

I hover my lips over hers. She smells so delicious and she's so soft in my arms.

"I haven't kept any secrets from you, Miss Hector. Although I do have something to tell you a little later."

She pouts, her plump lower lip sticking adorably out. "Tell me now. I hate surprises."

"Mmm," I say noncommittally. "I love when you get bratty. It makes me want to dominate you in the best of ways. Maybe teach you a little lesson about obedience."

"Obedience, huh?" Wren deadpans, wrapping her arms around my neck. "You should know, none of the Hector sisters are great at obedience. When Lou gets here, she'll be even worse than the rest of us combined. Obedience isn't in our nature."

"You'll learn to love it," I counter. "Because when I demand your obedience, when I ask you to bend your femininity for my masculinity, it'll be the freedom you never knew you needed."

"Sounds intense," Wren whispers.

"It will be." I suck her plump lower lip into my mouth. Her answering groan has me pistoning my hips to shove her harder into the tree. I'm dancing right on the edge of a rut and I don't even care. I might go into it in the middle of the game, and I don't care about that either. If I do, I'll leave and sweep her into my bedroom for days. I'm fine with that, more than fine.

"Ohken!" Someone shouts for me in the distance.

Wren groans and crosses her arms. "It's not that I don't love people, but it would be awesome to curl up under the bridge right now. I could use some troll whip from the source."

I manage a grunt of acknowledgement. She can't suck me off the way she wants to quite yet, but I can't wait until she does. She makes up for our currently inconvenient size difference with unbridled enthusiasm.

"You are perfection," I whisper before dropping her to the ground.

She tosses her hair over her shoulder and gives me a saucy wink. "I know. Let's go."

I can't hold back the belly laugh at her confident words. I didn't know what sort of female the gods would bring into my life one day. I just knew she'd have to be remarkable—kind, courageous, thoughtful, stunning, sensual. Wren is all of that and more, and tonight I'm going to tell her exactly how I feel.

"You can do it, Hern!" Wren shouts next to me, whooping for my friend as he tosses a giant log down the field. It lands with a thud several feet farther than the prior contestant's. Everyone's drinking mead—Wren included—and the Trolliday games have been going on for nearly two hours.

I sit on a stump with her in my lap, watching her obvious enthusiasm for the way we play. She's met nearly every troll here at this point, and as far as I can tell, she's having a ball. Her cheeks are flushed and her lips set into a permanent smile.

Hern trundles over and slaps Wren's palm when she lifts it for a high-five. "Only managed that with your support, lovely friend."

Wren snorts. "Seems to me that and a little mead helped you along. You can stop flirting now, though. I told you—my hole is well cared for."

Hern guffaws loudly and claps himself on the chest, green eyes moving to me. "Don't let this one out of your sight, brother. What a catch!"

Wren shimmies in my lap, rubbing her back to my chest.

I tilt my head to acknowledge Hern's statement, but he's already off to his subsequent adventure, shouting for the next contestant to take their turn already.

Wren looks over her shoulder at me. "This is so fascinating, Ohken. They go like this all night?"

Laughing, I reach around to collar her neck. "No, my sweet. They're wrapping up now. Nobody can beat Hern's distance. Next we'll do a sharing of power. The trolls who came of age this year will all show their power, and then we rotate in a circle to build on top of their gifts. By the time we're all done, there will be a new bridge here in the clearing.

It'll go into a raffle and be gifted to a troll who's ready to live on their own."

"God, that's so sweet!" Wren turns halfway around and reaches up to stroke my jawline. "Is that how your bridge originally came to be?"

"Don't know," I murmur, lost in her beautiful eyes. "But I redid the inside exactly how I wanted when I moved to Ever." More important words are on the tip of my tongue, but she gives me a saucy look.

"And what if I want to change something about it? What would you do?"

"Change it to be precisely what you want." I pinch her lips together and plant a tender kiss on them. So damn soft. Her snarky expression falls, her green eyes searching mine. She must sense my serious tone.

I collar her neck and kiss her again, and this time it's hungrier. I slick my tongue into her mouth, tasting her. She meets me and turns fully, rising up onto her knees just long enough to straddle me and deepen the kiss.

Thick thighs squeeze me tight, her breasts pressed against me. My mind helpfully supplies vision after vision of us in bed. I'm lost to her sugary bourbon scent, to the flash of mischief in her green eyes, to the way her fingers play with the buttons on my shirt.

I'm lost to the words I'm about to say.

Pulling back, I smile. "I'm falling in love, Wren. I wanted to tell you tonight, because this night is so significant to trolls. It's a night to celebrate family and community, and I want you to be part of that."

Her expression turns joyous, her smile so broad I can see all her teeth. She brings her forehead to mine, her voice a mere whisper.

"I'm falling too, and it's perfect and terrifying. I've never cared for someone this deeply this fast."

"And here I thought trolls were slow moving." I lift a brow.

She laughs and pinches my lips together like I'd just done with hers. "You could have taken those first steps a little more quickly. I wouldn't have cried about that. Instead, I had to pine after you for weeks and weeks."

"Most trolls would have ogled you for far longer." I laugh. "You've just experienced the troll version of speed dating, if I'm honest."

Wren snorts. "I could do with speedier. Speaking of which, tomorrow's my last potion, right?"

"Gods, yes." I run both hands over her plump ass, squeezing her tight so I can press her hips closer to mine.

"Was that a whine?" Wren laughs. "You're always so perfectly controlled, but you sound nearly distraught, Mister Stonesmith."

I rock my hips once, knowing she can feel my hard cock through my dress pants. "My rut's coming, Miss Hector. Within a week, I'd guess."

"Sorry I don't have a troll pussy so you could have just slid into day one." She grins at me. Sassy bitch.

Two can tease at that game. "Sorry my dick is enormous and I had to cook up a potion in order to fuck you properly." I dig my fingertips into her luscious ass. "I'll never want anyone else, Wren. Trolls are monogamous until we die."

Wren's smile becomes a frown. "Speaking of which, if you're seventy, and I'm not, how does that work?"

I open my mouth to explain how our lifelines will sync, but Hern steps to the middle of the clearing and raises his voice. "Hear me, friends! We'll begin the sharing of power now, calling forth those who came of age this year. I believe we've got nearly a dozen souls to celebrate! Let's get a round of applause!"

The clearing fills with hoots and stomps and cheers. Every

Trolliday follows the same pattern. A dozen male and female trolls join Hern.

Wren turns around in my arms and watches them in silence as one by one, they swirl their hands and speak the incantations of our people. Little by little, the outlines of a bridge form. By the time all dozen are done, a stone frame sits there.

I shift off the stump and set Wren gently down. "My turn, Miss Hector." Striding into the clearing with the rest of my people, I place my hands on the bridge and murmur the words trolls have been speaking for thousands and thousands of years. Others join me, and stones begin to form along the bridge.

When I'm done, I step back to give another troll space. Wren folds herself into my arms and smiles. "I wish I could help."

I stroke chocolate waves away from her face, swirling one peach-tipped lock around my finger.

"They would welcome your magic, my love."

Her brows rise. She looks doubtful. But then they dip to a vee and determination fills her gaze. "What if I blow it up?"

"Then I'll spank you for being a terror."

Wren snorts. "I'm serious, Ohken."

"There's no pressure to join in," I remind her.

"I'd like to, I think."

"Then I'll be right by your side." I reach for her hand. She threads her fingers through mine and allows me to guide her to the bridge. I place her palms on the stones. The bridge itself is constructed now, and the spells are simply aging the stones and strengthening them.

"You've got this," I murmur into her ear. "And I'm right here."

"I've got this," Wren mutters. It sounds like she's trying to convince herself more than me.

I press myself to her back, one hand around her waist and the other covering one of hers on the bridge. I will all my strength, all my confidence, to flow to her.

There's a gasp from a troll next to us, and I look down to see a vine curl up out of the ground, its tendrils digging into cracks in the bridge's foundation. Wren makes a pleased noise, and the plant springs up higher. Blue spikes begin to protrude out of the vines, and then they unfurl into blooms the size of dinner plates.

"A green witch," Hern says somewhere to my right. "Praise the gods." There are gasps and hushed whispers, and then a circle of trolls surround us.

Wren looks up and away from her vine, and a bloom pops, disintegrating into nothing.

"No!" she says. "Damnit."

I sense her refocus, and the vine grows faster, curling along the entire base of the bridge. Wren's muscles quiver in my arms.

"Easy, love," I whisper in her ear. "You're doing amazing."

She lets out a cry. Every single bloom pops and evaporates to nothing. The bright green vine grows dark and shriveled and then turns to dust as well. Wren lets out a disappointed sounding wail, her hands still on the stones.

Hern pushes through the crowd to join us. "Pay your magic no mind, lovely. It'll come when it comes."

I know he means that Trolliday is low-key and that she hasn't ruined anything.

She nods, but when she turns, she's scowling, her cheeks flushed an angry red.

I give Hern a look and he pushes the onlookers away from us. "Nothing to see here, brothers and sisters. Let us finish so we can gift this magnificent bridge!"

His words trail off as I look down at Wren. Her arms are crossed over her chest, her eyes shining with tears.

"Wren." I reach for her, but she tenses, so I drop my hand. "You're still—"

"Still learning, I know." Her tone is bitter. She's angry, I get it. But learning isn't linear. Not that that'll make her feel any better.

"Why don't we head home," I offer. "I can make you a lovely late meal or take you to Scoops or Miriam's."

Wren's lips purse together but she nods. When she looks up at me, her expression is heartbroken.

I pull her to me, wrapping both arms around her. "My beautiful, talented, sweet girl. Everything about you is perfect."

"Tell the Keeper that," she says under her breath.

I pull back. "What does he have to do with it?"

A tear slips down Wren's cheek. "I don't want to let him down."

A scowl pulls my lips into a sneer. "It's not your job to do so." I let out a growl. "It's not even a fair ask, Wren. The pixies are already working on it, and—"

"It's not the same as if I did it, though." Wren's tone is mournful. She looks down at her hands, then back up at me. "They can only tie the vines back up to the hedge. They need time or someone like me to get the vines to reattach, ideally before the Hearth people get here."

"You've got this, sweet girl," I encourage her. "And I'm here for you. We'll figure it out together, okay?"

CHAPTER SIXTEEN
WREN

The following morning, Morgan and Thea walk with me to meet Miriam in the garden. The sky is a cotton candy mix of pinks and purples. Most of the pixies are still sleeping after some crazy party they had last night, which is a good thing, because it wasn't that long ago they asked me not to practice here.

Still, I woke up this morning determined to do better than I did last night at Trolliday.

When Ohken and I went back to the bridge after my failed attempt, we cooked dinner together and made out for two hours. It was perfect. He reassured me a thousand times and showed me everything he loves about my body and mind.

He's great.

It's me that's the problem. And I am goddamn resolved *not* to be the problem. I'm typically a very go-with-the-flow type gal, but this feels so much more important than anything else I've ever tried to learn. I've never struggled this hard to pick something up, and the skyball tournament is only two days away. The Keeper asked for my help, and I have to believe he did that because he believes I'm capable of, I dunno, helping.

We pass through the hedge into the garden, and Miriam pops into large form, waving tiredly with a cup of coffee in her hand, eyes half-lidded. I hold back from teasing her, though, because I'm sure I'm not looking my best either. Ohken kept me up for ages and then I fell asleep in his arms. I woke up at two a.m. drooling on his sexy stacked pecs.

Miriam walks up the crushed shell pathway and slings her free arm around my waist. "G'morning Hectors. You three look beautiful today."

Morgan snorts. "Thea and Wren are always radiant, but I haven't combed my hair or put on a stitch of makeup."

Miriam rests her head against mine and yawns. "And yet you're gorgeous every day."

My sisters fall silent. I comm'd them both at four a.m. asking if they'd come to the garden with me. It was way too early to be bugging them, but I really felt like I could use their support.

We traipse quietly through the garden to the injured moonflower vines. The flowers hang sadly, held onto the hedge with loose string.

"I thought about this all night," I say, pointing to the hedge. "I'm a naturalist; it's my job to understand how the natural world fits all together, and I think we're going about this backwards. I'll try to grow the moonflowers, but it might be easier to just grow part of the hedge to support them."

Miriam gasps and claps her hands together, which jolts her coffee cup and sends coffee all over her shoes. She doesn't seem to notice. "That's brilliant, Wren!" She turns to give me a snide look. "I won't tell Ohken you were busy thinking about plants during your date."

Thea snorts. Morgan laughs. But I give Miriam a superior look. "I didn't start thinking about it until two a.m. thank you very much. And I called you all at four."

"I know," Miriam grumbles. "I had just gone to bed. We

had a rager with the king and queen last night. For being in their hundreds they sure do throw a good party."

"I want to hear all about it later," I say, "but let me concentrate on the hedge right now. That way the pressure's off on blowing up the moonflowers, but I can"—I make air quotes with my fingers—"maybe still do this."

Morgan slides her arm around my waist and squeezes me tight. "I believe in you, Mary. Channel the shit out of the Sandersons. They were badasses and you are too."

I blow out a steadying breath, turning to smile at her. "Alright, Winnie."

She curls her lip down on one side like Mary does, but lets go and takes a step back. Normally that move makes me laugh. Right now I'm nervous as hell.

Closing my eyes, I shove away the realization that there are hundreds of pixies living in the garden right now. I push Kiril's grief and sadness away. I let go of my focus on my sisters and Miriam, although I sense them here with me.

Instead, I focus on the tall manicured hedge that forms the outer wall of the garden. Earthworms crawl across my consciousness, but it's not disconcerting. More than anything, I recognize their work as a critical part of the garden's ecosystem. Small but mighty.

Smiling, I move past the worms and think about the hedge itself, seeing every root, stem and leaf in my mind's eye.

There! I can sense the moonflowers, but they're peripheral to the hedge itself. Focusing, I push energy into the hedge, willing the shrubs' branches to push out farther. I sense that they do, jutting up toward the sky and gathering the moonflowers in their prickly embrace.

A small noise nearly distracts me, but I recenter myself on the bushes. Their branches reach and pull until finally, someone taps me on the shoulder.

I blink open my eyes. Miriam and my sisters stand gobsmacked in front of me. A giant lattice of interwoven twigs and branches holds up the moonflower vine six feet in both directions. The moonflower petals still look a little sullen, but they're up.

Miriam turns to me with wonder in her eyes. "You did it, soulfriend. My gods, I've never seen anything quite like this."

I let out a whoop and pump my arms up in the air. Holy shit!

"A green witch? How useful." A silky voice interrupts my celebration.

My sisters and I whirl around at the sudden intrusion. A gorgeous pixie stands at the edge of the tomato bushes, iridescent white wings fluttering behind a graceful, lithe figure. Her hands are clasped in front of her waist. Even this early in the morning, she's impeccably put together with a tall coif of white-blonde hair and a silky blue gown.

Miriam drops to a knee next to Morgan, bowing her head. "My queen…"

I throw my hands up, unsure if I should bow like Miriam or what. "I hope we didn't wake you. I'm so sorry if I did, it's just that—"

She waves my excuse away with a gentle smile. "Do not worry about that, child. Miriam has told me all about you three, of course. But to see your green magic in action has me in awe. You've been learning for what"—she looks over at Miriam—"a few weeks?"

Miriam nods. "That's right my queen." Fuchsia eyes flick up to me and she rises off the ground, smiling. "Wren is amazing."

The pixie queen smiles. "Your Keeper spoke highly of you, of course, but to see it with my own eyes is a blessing. Ever is lucky to have a witch like you to work with Ohken and the pixies."

Miriam coughs. "She's doing more than just working with Ohken."

I sputter. Thea slaps Miriam on the back of the head, scoffing.

The queen laughs. "Oh, it is not at all uncommon for witches, pixies and trolls to mate. Being so focused on the natural world makes us good partners." She looks toward the garden gate, pink lips pulling into a smile. "Would you look at that…"

I turn to follow her gaze, and the hair on the back of my neck lifts.

Ohken stands there in jeans, a collared shirt and vest. His glorious auburn hair is piled high on his head, tendrils snaking down over his ears. He's rocking a kick-ass five o'clock shadow, which accentuates the pearly white tusks jutting up from his lower jaw. Emerald lips split into a smile when our eyes meet, and he stalks toward us.

"Here we go," Miriam whispers. "Time for us to head to Higher Grounds and get out of their way!"

Morgan and Thea give me quick hugs before heading toward the garden's exit with Miriam and the pixie queen. I barely have eyes for them, though, because the troll crossing the garden stares at me like he can't get enough, like he's starving and the only thing that will sate him is me.

Not gonna lie—it's a really good feeling.

Ohken stops in front of me, russet eyes flicking to the moonflower vines. His smile grows proud, wrinkles appearing at the corners of his eyes as he reaches out to touch the lattice of growth.

He admires it for a moment, then turns to me. "Well done, Miss Hector. I knew you could do it."

A rising flutter of pride swells in my chest, and I beam from ear to ear.

He steps closer, reaching out to collar my throat with one

big hand. He squeezes lightly and pulls me to him until my chest hits his.

"Last night, I took you to Trolliday, and we left with you feeling *less* than those around us. But I'm here to remind you that everything about you is perfect, Wren Elizabeth Hector. *You* are perfect, and you're perfect for me." His eyes shine bright, his gaze never wavering from mine.

Tears fill my eyes even as heat builds between my thighs. I ache to touch him, to finally take this further.

"I want you," I whisper. "So badly. I don't want to wait."

Ohken lets out a needy rumble and dips his head to brush his tusks against my lip.

"Let me take you to breakfast and then we'll go home and play. What do you think?"

His tongue snakes out, tasting my lower lip. My entire body tenses as I grip both his muscular forearms.

"Skip the breakfast," I gasp. "Just take me home." I'm riding a high from my power, intensely proud. I'm feeling really fucking good. And I want him to feel good too.

Ohken drops his grip on me and snarls, his upper lip curling back to reveal smaller pointed upper tusks. I want those teeth at my throat, bringing me pain and pleasure. I want to surrender to him in all the ways I sense he needs.

He grips my hand and pulls me toward the exit. We practically jog toward Main Street, crossing over and heading for the bridge. By the time we get there, I'm almost running, my chest heaving. Anticipation coils in my stomach, my clit throbbing.

"Not fast enough," Ohken snaps, swooping low to pick me up into his arms. It's on the tip of my tongue to caution him against trying to carry me, but who am I kidding? He's three hundred pounds of muscle. I weigh nothing to him.

I slide a hand inside his shirt and stroke at one hard nipple.

His grip on my outer thigh goes tight, nails digging into my muscle.

"Wren," he gasps. "We're almost there. Please."

"Please what?" I pinch his nipple. His knees buckle and he drops us down to the ground. I nearly fall out of his arms but the bridge is just ahead. Getting an idea, I shove away from him and take off toward it.

The laugh that rings out after me sends goosebumps down my arms and legs. It's low and confident and fucking feral. I pump my arms and legs faster, leaping down the few steps to the riverside and sprinting toward the bridge. It's just ahead, but already I hear the pound of heavy footsteps behind me.

Around us, the forest is quiet, like it senses a predator chasing its prey.

I push faster, I'm almost to the door.

Wham! A body barrels into me as soon as I get under the bridge, tossing me up against the door, sending the air whooshing out of my lungs. Ohken's enormous figure presses hard against mine, smashing me into the cold stones. He grabs my hand and shoves it against his enormous erection.

"You drive me wild, Wren. Feel that? That's for you my sweet."

Closing my fingers around his length, I stroke, loving the way his head falls back, his eyes closed as his lips curl into a snarl.

"Seems to me like you're slowly losing your mind, Mr. Stonesmith. Maybe your sweet witch is going to throw you into the deep end of your rut a little early. What do you think? Sounds fun to me."

Ohken's head snaps forward, amber eyes flashing as he brings his mouth to hover over mine. One big arm cages me in, and the other keeps my hand moving on his cock.

"You're not ready, Wren. We can't do this until tonight."

"There's a lot we can still do," I counter, sinking down to

my knees. He brings his other arm up onto the wall, never looking away from me.

Ripping his pants open, I pull his cock out and lick a stripe up the underside of it.

Ohken grunts, brows furrowing.

"I want to shatter your control," I admit. "I want to be the only one who gets to see you wild."

He growls and brings one hand down to fist my hair.

"Then suck, witch."

I don't need any more of a command than that. Wrapping my lips around the head of his cock, I take as much as I can into my mouth and hollow my cheeks. His responding groan tells me it feels good. I dip my tongue into his slit, gathering up the sugary moisture there and swirling it over the bulbous head.

My hands move in rhythmic strokes up and down his length.

Soft panting turns into a long, drawn-out groan. Cum spurts into my mouth, dripping down over my lips.

I pause just long enough to give him a heated look. "I want you to cover me in cum, Ohken. Can you do that for me?"

He nods, the fingers in my hair so tight I can barely move my head.

Big hips begin to thrust slowly, rhythmically to meet my lips. His cockhead draws away, then presses into my waiting mouth.

"Wren," he groans. "I'm about to fucking explode."

"Good," I snap.

"Need more." His voice goes low and gravelly the way it does when he wants to take charge.

"No!" I yowl, but he presses his hand to the doorway and we fall through in a tangle of arms and legs.

Ohken's claws come to my clothes and shred them. He tosses the fabric away and rolls, pulling me on top of him with his dick nestled between my thighs. He props himself up on one elbow and puts his other hand on my thigh.

"Ride, witch." The command sends my hips moving of their own accord. Every rock of my body drags his huge cock through my thighs. The ruffles under his head stroke my clit with every pass until I'm dying from pleasure.

When he starts to piston his hips to help me, I gasp.

"That's it, Wren," he croons. "Lose yourself to me. Come all over me, my love."

It's that last word that does it.

Love.

I shatter, soaking his cock with release as I throw my head back and scream. Ohken grunts, but it morphs into a howl of triumph as he spurts all over his shirt and my thighs, covering us in green cum.

He rips pleasure from my body until I fall limp against his chest, gasping for air and quivering from the feel of him.

The only sounds are his heavy breathing and mine. Eventually, I recover enough to slap his chest.

"How are you still fully clothed? Very unfair."

Ohken laughs and shifts forward, pulling me back into his arms as he stands and steps out of his pants. He kicks them to the side and turns to carry me up the long hallway toward the cave entrance. The engraved wooden door waves us through, lights popping on as soon as we enter the main room.

"Bath. Food. More sex." Ohken grins at me. "That's the order of things today, my sweet."

"You mean your love," I correct. "You called me that in the throes of ecstasy, you know."

Ohken looks down at me, dipping to brush his lips to mine. "My love," he repeats.

CHAPTER SEVENTEEN
OHKEN

I leave Wren napping in my bed and stride to the kitchen to comm Taylor. He picks up on the first beep.

"Everything ready?"

"Yep! Fleur is just about out of flowers at this point. But everything's set up just like you asked me to do. I'd ask a little more about what you have planned, but it was more or less obvious, so I threw some extra towels and blankets by the showers. They're there if you need them."

I hold back a laugh. It was thoughtful of him to foresee what we might need tonight, but I'm not letting a single stitch of fabric cover Wren's body from my view. I'm headed fast toward being an outright savage. Thanking Taylor, I click off and place my palms on the cool island countertop.

The countertop shimmies, and the cave sends a pitcher of water my direction.

I take it with a wry laugh. "Thank you, old friend."

Pictures on the walls clatter. She's laughing at me.

Closing my eyes, I focus on what I'm feeling. I'm jittery like I've had too much of Alessandro's espresso. My stomach rumbles painfully, and I lick my lips. Even my hands quiver slightly. My rut is almost here, but the skyball final is tomorrow.

I want my witch, and I can't wait to show her what I have planned for this evening. She'll be ready for me in a few hours, and I plan to make our first time memorable. I'm half tempted to pounce on her right now, but she could use the rest. Plus, our potion won't have completed its magic for a few hours yet.

I groan and grab the pitcher of water, rounding the island and flopping onto my oversized sofa. My cock is rock-hard, standing at attention and dripping like a faucet. I rock my hips and close my eyes, imagining how fucking delicious it'll be when Wren seats herself on my cock. The wait is killing me.

By dinnertime, I'm almost mindless with need. Sweat pours down my face as I toss and turn on the sofa. I rise and jog to the bathroom, taking a quick cold shower during which I rub my cock until it spurts. It's not enough, not nearly enough to slake my need for her.

When I leave the bathroom, Wren's slowly waking up, her legs tangled in the bedsheets as she stretches long arms over her head. The sheets slide down her chest, revealing pert dusky nipples.

My strides eat up the distance between us. I grab her soft hip and roll her onto her stomach, raking my tusks over the lush roundness of her ass. Wren laughs, but I kiss and bite until her laughter turns into soft panting.

I lick a stripe up the side of her ass cheek, marveling at the indented lines there. The lines are a paler shade of her natural skin color. Pressing a kiss along the length of one, I pinch her thigh playfully.

"I didn't know humans came with stripes. I didn't notice these before."

She laughs and rolls onto her side, which puts her pussy

right at my eye level. She throws a wink in my direction. "They're stretch marks, baby. Happens to humans when we grow too fast. Usually, humans don't like them."

I lean forward and nuzzle her pretty fat thigh, noting how the stripes zigzag along the outside of it. Reaching up, I trail my fingertips alongside her inner thigh until I reach the juncture, stroking softly.

"Disregard anything a human ever taught you about beauty, Wren. You're stunning, your stripes are stunning, and I've never met a woman as beautiful inside and out as you."

Her smirk turns into a full-on grin, and she props her right leg up, giving me the perfect view of her pussy. She's soaked for me and still coated in cum from our earlier play.

A feral snarl tumbles from my lips, and I dive in tongue-first.

Earlier today wasn't enough. It'll never be enough. I need all of her.

Her head falls back, hips rolling to meet my mouth.

I shake my head from side to side, swirling my tongue over her clit.

"Yes!" she shouts. "Don't stop, that's so fucking good!"

When I suck hard and then shift off the bed, she lurches upright, scowling mightily. "Ohken Stonesmith, you better get back here and finish what you started or I am going to fuck with you for the rest of your life. I hold a grudge like nobody's business."

Grinning, I slide off the bed and head for the shower, glancing over my shoulder at her.

"That was a tease, Miss Hector. The potion's done its work, and I have plans for us tonight. Come wash off with me; it's almost time to get dressed and go."

"Away from the bed?" Her brows arc up into a desperate vee. "I thought we'd be here. I don't wanna leave."

"It's a surprise," I call out. "You love surprises."

Wren mutters something under her breath, but moments later I hear the soft pad of feet.

I reach into the shower and turn it on, then swivel around to watch her join me.

She leans in the doorway, both arms crossed and a resigned expression on her face.

"This better be an absolute banger of a surprise, baby. You know I hate surprises."

I reach out and rub my fingers over the aragonite stud in her ear. "But I love giving them to you."

CHAPTER EIGHTEEN
WREN

It's true that I hate surprises. But it's also true that I love gifts. So, if one leads to the other, I suppose they cancel each other out. No matter how much I beg, Ohken refuses to tell me what we're doing tonight. I don't want to leave the cave though, because tonight is *the* night.

His sex potion has done whatever it needs to do, and we can finally take things further.

And further.

And further.

Because his dick is about fifteen inches long.

He squeezes my fingers as we walk up Sycamore away from downtown. As far as I know, there's nothing out here but the stadium, so I'm guessing that's where he's taking me.

"You're quiet." I risk a look up at him. He's barely said two words this entire walk, and it's been a solid half hour. Plenty of time for me to psych myself out about if his magic pussy-expanding potion is gonna work or not.

He lets go of my hand and slings his arm around my waist, pointing ahead of us with the other hand. "I'm just excited. We're almost there, so I'm sure you can guess what I planned to show you, but I wanted you to be the first resident to see the inside."

I grin like the Mad Hatter, picking up the pace as we get to a bend in the road. We round it and a huge structure rises up in front of us. It looks exactly like a football stadium with huge curved walls and giant floodlights around the top of the exterior walls. It's made of flat black stones, giving it a sort of Monty Python medieval feel. Big open doors dot the wall every ten yards or so.

Perfectly flat, grassy fields surround the stadium. Ohken gestures ahead. "The fields will start to fill up with pregamers. By the time the final starts, everything you see will be covered with cars and motorcycles and tents."

I slide my fingers down the inside of his forearm before slipping them through his. Goosebumps follow my touch, and when I look up, his jaw is tightly grit.

Anticipation thrums in my chest. I can't wait to see what he's cooked up for this evening. He makes everything special—every look, every touch, every comment. Every date. I've never felt so damn cherished in my life.

"I didn't realize how much I needed you until I had you," I murmur, stopping in front of one of the arched entryways.

Ohken turns toward me and fists a hand through my hair, guiding my head back. "Good. It's my goal to make you crazy about me, so if it's working, I'll consider it a job well done."

I shrug and slide a hand inside his shirt, tickling his thick abs. "Well, we'll see what happens after the relations. What if we have terrible chemistry?" I barely hold back a cheeky grin.

Ohken chuckles and leans down, nipping at my lower lip with his. His lips are so warm, so demanding. He grips my jaw with one huge hand, angling his mouth over mine, forcing me to open for him. He moves, pushing until my back hits the wall. Big arms slide down the back of my legs and hoist me up. His mouth chases mine, his kiss growing hungrier until he rips himself from me with a whine.

"You drive me to distraction, witch." His voice is frayed, the words tumbling from his lips. "I wanted to give you a tour, but you are utterly bewitching."

"How fitting." I chuckle and run my fingers down his throat, marveling at how fucking manly he is.

Ohken chuckles and sets me down. Grabbing my hand, he pulls me through the entry hallway. "Let's get this tour done, and then we're christening this place together. What do you think?"

I stop, biting my lip. Because I have an idea. A sexy, devilish idea.

"I want a naked tour."

Ohken whirls around, one auburn brow slanted upward. His look of surprise morphs into something darker. He slides his hands into his pockets. "Get more specific, Miss Hector."

I step closer, unbuttoning the topmost button of his black collared shirt. "Every few minutes, you should lose another piece of clothing. Because I'd really love to stare at your incredible body while you tell me all about how you constructed this place."

He chuckles. "Are you going to remember anything I say if you're busy staring at my dick? Because that's what it'll be, Miss Hector. I'm already hard, and we both know you want it."

I give him an indignant slap on the stomach. "I'm sure I'll manage."

He lifts his chin and swiftly undoes the rest of the buttons. When he slides the shirt off his bulky shoulders, I hold back a whine. God, he's got the most gorgeous body. He tosses it to the ground and reaches for my tee. "Your turn."

I take a step back. "No way. One at a time. Tell me about this beautiful stadium you built out of thin air, and I'll take my shirt off in a minute. Plus are we going to have to traipse back through here to find the clothes afterward?"

He growls, tugging me to him by the belt loops. "I'll do the traipsing. Shirt off, Miss Hector. I like your game, but it's moving a little slow for me. Every time I lose an article of clothing, you will too. As much as I want you to look your fill of me, I need to look my fill of you. This is nonnegotiable."

"Jesus, you're bossy," I mutter.

"*The* boss," he agrees, leaning down to drag his tusks along my collarbone and over my shoulder.

"Mmm, feels good when you do that." My head falls to the side to make room for his attention.

His wet tongue comes to the shell of my ear, and he laughs low and devious. "It'll feel better when I bite you with my cock buried in that sweet, tight pussy."

Fuck me, I want to skip to that. But I just came up with this damn tour game. "Noted," I gasp out. "Let's keep the tour short."

Ohken grabs my hand and presses it to the front of his pants, running my palm over his hard cock. "Are you desperate for this, my sweet? Anxious for your first taste of troll dick?"

I don't bother holding back a whine when he bites his way down my shoulder, dragging my bra strap down with his teeth.

"Get on with it already," I snap, turning to give him a saucy glare. "You're the biggest tease on the planet."

He stands, his expression thoroughly pleased. "Part of being a good Dominant is making sure your partner is ready. I take pride in making you gush for me, sweet witch. I want those panties soaked through by the time I take you."

For a long minute, we stare at one another like we're standing off. Ohken's russet gaze never flickers, never fades in intensity. If anything, it's like he's daring me to look down or submit. Except that the sexy lessons he's teaching me are finally sinking in. Submission isn't about giving in, just like with my magic. It's not something to lose myself to. Submission is about not trying to control something. It's about letting go and trusting.

I drop my eyes and smile.

"Beautifully done," he murmurs, reaching for my hand. "Come with me, Wren."

I glance up to find the smirk back on his face. He leads us down a hallway, pointing at big cutouts in the stone on the inner side.

"This hall runs around the entire outside of the stadium. Each of these cutout sections will hold a vendor or pop-up restaurant. It's modeled after human stadiums the Keeper saw when he lived in the human world."

I stop in my tracks. "Wait a sec. I knew he'd lived outside of any haven for a bit, but he designed this place?"

Ohken nods. "He's a prodigious design talent. He designs almost all of the new havens. It's not something he'd mention because he doesn't like talking about himself, but he has a knack for community and building design."

I fall silent, mulling over that bit of news.

Ohken tilts my chin up. "Miss Hector. I'm fucking done with this tour. I can't stop staring at your gorgeous tits, and I'm ready to rip your bra off with my teeth. Let's get to the good part, shall we?"

He opens his arms and I hop up into them with a joyous laugh, wrapping my arms around his neck. He peppers my face and neck with kisses, stalking down an offshoot of the main hallway. We duck into a smaller hallway and hop into an elevator. Ohken presses a button and we jolt upward for a few seconds. When we step out of the elevator, I gasp. We're in a long skinny room with lockers and benches on each side. But flickering candles and flower petals cover every surface.

"My God." I release a held breath.

Ohken sets me down and stalks into the room, waving a hand around. "The one thing the Keeper hated about human stadiums is the basement locker room. He wanted the players to join in the fans' excitement. And I wanted you to see this first." He turns and walks to the far wall, pressing his hand to it. The whole thing goes transparent like a window, giving us an incredible view of the stadium's interior.

I jog to meet him, mindful of the candles. Stepping carefully around them, I press my hand to the glass and marvel at the huge soccer-like field below us. Rows of bleachers encircle the field. If I didn't know it was for a monster sporting event, I'd guess it was a beautiful soccer stadium somewhere in Europe.

"This is stunning," I murmur, turning to look up at Ohken.

His eyes crinkle in the corners as he smiles and leans against the glass. "Stunning." His voice pitches low and soft. He raps on the glass with the back of his knuckles. "It's one-way glass, so we can see out but from the exterior it appears to be a wall like any other." He flattens his palm to it again, and the whole thing shimmers and turns shiny. "And there's a mirror mode as well."

I grin. "How convenient."

"Indeed."

"I take it you want to fuck me in front of this mirror?"

"No." He laughs, devious and confident. "I want to fuck you against this mirror. And you're going to watch me do it, Miss Hector. Right now."

I struggle to breathe around nerves jangling in my stomach.

Ohken reaches for my bra and unclips it, tossing it away.

I wave around at the hundreds of candles with a cheeky grin. "Don't set the building on fire."

Ohken's eyes come to mine. "Don't think for a second that

this isn't all exactly how I planned. I won't let you get burned, my sweet, not unless you want a little bit of pain with your pleasure."

"Mmm." I won't deny that a little pain can be fun. He proved that by rolling thorns over my goddamn nipples. I'm not saying no to a damn thing he wants to try.

He reaches for my jeans next, dropping to a knee to slide them over my ass. He tugs hard, pulling them down my thighs as he plants a line of kisses down my soft stomach.

"Perfection," he murmurs. He nuzzles my pussy with his nose, sliding my thong down before helping me step out of my boots and jeans. Then he stands and takes a step back, leaning against the mirror again. "Undress me, Wren."

I don't need to be told twice. His upper body is already bare, and it's fucking delightful how his big chest rises and falls with deep, fast breaths. He widens his stance and brings his feet forward, giving me room to obey.

I slide both hands up the fronts of his thighs, running them over his impossible length.

"I don't know how the hell this is gonna work," I mutter, undoing the top button.

Ohken lets out a soft growl. "It'll fit, sweetheart."

I glance up as I shove his pants down, gripping the waistband of his boxers to push them down at the same time. "You calling me sweetheart is hot."

"It's uniquely human." He smiles. "I learned it in one of the historical society's volumes on human pleasure."

I glance down, cupping his heavy balls and pulling gently on the skin between them. "Well thank God for research. This is anything *but* human, however. Tell me, Ohken, how you like to fuck."

He groans, squeezing his eyes closed as his head falls back and hits the mirror.

"Thoroughly, Wren." His voice is pure gravel, his fists

balled and tense. There's a slight quiver to his huge muscles. My man is on edge.

"I was thinking of teasing you," I admit. "But you look ready to burst." He lets out a strangled choke when I fall to my knees and suck at the tip of his cock. But unlike before, my jaw hinges and drops wider, and his entire cockhead slips between my lips.

I back up, shooting him an amazed look. "Holy shit. Did I just...am I imagining that I was able to do that?"

Russet eyes darken, and my big troll grins like a maniac. "You can do a whole lot more than suck on the tip, Wren. Magic is a beautiful thing."

Fuck yes. Opening wide, I swallow his cock to the back of my throat and farther.

Ohken roars and brings one hand to the back of my head, fisting my hair to guide me off his dick. I suck at the soft, frilled edges that surround the mushroom head, loving that I'm able to finally do this. Any worry I had about our fit is gone in a rush of heat and desire that spins my head.

I shift forward, taking him to the hilt. A desperate whine echoes in the big room around us.

"Enough." Ohken pants. "Give me a moment, Wren."

When I don't stop, he tugs lightly on my hair.

"Miss Hector."

I pull gently on one of the ruffled edges around his dick, totally avoiding eye contact. I'm having too much fucking fun.

He hisses and yanks my head back, dropping to his knees in front of me, spinning us so I'm pressed to the mirror. He covers me from behind, his dick nestled between my ass cheeks. He pulls my hands above my head and holds them there, his free hand coming around my stomach to squeeze the soft rolls.

"You are the brattiest of brats, Miss Hector. Do you know what happens to brats?"

I pant when he scrapes his tusks along my shoulder blade.

"They get spanked? God, I hope they get spanked!"

Ohken's hand strokes down the dips and valleys of my stomach and over my mound, rubbing gently at my clit. He moves behind me, guiding his cock between my thighs. When he rocks his hips, his cockhead rubs along my slit, lighting up every nerve ending. Concentration obliterated, I rest my head against his chest.

"No," he snaps. "You're going to watch every moment of me taking you for the first time. I'm going to bring you to the edge over and over, Wren. You'll be begging by the time you get off."

I shove my ass against his hips, squeezing my thighs around his length. "Or maybe I'll feel so tight and delicious you'll combust the second you slide in."

"Maybe," Ohken murmurs, thrumming his fingers on my clit, the slow pump of his hips methodical. He shifts backward and presses my right hand to my thighs. "Keep your hand there, Wren. Don't move it until I tell you to." The other remains flat on the mirror above my head.

The picture in front of me is intoxicating—I'm spread wide with Ohken dwarfing me from behind. His cock peeks out from between my thighs now and again, stroking every sensitive spot. He's got one hand on my clit, but slides his fingers down so when his cock pokes through, he can stroke his own folds.

His cheeks are flushed dark green. He's watching his cock disappear into me from behind.

I'm not an obedient woman. But he was right about one thing. I'm about to start begging because this tease is for the damn birds. I want him inside me, and I want it now. But I know I can't demand that of him. He doesn't work that way.

So instead, I begin to work my hips to meet his, shoving backward when he pumps forward. The move drags my pussy lips along his thickness. The green flush of his cheeks grows darker, his mouth falling open as his brows furrow in concentration.

I drop my hips lower and angle back, and the head of his cock presses up against my pussy entrance instead of sliding through my thighs.

Ohken grunts, then runs one hand up to my breast to pluck my nipple hard.

"Naughty witch. You're determined to speed this up, aren't you?"

"God yes!" I cry out, pushing back. But he redirects himself and takes up the slow torture again, rubbing and pumping and touching himself until I think I might die of need. A slight coating of sweat covers my skin. My breasts grow heavy and achy as he plays with them, his touch growing rougher and more demanding.

"Please," I beg. "I can't take this anymore Ohken!"

He laughs, and I can't even sass him about how fucking triumphant he sounds.

"You win, please!"

Ohken growls and rocks back onto both heels, drawing me away from the mirror and placing my other hand on my thigh. "Leave it there, Wren."

"Okay!" I'm practically sobbing at this point. If I don't get him inside me I'm going to lose it.

He guides my thighs farther out around him and reaches down, notching himself at my core. Russet eyes meet mine in the mirror. "Ready yourself, my sweet. Even with the magic, I'm big."

I can't tear my eyes from the scene in the mirror. His plump tip disappears between my thighs and presses against my pussy lips. The very first inches slide in, stroking me from the inside out.

"Jesus fucking Christ the goddamn ruffles!" I shriek.

He chuckles. And he slides farther in, bringing his other hand underneath my left thigh. He holds me spread wide as he rolls his hips up, his cock disappearing into my pussy. I struggle against the intrusion. He touches every place inside me that aches for pleasure.

He leans forward, biting a line down my shoulder. A growl demands my attention in the mirror.

"Watch that pretty pussy gobble up this big troll dick, Miss Hector. Don't you dare look away from us."

CHAPTER NINETEEN
OHKEN

Wren's pussy strangles me as I sink deeper inside her. She's tighter than I could have ever imagined, even with the magic helping us along.

"God!" she shouts and claws at her thighs.

"I'm almost to the hilt, my sweet," I croon in her ear. Her head falls to the side, granting me access to the expanse of her soft neck. I lick a stripe from her ear down to her shoulder, then rake my tusks along her back. Dropping her farther onto my cock, I resist the urge to roar when her ass meets my lap.

"You took all of me, my love. Well done."

"It's like fucking a goddamn tree trunk! This is never gonna wor—" Her words die when I lift her up off me and slide her back down again. Blistering, ragged pleasure screams through my system. My balls are full to bursting, aching to unload deep inside her.

But I promised teasing.

"You feel so goddamn good." I growl the words into her ear.

She clenches around me, a whine echoing off the mirror in front of us.

"Big. Really fucking big," she cries out.

"And you're taking every inch," I remind her, circling her clit with the heel of my palm.

I pick up a steady pace of pulling her off my cock and dragging her back down onto it. Wren's cheeks turn bright pink, then red, her brows furrowed in the middle, pink lips parted in a desperate 'o.'

I roll my hips a little harder, testing how it feels for her. She cries out.

I can't hold back. Shifting forward, I guide her hands back onto the mirror and grip her hips, pummeling into her from behind. Big tits sway, her nipples two hard peaks. I told her not to let her eyes close, but I'm too fucking far gone to chide her for it now.

Her thighs begin to tremble, her muscles tensing. Her pussy clenches hard around me as we chase that sweet high of ecstasy.

With a yowl, she spurts creamy honey all over my cock, her muscles fluttering around me. Every contraction of her pussy teases my dick until I'm riding a never-ending wave of bliss, right on the edge of release.

Wren screams my name on repeat. I can't tear my eyes from how fucking beautiful she is in the mirror. She tightens further, and liquid squirts out of her, coating her thighs and my cock, dripping down my balls. And that sends me barreling over the edge. My sack draws up tight as I shoot a load into her, filling her with seed. The sound of me fucking her turns wet and sloppy, and cum drips from her pussy to cover the floor and the backs of her thighs.

"Oh fuuuuck!" Wren shouts, jerking in my arms. She comes again, and again. And every time she comes she drags me with her until I'm wrung out from the pleasure of fucking my mate.

After a half dozen orgasms, she slumps forward onto the

mirror. The floor around us is slick with her sweet honey and my cum. Hunching over her, I kiss my way along her spine, reveling at the fact that this woman is mine.

Wren's emerald eyes meet me in the mirror. She gives me a thumbs-up. "Consider the stadium christened."

I throw my head back and laugh before meeting her sated gaze in the mirror again.

"I'm not done, Miss Hector. Not by a long shot. Come here."

Green eyes drop submissively, then dart back up to mine. "Yes, sir."

~

The following morning, I leave the kitchen and head for my bedroom. Opening the door, I marvel at the vision I'm presented with—Wren naked in the middle, arms and legs flung out like a starfish. I lean against the doorframe and admire the view. The way she's spread means I get a hint of swollen pussy lips and a tease of her back hole.

"You gonna stand and stare at my ass all morning or did you bring coffee?"

Laughing, I walk across the room and around her side of the bed, sitting down with the coffee in hand.

Wren flips over and shoves her way up to the headboard—the headboard I tied her to last night while I ate her out—and reaches for the coffee.

"Mmm, troll whip." She laughs as she takes the mug, but the smile dies and she looks back up at me. "I've been thinking. I don't want to deprive everyone of this just because I was jealous. You should start providing it to Higher Grounds again."

I wave the comment away. "Already taken care of. I was able to arrange for a troll from another haven to take over."

"Oh really?" Wren's voice is skeptical. "And how does that conversation go, exactly? Excuse me, sir, would you mind jacking off and sending me the jizz so I can give it to Alessandro for coffee?"

"Something like that." I grin and slide a hand up her plump thigh. I look down to admire it. "You're stunning, Wren." I'll never stop admiring how soft and luscious she is.

"I suppose you've got a thing for full-bodied women, huh?" She chuckles as she takes a sip of the coffee, troll whip covering her upper lip. I want to lick it off.

"Nope. I've got a thing for feminine women, and you're the most lusciously feminine woman I've ever met."

"Mmm," she muses. "Are you one of those men who finds pregnant ladies hot?"

Heat streaks through me. We haven't talked about children. We've really only talked about my rut, which is the last step a troll male takes before having a conversation about a bonding tattoo.

I stop stroking her leg and look into her incredible green eyes.

"I am. I'd love nothing better than to experience that with you, one day, when we're both ready."

Wren's sassy smile morphs into a full-on grin, and she sets the coffee down on the bedside table. Both arms come around my neck, and she pulls me on top of her.

"I don't know if you'll be exhausted after skyball, but I was thinking maybe afterward we could—"

"Yes," I demand. "Yes to that plan."

Her pink lips turn up in a smile. "Good." She glances down at her comm watch. "Shit, I told the girls I'd meet them for breakfast this morning. What are your plans for the day?"

I'm admittedly busy all day, but we make a plan to get

together prior to the game. When I start nipping at her breasts, admiring the way they spill from my hands, she yowls and pushes away from me, citing her breakfast date with her sisters.

I laugh and stroke my cock as she dresses in one of my big shirts. Eventually, she manages to escape me, but I feel the pang of her loss. Even the cave is different without her here, morose and quiet and not her usual helpful self.

Heading into the bathroom, I shower, but all I can think about is how we're physically compatible now—more than compatible—and I want to spend my evening focused on her. I dread playing in the game, because knowing she's going to be sitting in the stands, thinking about riding my cock, has me worried I won't be able to concentrate. Although, I know more than a handful of Evertons have money riding on this game, and they're counting on me to help our team win.

Once I'm ready, I comm Richard, the pack alpha for the werewolves.

"Ohken, how are you?" His deep voice is tinny through the watch's small interface.

"All good. I wanted to make sure you still feel good about security for the tournament?"

The shifters have far greater numbers than the Keeper, the gargoyles, and me. They'll be stationed throughout the stadium to keep an eye on things. It's not that we're expecting trouble, per se, but Wesley was able to coordinate a targeted attack twice in the last few weeks. I wouldn't put it past him to do so again.

"Yeah," Richard says. "Most of my alphas are out at the stadium already. I'm told there's a fair bit of tailgating that's already started. They've broken up a few fights."

"Great." I groan. "By the time this is done, we'll be praying not to host the tournament for another hundred years."

"It's gonna be great as long as you secure us the win,

brother." Richard laughs. "I'm past my playing days, but I'm half tempted to try anyhow." That's almost laughable. Richard's nearly as big as I am and all muscle. He'd be a great player, but an injury two tournaments ago stopped him from playing more.

We sign off and I leave my cave, heading to find the Keeper. We've got quite a few things to go over this morning. When my comm watch pings again, I expect Richard, but it's the Keeper's name that pops up.

"Ohken, come to town hall, please. Hearth representatives would like to meet with us prior to tonight's festivities."

I open my mouth to respond, but he clicks off. Sighing, I pick up the pace and jog toward Main Street, hitching a left and making my way the three or four blocks to town hall. Just like the rest of Ever's town council, I technically have an office here. I'm never in it, though. Town hall is a sad building to me —the gazebo in front of it gets frequently used for town meetings, but we rarely go into the building itself. Every time I do, I feel…depressed.

That building is missing something, and I've never quite figured out what it is.

Alo's standing out front when I arrive, big arms crossed over his broad chest. He gives me an irritated look. "The fucking Hearth assholes showed up this morning and demanded a meeting with the town council and protector team. Can't wait to see what this is about."

Great.

I give him a quick look. "Should Thea be here? She's officially part of the protector team now."

Alo shakes his head. "She had plans already, but she's aware. Shepherd's going to catch up with her afterward. I don't think he was anxious to put her in front of the Hearth since she hasn't registered with them yet." He looks up at me. "Has Wren?"

Shit. I hadn't considered that, but with Wren's power growing and Thea doing so well with hers, they'll have to register soon.

"That's what I thought," Alo grumbles as he opens the town hall's double front doors. "I imagine we'll get shit for that."

We stride down a long tiled hallway to the far left office—technically the Keeper's office. Although, like me, he's rarely here. When we open the door, the Keeper and Shepherd are just inside. At the window stands an elegant woman, dark hair coiled high on top of her head. Angular cheekbones give her a haughty look. Next to her are two men. They could be twins with how similar they appear. They're cut from the same cloth as the woman. Willowy but athletic.

Vampires.

I haven't seen this trio since the Hearth came down after Wesley's first attack.

The woman looks over at me, turning from the window to slowly incline her head in greeting.

The Keeper leans against the room's fireplace, one arm up on the mantle. A tick in his jaw tells me they've likely already been arguing.

I reach out and shake the hands of the three vampires. "Evenia, Aberen, Betmal. It's been many years."

"That it has," says the woman, her tone dripping with disdain. "We would not have come at all, were it not for the recent attacks." Her eyes drift to the Keeper. "And your unregistered residents."

A muscle works in the Keeper's jaw. "I've already told you, Evenia. The Hector triplets haven't officially decided to stay in Ever. Once they do, I'll reg—"

She waves his remark away. "And yet one has already mated Shepherd Rygold, is that not right?"

Shepherd rises to a stand, his face carefully neutral. "Only just. We've got the registration paperwork; we'll fill it out after the tournament is out of the way."

"See that you do," Evenia commands. "New witches? We need them on record in case their services are called for elsewhere."

"I don't think so," the Keeper snaps. "The Hectors are just getting settled here. They wouldn't want to be pulled into your endless programs and policies in other havens. Leave them alone."

One of the males snarls. "Why so protective, Keeper? Perhaps because you called them yourself? You've registered one as your mate, breaking your betrothal to Moira Finher. There can be no exceptions to our rules, not even for you, child."

Before any of us can say anything, Evenia barrels on.

"That brings us to the reason for our meeting this morning. You've had two attacks in just as many weeks. You'll remember the Hearth's three-strikes policy, Keeper?"

"Naturally," he grits out. "How could I forget with you calling to remind me every other day?"

She nods again, giving him a superior look. "Well, let us ensure nothing happens during skyball, because it would be terribly inconvenient to have to place another Keeper here if you fail in your duties."

I hear the crack of the Keeper's teeth at her veiled threat.

I've had enough of this. Turning back toward Evenia, I cross my arms. "We're facing unprecedented challenges, Evenia, as you're well aware. Wesley's back, which means we can expect further issues from him. It's only a matter of time before he tries this at another haven, once he realizes he's not going to be successful here."

"Perhaps." Aberen laughs, red eyes narrowed. He opens his thin arms wide, black nails glittering in the early light. "The reality is, he *hasn't* attacked any other havens. Just this one."

Red glittery eyes flit over to the Keeper. "Perhaps he senses weakness, and that is why he focuses here."

Alo flares his wings wide, spines emerging along his shoulders and down his forearms. The vampires take a step away from him, Aberen and Betmal moving closer to their mate.

Alo practically shouts at the Hearth representatives. "The Keeper put himself at risk to determine who was behind the first attack, willingly taking a second mark on his record. He's behaved with the utmost regard for his haven and its residents. You should be giving him a godsdamned award."

One of Evenia's brows lifts, but her expression remains skeptical.

"We're done here," I state, reaching behind me to open the office door. "This town council has things to take care of today, and they don't include verbally sparring with the three of you. Please, go and enjoy our lovely town. Spend gobs of money at our businesses. I don't care what you do, but get the fuck out of town hall."

If the vampires are surprised at my vehemence, they say nothing. The two males glide gracefully through the door into the hall. Evenia slips across the room to stand in front of the Keeper, her ruby-red eyes focused on him. The look she gives him is almost tender, but it's all a mask. She's one of the cruelest beings I've ever met, and I've had the misfortune of meeting her a number of times.

Reaching out, she strokes a black-clawed hand down the Keeper's scar. He jerks away and bares his teeth at her, snapping at her hand.

She laughs. "Don't disappoint your fathers and me, Abe—"

"It's Keeper, now," he snaps.

Evenia chuckles again. "You're still my son, and if you fail, you'll be the first Keeper to ever be removed from his post. I won't stand for that embarrassment to our house, do you understand me?"

If the Keeper is worried about his mother's pronouncement, he doesn't show it. Instead, he takes a step closer to her, fangs sliding farther down from his upper jaw.

"Get the fuck out of my office," he snarls, his voice low and deadly.

Evenia chuckles, giving him one last look before sauntering out the door to join her husbands.

The Keeper turns to watch me close the door, then slumps against the fireplace. None of us say anything. After a tense moment, he stands tall and shrugs his shoulders.

"Don't let the Hearth distract us from our jobs today. We've got a good plan for keeping Ever safe. We—"

"Keeper," Alo murmurs.

The Keeper looks away, sucking at his teeth like he can't bear to look at us.

Alo's voice is gentler than I've ever heard it. "Do you want to talk about it? We're in your corner, always. Without fail."

The Keeper glances at us, and it's the most fragile I've ever seen him. He looks like he's about to crack.

I take a step closer to him. "What do you need, Keeper?"

A neutral mask falls over his face. "Nothing. I'm on my way to visit with Moira. She's in town for skyball. I need to speak with her about teaching the Hectors once they reach the limits of the instruction we can provide here."

I cross my arms. "Did you see what Wren did with the moonflowers yesterday?"

The Keeper nods. "I'm grateful, and I'll tell her so myself at some point today."

The room falls silent.

Finally, he puts his hands on his hips and stares out the back windows. "I hope to gods the tournament goes off without a hitch."

Fuck. I do too.

CHAPTER TWENTY
WREN

Thea's mouth drops open. "A baby arm holding an apple?! Are you kidding me? I thought you were joking!"

Morgan smirks and crosses her arms over her knees. We're sitting out front of the Galloping Green Bean waiting for a table to open up. It's hella busy with the tournament, even though it's still early-ish in the morning.

"Hence the potion," I say with a deadpan look. "Apparently that's how it works when trolls mate outside their species."

"Jesus," Thea grumbles. "And it didn't hurt going in? Is your uterus obliterated? Are your insides rearranged?"

I laugh out loud, although her comment does make me wonder if my insides look like a car crash.

Morgan snorts. "Just don't ask me to weigh in as a physician, because I have no scientific training to support a theory about this shit."

Thea dissolves into fits of laughter.

Alba pokes her head out the front door, nickering softly. "Hectors, get in here—your table's ready." She disappears back inside.

Thea scowls at the door as it closes. "You'd think we'd been lollygagging out here for half an hour or something."

I pull the door open for my sisters, smacking Thea's ass as she sails through.

She hisses like a cat and swats at me, but slides her arm around my waist as we follow Alba.

I marvel at how busy the diner is. It's early, but every table is full, and some monsters stand at the bar with no chairs. They scooch out of the way when Alba sashays along the bar toward the booths that face the front of the diner. Somehow, she manages to get us into the same booth we always sit in.

She winks at me when I slide in next to Morgan. "I'll grab coffee. I'm out of troll whip, though, so don't ask for it. Although," she cuts me a salty look. "Something tells me you already know that."

I'm about to let her know that Ohken made other arrangements, but Miriam sails into view with Alo's son Iggy propped on her shoulder. He hops off and sidles up next to Thea, rubbing his horns on her arm.

Thea rolls her eyes but opens her arms. Iggy hops onto her thighs and sits down, resting his arms on the table.

Alba leaves us but returns a minute later with four coffees (sans troll whip) and a hot chocolate for Iggy. He dives right in almost before she sets it down, jolting the cup and sending chocolate all down the sides.

Thea laughs and strokes his chocolate hair away from his horns.

"God, you two are adorable." I lift my coffee cup in a toast to my sister. I've never seen her this happy, even before Mom and Dad's accident.

"Hector triplets? Is that you?" A high-pitched voice has us all turning on the bench seats. Walking up the aisle toward us is Moira, the Keeper's betrothed and the one who identified us as witches. Seeing her in real life, rather than through a hologram, is an otherworldly experience.

She waves one winged arm. The Keeper trails behind her, looking intensely uncomfortable.

Morgan goes stiff as a board in the booth next to me, shoving herself right up against the window.

Moira and the Keeper stop at the end of our booth and the bird-lady smiles, feathers on her head fluffing up and then smoothing back down. Her humanoid eyes crinkle at the corners.

"My goodness, it's lovely to meet you three in person. The Keeper has told me so much about the progress you're making."

"Has he?" Morgan questions. I kick her under the table.

Moira pauses and gives Morgan a look I can't quite decipher—it's like she knows this is awkward as fuck what with her being betrothed to the Keeper but Morgan being his mate. Still, she seems determined to be friendly. She looks around and gestures at the busy diner. "We were planning to grab a quick breakfast, but it's busy here." Her eyes drop to the open spots next to me and Miriam. "You seem to have a little extra space. Could we join y—"

"Let's not bother them, Moira," the Keeper says. A pink blush crawls across his cheeks. He reaches up and tugs at the top of his turtleneck.

"Nonsense!" Morgan chirps happily. "We'd love to have you join us. Please sit."

Oh shit. What is my sister up to?

The Keeper stares at Morgan. Morgan stares at the Keeper. Moira looks around at the rest of us and then takes a seat gracefully next to me. Golden brown feathers ruffle up on her forehead, making her look like a humanish parrot.

I shift closer to Morgan to avoid smashing Moira's feathers. She crosses her legs toward me. Chicken legs. Her legs are chicken legs. Her arms are wings. She still has fingers at the very ends of the wings.

I'm so confuckingfused.

The Keeper clears his throat and drops into the booth next to Miriam, who grabs her coffee and sips it. Her brows are all the way up in her damn hairline. I don't think she could be any more obvious, and I kick her under the table.

"That was my leg, Miss Hector," the Keeper snaps.

Heat flushes along my cheeks.

Nobody says a word.

Conveniently, Alba shows up to take our order. I'm fascinated when Moira doesn't order like, a plate of worms or something. She gets chocolate chip pancakes just like Thea and Iggy.

Half an hour later, we're all in hysterics as she tells us about a time the Keeper was trying to help her sort out a problem with a boy, but ended up scorching all his feathers off so he looked like a bald chicken. Even Morgan's laughing, and that's saying something given how close Moira and the Keeper obviously are.

Somehow, it's not as awkward as I imagined when they sat down. Until Moira brings up registering with the Hearth.

"You really should, now that you're mated." She gives Thea a pointed look and sips at her coffee. How the hell is she holding? She's only got two fingers on the tips of her wings. God, it's weird.

"I've got the paperwork," Thea responds noncommittally.

I partially turn so I can look at Moira. "What does it really mean to register with the Hearth? Everyone seems super keen on us doing it quickly, but the welcome packet was vague."

Moira glances over at the Keeper, but he gives her a look that screams "Go ahead."

"Well," she says. "Registering allows the Hearth to better track each haven's growth over time, which helps them plan long-term programs. Think of it like the human census."

Morgan snorts. "The census is riddled with bias and inconsistency. Is yours any better?"

Moira's expression softens. "I'd like to think so. Registering allows us to track what powers lie where. If a haven needs assistance, it's easier for the Hearth to suggest a monster relocate, for instance."

"Like, forced?" I don't mean to bark out the question, but I have a sudden vision of being dragged away from Ohken and my sisters.

"No, of course not." Moira is quick to clarify, glancing at the Keeper like she wants help.

He sets his coffee cup down and crosses his long muscular arms.

"The Hearth controls many things, as the original creators of the haven system all those centuries ago. They control formal education, Keeper and protector team identification and assignment, even interhaven travel." He gestures around at the busy restaurant. "Sporting events too. They've got their sticky fingers in everything, and they like to know everything about everyone. Hence registration."

Moira's feathers puff up and she crosses her arms, then turns in the booth and rolls her eyes at us.

"The Keeper's point of view is unnecessarily negative, in my opinion. You can make up your own minds about the value the Hearth brings. It's not a perfect organization, but without it, I would never have been allowed—really, encouraged—to teach."

"Why?" Morgan's voice is soft.

Moira smiles, which pulls the sides of her beak up like human lips. "Most harpies don't live in havens. We're generally very solitary and many of the older generation are cannibalistic and dangerous. They live outside havens because they don't want the structure of societal constraint."

Morgan shifts forward, putting her elbow on the table. "I could have sworn I saw another harpy the day we arrived. She looked just like you."

Moira's smile grows bigger. "Celset, yes! She's lovely. Like me, she's more progressive. She has lived in Ever for many years, well, since the Keeper took over."

"How did the Hearth encourage you to teach?" I'm fascinated by her unexpected story. Literally everyone we've met so far has been kind and accommodating, it's odd to think of a whole monster species as being anything but that.

Moira glances over at the Keeper, her smile falling. "Ab—the Keeper was at the Hearth school for training, and I kept trying to sneak in and learn. He caught me and grilled me within an inch of his life. But he saw something in me that day." Tears fill her eyes, but she doesn't look away from him. I'd say it was a tender moment if I wasn't seated between her and Morgan.

"When I told him I wanted to learn to teach, he petitioned the three heads of the Hearth to allow it. It took a lot of questioning and they tested me in a variety of ways. But I passed." The feathers on top of her head flutter upright and then smooth back down. She looks over at Morgan and me again. "So without the Keeper and the Hearth, I would still be living alone in the wild. I am eternally grateful."

"You deserve every success, Mo," the Keeper states. Morgan and I turn to look at him, but his eyes are locked onto the bird-woman. He looks almost...fond. Which I suppose he should be if they're supposed to get married.

I should want to hate her for being the Keeper's betrothed, but I can't find it in me. Moira's story compelled me.

Morgan shifts back onto the bench next to me, picking at her pancakes. I suspect she'd like to hate Moira too, but just like me, it's nearly impossible to not like the kind-hearted harpy. Even so, Morgan's my sister and one of my best friends in the entire world. Where does all of this leave her?

CHAPTER TWENTY-ONE
OHKEN

The day passes in a blur. I take turns patrolling town and the stadium with the Keeper and gargoyles. I sense nothing amiss; everyone appears to be having a wonderful time. Main Street is busy. The pop-up shops along either side are booming. Every business is full of customers with lines out the door.

I have extra staff on hand for both Fleur and the General Store because I knew I wouldn't be able to work shifts this week. Everything is taken care of, which is good, because my thoughts keep heading straight back to Wren.

Her sweet cries as I punished that slick pussy in front of the stadium mirror. The way she jerked underneath me when she came. How voluptuous she looked tangled in the sheets.

I'm obsessed. No. I'm past obsessed.

I'm in love. It's happening fast, too—faster than I expected. I've watched other trolls fall in love over the years. It's usually such a slow and tender build until the rut. But Wren has taken the usual process and accelerated it.

Bringing my wrist up, I direct my comm watch to call her.

Moments later, her throaty voice rings out of the small interface.

"Hello lover."

My lips curl into a smile as pride blooms hot and hard in my chest.

"Hello Miss Hector. Are you still free for a few minutes? I've got to head to the stadium soon."

"Hell yes I'm free!" There's a round of laughter behind her; her sisters, if I had to guess. "I'm in the garden with Miriam and Mor. Come see me?"

Hmm. I'd prefer something quieter and more secluded, but I don't have time to do the things I'd like to do to her.

"Be right there," I say, scowling at the busy Main Street. People are slowly making their way toward the stadium. The game starts in two hours, and I've got to meet the team in the locker room soon.

Monsters shout and wave at me as I head toward the garden. The scent of troll mead is strong up and down Main. Half the pop-up restaurants are bars since Ever doesn't really have one.

"Ohken! Crush those Fevers!"

I glance over to see Alba's nephew, Taylor, with a flagon of mead in both hands. He lets out another shout and raises both cups high above his head. Mead spills down the sides. I chuckle and pump both fists in the air. Beings stop me another half dozen times before I make it to Sycamore, turning left toward the garden.

My heart pounds when the garden comes into view. I can't wait to see Wren. People slowly walk up the wide street toward the garden. By the time I get to the garden's opening, my body is tense and tight. I recognize the signs of an impending rut. I'll be there in a day, max. Choking back a groan, I duck through the opening in the hedge and look for

Wren. If I can just get my hands on her, everything will be better.

The anticipatory butterflies in my stomach rocket around, smashing against my insides when I see her. Her long hair is half-pulled up in twin buns on top of her head. The part that's down falls in gentle waves to her shoulders. She's hunched over the damaged moonflower vines, both hands on the lattice she magicked earlier this week. Miriam and Morgan stand quietly by her side. Morgan sees me first, pointing to Wren and then giving me two excited thumbs-up.

My chest fills with pride. That's my woman right there, serving her community, surrounded by her family and friends. I love everything she stands for, everything that's important to her. Wren's puzzle pieces fit mine so perfectly.

I cross the garden and stop to one side, not wanting to distract her. I have the perfect angle to stare at her beautiful profile, at plush pink lips she wrapped around my cock last night. I don't mean to let loose a growl, but I can't hold back the appreciative noise.

Wren glances over, green eyes blinking open. She lifts her chin proudly and gestures at the vines. "I did it, baby. I grew the actual moonflowers for the first time instead of just the hedge around them!" She rocks onto her heels and stands.

I pull her to me and wrap both arms around her body, sliding my hands up her back into that luscious soft hair. Completely ignoring knowing looks from Miriam and Morgan, I bend down and kiss Wren, losing myself in her scent and taste. It's a tender kiss, something gentle for a soft moment.

Miriam grips one of the moonflowers and holds it up on the vine for me to see. "Look at the size of these flowers, Ohken. Wren did that just now. We'll be drowning in pixie dust soon!"

Wren looks up at me, and her smile turns into a full-fledged grin.

"I'm so proud of you," I murmur, stroking the shell of her ear and down her neck. "So damn proud."

"I'm proud of myself," she snarks. Stepping back, she grabs the front of her tee and holds it out so I can read the writing. I hadn't even noticed it yet, but I laugh the moment I see it.

"Badass Misfit" is painted on the front in big gold letters.

Wren laughs and turns to point at Morgan, who's wearing the same shirt.

I cross my arms. "Where did you ladies get those? I don't recall ordering them for the store."

Morgan winks at me. "Oh, we've been crafting with Catherine. She is hella handy with stuff like this." She looks at Wren and then bumps Miriam with her hip. "Wanna head to the stadium, Mir? Thea and Shepherd are on their way."

Miriam gives Wren an exaggerated wink and drops the moonflower. She links her arm through Morgan's and they walk toward the front of the garden. Morgan looks over her shoulder and lets out a little tsk.

"Wrennie don't keep him too long. We need that big man of yours to win this game!"

Wren laughs, but any response to her sister fades when I dip my head to take her mouth. I'm hungry for her, my lips devouring hers. Like every time we kiss, she returns my fervor tenfold, her tongue sliding past my lips to tease me. It's a soft reminder of just how good she felt in my arms last night. And this morning.

When we part, she rubs my chest in gentle circles. "You seem extra needy, baby. Are you gonna make it all the way through the game?"

I bring my forehead to hers. "I don't know," I admit. "I'm close, Wren."

"Oh my God," she says. "What if you collapse midgame

because the rut overtakes you and I have to sprint onto the field for an emergency blowjob?"

I bury my head in the side of her neck and laugh. "That would be the show nobody knew they needed."

"Well, if that happens I'll do my best to get you home before I service you."

Hunger claws at my gut, every muscle tensing at her seductive words.

A possessive, needy growl rumbles out of my throat.

"You don't know what those words do to me, Miss Hector."

Green eyes flash with mischief. "Oh, but I do, Mr. Stonesmith. You like to be teased a little, don't you?" She bats her long black eyelashes. "You love the idea of being tied in bed while I—"

I whip out a hand, squashing her lips between my fingers and using that grip to haul her right against my body. "You got half of that right, Miss Hector. You'll service me, but you'll do it at my command." I reach one hand around her back and slide it down her jeans, resting two fingers between her ass cheeks. "I might collar you during this rut, Wren. What do you think?"

"Hoboy," she deadpans. "I'm not sure I'm going to be as compliant as you hope." Her brows curve up, her expression haughty.

"Good," I snap, dropping my grip on her pouty mouth. "I prefer to dominate you into submission, sweet girl. You'll be begging me to put an end to the teasing by the time I'm done."

Wren laughs. "I thought you promised to be wild during your rut. I was really counting on seeing that."

"Wild," I counter, "is not the same as out-of-control."

She plants both hands on her round hips. "Well shit, I was hoping to see you raging."

I reach for her hand and bring it to the front of my pants,

stroking my cock through the fabric. Letting out a needy growl, I crowd into her space. "I need you, Wren. When this game is done, I'll find you right away. Deal?"

She's breathless as she strokes. "Deal, baby."

I like my new nickname. It's uniquely human, but it suits her and I adore hearing it roll off her tongue.

Green eyes flick past me to the garden's entrance, and she groans. "Shit, the traffic is picking up. We need to get you to the stadium, right?"

I glance down at my comm watch. "I'm supposed to be in the locker room in five minutes, and we're a solid half hour away."

"Yep," Wren chirps. "Time to go, lover." She threads her fingers through mine and pulls me toward the street.

I know one thing with absolute certainty—I'd follow this woman anywhere.

～

Half an hour later, I stride into the locker room in the belly of the stadium.

A big centaur, Senza, glances up from where he's binding his forelegs with a protective wrap. "Glad you could join us, troll."

I roll my eyes. He's not mated or anywhere near being mated. He doesn't get it, but he will one day if he finds his other half.

The Keeper emerges from a door on the other side of the locker room, tossing me a head nod when he sees me. "Good of you to join us, brother."

I open my mouth to bark out a retort about how I'm only a few minutes late, but the Keeper continues.

"Let's kick some ass tonight, okay? The Fevers are talking a lot of shit out there, but we're going to crush them."

TANGLING WITH TROLLS

A chorus of whooping goes up around me. The four centaurs stomp their hooves and the shifters howl. I'm the only troll on the team, but with the size of our monsters, we've got a formidable defense.

Offense could be an issue, but we're all counting on Reddek the pixie to be fast on his feet and wings.

The Keeper will be patrolling during the game, so he won't be down on the field with us. I know he's worried about security, but at this point, we've gone over every inch of the stadium. Richard and the shifters are patrolling inside and outside the building. There are even a few shifters in town keeping an eye on Main Street.

It's time to enjoy skyball.

I change into my uniform, tugging tight green shorts over my thighs. Nearly my entire leg is exposed. Wren is going to get a kick out of that. I'm a fan of beautifully tailored clothing. Shorts are not in my vocabulary.

Except for tonight.

I reach down to adjust my cock, hating the way the fabric constricts me. One thing's for sure—these shorts are tight enough that the whole stadium is about to get a view of my half-hard fat cock. Because it hasn't gone down since I touched her in the garden, and I don't think it will at this point.

Once we're fully dressed, our team leaves the locker room and heads down the elevator and short hallway to the field. Faint chanting becomes a thunderous roar when we emerge inside the stadium. Overhead lights flood the long field with artificial sun. Thousands of monsters line both sides of the pitch, seated on wooden bleachers that rise forty rows high on either side. Green-and-gold flags wave at the opposite end— that's Ever's goal area. We jog to the middle of the field and I raise my hands high, cheering with the stadium.

The stadium is full, but I search every front row—I got

Catherine and the triplets seats right up front so I can stare at Wren. She waves when she sees me, shouting my name while she hops up and down in place. Morgan, Miriam, and Catherine cheer too. They're all dressed in Ever's signature green and gold colors. Thea's not there, but I know she's patrolling with Shepherd for the beginning of the game.

A thrill snakes down my spine. I've been so focused on courting Wren that I'd forgotten how much I love skyball. I've missed half our practices, but I'm fucking ready for this game anyhow. In front of us, the opposing team stands tall in their black and blue colors.

A big minotaur looks toward Wren and her sisters, his lips splitting into a big smile that pulls the gold ring in his nose. "Pretty little things. One of those yours?" He pounds a beefy fist into his palm.

Senza elbows me in the side. "Ignore him, he's just trying to get under your skin."

I grin back at the minotaur. I know exactly what he's doing, and I'm not the least bit worried. My witch is going home with me tonight and nobody else. Still, I make a mental note to knock out a few of his teeth if I can.

"I'll give her a little kiss when we win," he goads, winking at me.

Like hell you will, I promise him silently.

CHAPTER TWENTY-TWO
WREN

This is so fricking exciting! The stadium is lit from above by huge floodlights, illuminating the long green field. Bleachers soar behind and across from me, filled with monsters of all sorts screaming their heads off.

I still can't believe Ohken was able to build this in just a few weeks under the Keeper's direction. It's packed full of all sorts of monsters. We've been monster-watching like crazy and it's fascinating. A pack of gryphons flew in and took over a bunch of seats at one end. They seem like the bros of the monster world—backward-hat-wearing dudes double-fisting mead and engaging in ridiculous antics.

Then there was a whole group of naga who slithered in and took up the row just behind us. Not gonna lie, having humanoid upper bodies does not at all make me feel better about their bottom halves being a snakes. Any of them could wrap me up like a tootsie roll and crush me flat as a pancake. It's a smidge disconcerting.

A huge roar draws my eye back to the game, by which I mean my man. Because good God—he is looking fine in his uniform. Dark green shorts do nothing to hide his muscular thick thighs. When he turns to face a referee in the middle of the field, I get an eyeful of beefy troll ass. I could bounce a whole stack of quarters off that thing. I might actually try that later.

His jersey hugs his thick middle, but the top is stretched across his enormous shoulders.

A jarring elbow to the ribs yanks me out of my appreciative stupor.

"You're sighing," Miriam says with a grin. "Like, so loud." Fuschia eyes flash at me as she fails to hold back a cackle.

Morgan rolls her eyes at us but can't hold back a smirk. She whoops for our team. I bet she's loving this so much—she's so competitive.

The teams face off in the middle of the long field. Ohken was right—this looks just like a soccer field. Even the goals at either end have the same shape and net as soccer does. I'm just not sure what'll happen once the whistle blows, assuming they do that.

A human-looking ref stands between the teams. He says something to each team, although we can't hear him from this far away. Representatives from each team nod their agreement. A big pixie from the Misfits shakes the hand of a centaur from the opposing team. They back away and the ref flips a coin, catching it in his hand. He jerks his head toward the Fevers centaur and the opposite side of the stadium goes wild.

Our side responds with a chorus of boos that get cut off by a loud whistle. I don't know where the noise comes from, because I can't see any sort of loudspeaker, but its shrill beep echoes around the stadium. The ref drops the ball in front of the Fevers captain and they're off. A big minotaur shoves several Misfits out of the way as they barrel toward their goal.

Ohken comes out of goddamned nowhere and runs into the minotaur, knocking him off his feet as one of our guys steals the ball. I watch the minotaur's head hit the ground with a loud crack. Ohken pauses and winks at the guy, saying something I can't hear. Then he takes off to follow the Misfits as they rush toward our goal.

The minotaur shuffles upright and bellows, sprinting after our team. But moments later, Ohken's shoving three big shifters out of his way. Our pixie kicks the purple ball and scores the first goal!

Morgan, Miriam, Catherine, and I leap to our feet, screaming our heads off.

"Crush 'em, baby!" I shout, knowing Ohken can't hear me from this far. But I want him to know I shouted for him every step of the way.

Miriam turns to me with an excited hop. "Hand me my banner, would you?"

Realization slaps me in the face like the bitch she is.

Oh no.

Miriam must see that something's wrong, because her smile falls. "What is it?"

"Fuck!" I cry. "I forgot the damned banners because I got dickstracted!"

Catherine laughs, Miriam scowls, and Morgan slow claps for me. "Way to go, Mary!" She only uses my Sanderson sister nickname when I'm being particularly obtuse, and this is one of those times.

Catherine reaches around Morgan to pat me on the shoulder. "My car is parked just outside. Want to run back and get them?"

"Shit." I turn to look at the game. Our guys are running back this way. But when I see how distressed Miriam looks not to have her banners, I know we have to get them.

"Yeah." I nod at Catherine. "Miriam pixie dusted them to shoot off fireworks. We've got to have them."

Miriam shoos me out of our row. Catherine follows and

we sprint down the bleachers to the nearest exit. When we get to the field, I run after her. She got a fucking great parking spot. We hop in her tiny car and she throws gravel getting us out of the parking lot, zooming back toward town.

I slap myself on the forehead as the landscape whizzes by. "I can't believe I fucking forgot the banners. Of all days! Now we're missing the game!"

"Not a big deal at all, sweet Wren." Catherine laughs. "Plus I learned a new word—dickstracted. Thanks for that."

"Oh, err—" I let out an awkward chuckle. "Humans have all sorts of inappropriate terms related to sex, despite the fact that most humans are actually pretty weird about sex."

"Well," Catherine counters, "don't hold back on my account. I don't plan to ever be part of the human world, but a few new vocabulary terms might come in handy."

I snort. "I can just imagine you busting out with that one in front of the Keeper sometime. I feel like he'd drop dead of shock."

Catherine smiles, mirth flashing in her steely gray eyes. "The Keeper and I aren't in the regular habit of discussing my nonexistent love life, but if the opportunity arises to describe someone as dickstracted, I just might take it."

I grin as I look at my hostess and now-friend. "You're really fucking cool, Catherine. You know that?"

Her grin grows broader and she shimmies her shoulders from side to side. "I really am," she finally says, winking at me.

The Annabelle comes into view just ahead. Her white shutters flip-flop by way of greeting when we pull into the drive behind the house. Catherine and I hop out and run into the kitchen where we had been making the banners. Yes, they're still there! I grab them, but just as I do, an explosion rocks the inn and knocks me against the cabinets.

Catherine hits the wall next to me and slides down. She's up before I am, running toward the front of the Annabelle.

"Catherine!" I shout, struggling to a stand. "What was that?"

A harried shout echoes down the hallway from the lobby. "Annabelle! What's wrong?"

My wits come back fast, and I run, following the sound of Catherine's voice to the second story. I see the bottoms of her shoes as she runs up the stairs to the third story. I've never been up there, she's made it clear it's her private space, but something's wrong so I'm following.

The Annabelle heaves and shudders around us, and even though I can't speak her language, I sense she's horribly distressed. In front of me, Catherine bursts through a beautifully painted door. I rush through behind her, knocking into her when she stops dead. I grab both of her arms to steady us as I glance around.

I don't know what I expected her room in the attic to look like, but it wasn't this. Canvases cover every inch of two walls and a third wall is the most elaborate painting—it's downtown Ever. There are open pots of paint and cups filled with brushes stuck on every surface. But a gigantic hole opens the back wall to the outside. Black smoke billows and the inn shudders and heaves.

"Annabelle." Catherine's voice is nothing more than a horrified whisper. She pulls out of my grip and runs to a tall wooden armoire, reaching in and grabbing a handgun. She grabs another and turns to me when an enormous shadow casts darkness over the room. She and I whip around at the same time to see a huge centaur landing in the room. But this one isn't like Taylor and the others I've met. This one's a dark steely gray, but where the other centaurs' backs are smooth, this one now folds enormous wings flat against his back. Long hair is pulled back into an elegant bun, his features angular and harsh.

He hooks his thumbs in his waistband and inclines his head at Catherine. "Put the guns down, Cath."

Catherine sneers at him. "I think not Arkor."

The winged centaur shrugs, jerking his head toward me. "You won't win a fight against me. Not and have your friend make it out of this alive. We can give it a whirl though, for old time's sake."

Catherine's gray eyes flick to me, and then she slowly drops the guns to the ground and kicks them away.

I don't know who the hell this dude is, but I've got to do something. I don't know if there are more of them, or if he's the only one. There's a visual standoff happening between him and Catherine, but all I can think is that I need to call for help. Even if I can't outrun this guy, maybe I'll get far enough to let the gargoyles and the Keeper know what's happening.

Turning, I sprint back through Catherine's door as I lift my wrist to comm my friends.

But I run smack dab into a male who now stands in Catherine's doorway. I bounce off his chest and fall back into the room on my ass, bouncing hard on the plank floor.

The naga I just ran into slithers into the room but ignores me and snakes around toward the centaur. He's holding a glowing rope in one hand. Catherine reaches out for me to help me up off the ground. She wraps one arm around my waist and tugs me slightly behind her.

"Leave my home." Her command brooks no argument, but the males laugh like they're enjoying a joke at our expense.

The floor ripples under our feet, shoving the two males toward the hole in the window. It's the Annabelle, she's trying to help despite the huge hole in her siding.

The naga glances around, the laugh dying in his throat. "It won't be long before the inn rallies, Arkor. Let's go."

"Indeed." The winged horse-man glares at Catherine. "We had intended to grab you after nightfall, but this is mightily convenient, old friend. Come along. Your mate is anxious to see you."

Fury rockets through my veins. "And he can fuck all the way off," I shout. "We're not going with you."

The male chuckles, a low, possessed sound. He's unafraid of me, and why would he be? I've got no weapons and my power is useless here. He jerks his head at us, and the naga slithers closer.

"Easier not to fight, my sweetsss." Words end on a hissed rasp as he brandishes the rope at us.

Catherine and I both throw ourselves at him at the same time, but he moves faster than I could have imagined, grabbing us and smashing us together in his coils. Pressure crushes my chest as he squeezes his cylindrical torso tighter around us.

"I do enjoy a ssstruggle, though." He loops the glowing rope around us, and a sense of melancholy drops over me like a blanket. My focus goes fuzzy. Catherine slumps against me, her head lolling back against my shoulder.

The Annabelle shudders, every board on the wall clattering angrily. Canvases fall from their hooks and knock into paint jars, splashing color all over the room.

"Time to go," the winged man says. He turns and glances out the window, then leaps out of the hole and spreads his wings wide, disappearing from view. The naga slithers to the hole in the wall, grabbing us in one hand. He reaches for our comm watches and rips them off our wrists, tossing them into the room behind us. Then he transfers us to his back and leaps to the ground.

I try to scream, but it's hard to muster the energy to do anything.

We reach the ground where a nondescript van is parked on the side street next to the inn. Arkor opens the back doors and the naga tosses us in, nodding at the other male. "I'll meet you at the checkpoint, bossss."

Arkor claps the naga once on the shoulder, and then the snake-man slithers off into the darkness.

He slams the van doors shut, and darkness overtakes us.

I hear him speak again, although I can't see who's driving the van. One side dips as if a huge weight has been added to it, and then adjusts level again.

"Be watchful," Catherine whispers in my ear. "We can't be allowed to leave Ever, Wren."

I look around for something, anything to use to get us out of this situation. But the only thing I can even see is the faint glow of the ropes that bind us. And that sense of despair rushes over me again, so hard and awful that I hunch over and grit my teeth to try to fight it off.

But I can't, and as the van starts to pull away from the inn, I feel myself giving in to whatever magic the rope must be imbued with. I dig deep for the will to fight it, but somehow, I find I don't care all that much.

CHAPTER TWENTY-THREE
OHKEN

That damn minotaur has it out for me. I suppose he's not thrilled to have lost a front tooth when I rammed him, but I don't feel bad. He's talking about my woman, and all's fair during love and skyball.

He guns for me as his team sprints up the field toward their goal. Senza and one of the shifters intercept and trip their man, and punt the ball back in our direction. Despite the fact that it wouldn't help his team, the minotaur barrels for me anyway.

I turn and run after my teammates, shoving smaller monsters out of the way to clear a path for the Misfits. The minotaur's hooves pound the ground behind me. I dive out of the way at the last minute while Senza scores our second goal.

The minotaur roars, but I shoot him a triumphant look. He starts toward me with fists balled, but the ref jogs up and the bull-man stops. Stupid as he seems to be, even he knows better than to start a fight after a goal. He snorts once, spittle flying from his mouth.

I grin and swivel my head to see my girl. I find her spot in the stands, but she's not there. Morgan, Miriam and now

Thea are all cheering wildly for us, but Wren is gone. Catherine too.

Frowning, I look down at my wrist but I left my comm watch in the locker room. I jog back toward the middle where the ref will drop the ball again and a new play starts.

Fifteen minutes later, Wren and Catherine still aren't there. My stomach turns into a sinking pit. I trot to the side of the field, ignoring Senza shouting behind me. Stopping in front of the girls, I gesture to Wren's empty spot.

"Everything okay?"

Morgan looks over, her brow furrowed. "Yeah, Wren and Catherine drove back to the inn to grab the banners we made, but it's been a solid twenty or twenty-five minutes since they left."

Shit, she's been gone even longer than I realized. It's a long walk here, but a short drive because one of the streets cuts straight through. She should be back.

I don't know how or why I know something's wrong; I just know it is.

I give Morgan a look. "Call the Keeper, Shepherd, Alo, Richard. Call everyone."

Morgan's brows draw closer together. "What's wrong?"

Thea cocks her head to the side and then shakes it. "The wards are fine. I just checked. They're probably just—"

"No!" I snap. "Something's wrong. I can feel it." I leap over the stand and jog past the girls to the nearest hallway.

My team shouts my name in confusion, but I don't bother to look back. Miriam and the triplets rush after me. Thea comms Wren, but there's no answer. Catherine doesn't respond either. That horrible sinking sensation in my stomach grows heavier, and heat spreads across my neck.

"Shit!" Morgan shouts when we get outside. "We came in Catherine's car and you walked!"

Gravel flies as a truck barrels toward us. I've never been

more relieved to see the Keeper in my life. The truck skids to a stop and I leap into the bed. Thea jumps in with me and Morgan and Miriam jump into the back seat. Dark shadows swoop overhead—the gargoyles.

I faintly hear the Keeper shouting into his comm watch. Richard confirms everything's fine at the stadium and in downtown Ever. Nothing seems amiss in town. The Keeper's comm watch spits out a steady stream of data from the monitoring system. The data says everything's fine.

Except it's not. I know it's not.

Because deep in my chest there's a sensation of anger and terror. It's not mine; I recognize it as Wren's. And I feel that because she's mine and our connection runs so deep. Once we claim each other, I'll feel every emotion as strongly as she does.

Morgan shouts as the Keeper swings left on Sycamore, heading for the Annabelle. I don't see the smoke until we get close to town. There's a hole the size of a truck in the third floor of Annabelle's side. The inn is shuddering and shaking on her foundation, rocking and creaking. She's distraught.

Morgan and Miriam leap out of the back seat before the truck even stops, shouting for Wren and Catherine. But by the way the inn is swaying side to side, I already know we won't find them here.

"How the hell did the downtown shifters not hear a fucking explosion?" the Keeper snarls.

That's a problem for another time. I stand there with fists balled, watching the inn smoke as it shudders and thrashes.

Morgan comes flying back out of the front door. "They're not there! Catherine's room is destroyed, there's shit everywhere!"

The Keeper strides back to his truck and pulls up the computer screen I installed for him. He punches button after button as I join. The monitoring system shows nothing amiss.

Alo and Shepherd land next to us. Shepherd goes immediately to Thea's side, but Alo comes to stand next to me. "There are tire tracks on the side street. Someone took them in a vehicle."

"Fuck!" I shout, running my hands through my hair. I need to get to Wren. I need to save her, to protect her, to love her. And someone is trying to prevent that. My vision goes red until everything is tinged in darkness, my breathing going low and steady.

"Easy, Ohken," the Keeper murmurs. He slaps his computer shut with an angry huff. "The wards aren't designed to keep anyone inside Ever, only to keep thralls out. The monitoring system won't help us here." He turns to Alo and Shepherd. "Can you two fly over the side street and try to follow the tracks? We'll follow you and I'll get the shifters to block any roads out of town, assuming they're not already gone."

Alo nods and pushes hard off the ground, streaking up into the sky. Shepherd grabs Thea in his arms and does the same, bulleting after his brother.

I leap back into the truck bed and pound on the roof of the cab. "Let's fucking go!" Red covers my whole vision. I haven't raged since I was a teen and hormones began to make me more powerful. It's something most troll males only deal with at that phase of their life, or in times of war. But I haven't had cause to go into a rage since then.

But I'm in a fucking rage now, because whoever took my woman will pay with their life. If I have to leave Ever and scour the entire human world to get her back, that's what I'll do.

I'm coming, sweetheart. I'll get you back if it's the last thing I do.

CHAPTER TWENTY-FOUR
WREN

The van bounces along, too bumpy to be on a paved road. Shit, they're taking us somewhere off an actual road. That'll make it harder for our friends to find us—and that's if they even realize we're missing, which doesn't seem likely.

I nudge at Catherine as I try to clear the fog from my mind. "Catherine. We need options. Give me ideas."

Catherine's head lolls from side to side, but she manages to sit up straighter. "We can't let them take us out of town. Wesley is likely on the other side, and if he gets ahold of me..."

I shove that bit of info aside; it won't help us right this second. And it's clear they came here for Catherine. I have no idea what'll happen once they find me, or how they might try to use me if they discover I have power. I think back to the thrall's attack on the moonflowers. I can't let something like that happen again.

Focusing on the ropes that bind us together, I shimmy around, but they're tight as hell. There's no way I'll get them loosened. I cast around, trying to see if there's a way to focus outside of the van. They've got it partitioned so we can't see the drivers at all, we're inside a tiny dark box.

A tiny ray of light shines through from somewhere. When I squint, I realize it's a small line, maybe the bottom edge of a window with a covering on it. The sliver of an idea begins to come to me.

I nudge Catherine. "Let's try to get up. Push against me and we'll lean against the wall to my left. I think there's a window. If I can see where we're going, maybe I can use my power."

Catherine nods and presses her back to mine. I use the leverage to push against the floor and we rise to a shaky stand. The van goes over a bump and we slam into the side, but we both spread our feet to try to steady ourselves. I press against the ropes and eyeball the sliver of light.

"Hell yes!" I whisper-shout. "It's a window, it's just covered. Push me closer, I'm going to try to rip the cover off."

Catherine grunts and shoves me closer to the window, smashing my face up against it. It's uncomfortable as hell, but I angle my head down and drag my teeth along the edge of light. There's definitely a black film over the window, but it's not stuck on super well, and when I scratch at it with my lower teeth, it begins to peel up.

We bounce over bigger bumps and almost fall.

"Hurry, Wren," Catherine murmurs. "We're bouncing too much to still be on a main road." She pushes me harder to the window, and I awkwardly bite at the film and pull it up. It takes a few tries, but I'm able to peel a strip three inches wide off the film. I yank it with my teeth until it curls up and gives me a line to see outside.

"We're driving across a field," I whisper. "I can see the fucking ward off in the distance. They're definitely trying to take us out of town."

"We can't leave Ever." Catherine moans. "Wesley cannot gain access to my power." She lets out a frustrated growl.

I wiggle my hand, my fingers brushing hers. Threading mine through them, I try to focus. "Hold me against the window so I can see. I'm going to try to call the forest to poke at the wards. It'll notify the Keeper, right?"

The tight ropes around us make me feel empty, but I struggle against the empty, dull sensation.

"Yes, Wren!" Catherine's voice is tight with excitement. "The monitoring system will ping his comm watch! We just need to buy some time. Here, let me help."

I hear her plant her feet and grunt, pressing me hard against the side of the van. I spread my own feet wider and push back against her for leverage, focusing on the field I can see out the window. The sun is low in the sky, and we're tearing across a field toward the wards. From here I can see their shiny green glow. They're reinforced extra strong for this event, but they were never meant to keep anyone inside of Ever.

I focus on the forest ahead of us. I hear the worms and beetles and bugs. I sense the roots spreading deep around us, even outside of the wards. A tingling sensation spreads along my scalp, and every tree, every branch invades my mind's eye. I've never been able to see this much, but terror drives me to focus.

Power bristles in my fingertips and I push it toward the forest, calling it to twist and grow as I imagine a barrier in front of us. I watch the forest begin to shiver and shake, and then the trees shoot up into the sky, leaning and swaying against one another.

They twist and dive through each other's leaves. I'm weaving a lattice, and it stretches as far as I can see in one direction. There's muffled shouting ahead and the van slams to a halt. The shouting intensifies, but I try to continue focusing on the forest just inside the wards. I send power to the trees, urging them to poke at the wards. I watch them hit, their branches brushing along the film. It sparks an angry dark green and shudders. I know the wards are self-healing, but I'm not trying to damage them. I just need to stab them enough to send the Keeper a message.

A weight shifts the van from side to side, and I hear a door slam shut.

"Hurry, Wren!" Catherine shouts. "We have just a moment!"

I scream as I send power to the entire forest in front of us. Dark trees shoot up into the sky, a wall that goes higher than I can even see. Black stars dance across my vision, and melancholy steals back over me as I lose my fight against the ropes' dulling magic.

The back of the van rips open and the centaur stands there with a furious look on his face.

"Undo it, witch."

I hiss at him. "Bold of you to assume I had anything to do with it."

Black eyes flick to where I peeled the film away from the window, and he laughs. It's cruel and cold. I know in my heart that this male won't hesitate to kill me if we get out of Ever and they just want Catherine.

He steps up into the back of the van, his front legs so heavy they push down the whole thing. Catherine and I stumble and fall toward him, unable to keep ourselves upright. I scream as the male catches us. My gaze meets his, and the last thing I see is his head coming toward mine. Then pain blooms along my brow, and the dark stars become a thick blanket of black.

CHAPTER TWENTY-FIVE
OHKEN

I swivel my head from side to side, trying to see if I can locate any more tire tracks, but so far, we haven't seen anything. The good news is nothing indicates a car drove off the road. The bad news is we have no idea if we're going in the right direction.

The Keeper barks orders into his comm watch, but I can barely focus. Angry red rage coats the entirety of my vision. When I lay eyes on her, whoever took her will get a taste of a troll in battle mode.

The Keeper's watch flashes red and he yanks his computer open.

"Keep your eyes on the road!" Morgan shouts just as the Keeper swerves around a bump in the road.

Lights flash red across his computer screen. I know what that means because I helped him build the monitoring system. Something's attacking the wards. Based on the shade of red, it's a large-scale attack.

Alo swoops down, flying alongside the truck as he points off to our left.

"The trees are twisted into a huge barrier and they're stabbing the wards! It's got to be Wren!"

Pride blooms in my chest, filling me with renewed rage. I'd leap out of the truck and sprint for her, but the truck is faster. I clench the roof and shout for the Keeper to go faster. He swerves to the left and Alo veers away, flapping hard as he barrels through the sky. We follow, bouncing through a copse of trees that empties us into a field.

Sunlight is fading fast, but as we streak across the field, the forest comes into view. It reaches so high, I can't see the tops of the trees.

Wren, my love, well done. Hold on.

The Keeper's foot is flat on the ground as we follow tracks across the field. Shepherd swoops out of the sky and drops Thea carefully into the back of the truck. The moment she's out of his arms, he goes into battle mode, growing larger as long spines emerge along his shoulders, back, and tail.

As we get closer to the wards, a vehicle comes into view—a black van. There's an explosion, and a chunk of tree blasts outward.

"They're blowing up the forest!" I shout. "Faster!"

The males—a big naga and even bigger pegasus—spin around as soon as we're close enough for them to hear, rushing to get back in the van. They leap in and take off at an angle alongside the ward, tires throwing dirt back at us.

Alo and Shepherd bullet out of the sky, landing on top of the van. Alo stabs his claws through the van's roof and starts ripping back giant pieces of it. I can't hold back anymore. Climbing up over the top of the truck, I hunch down on the hood and leap. I launch through the air and slam down on top of the van, ripping a huge chunk off and tossing it away.

Catherine's gray eyes are the first thing I see. She's on her side, tied to Wren whose head lolls to one side. Blood drips from a wound along her hairline. Alo, Shepherd, and I peel back enough metal for me to drop inside and pick up the girls. I hand them up into Alo's arms and he streaks out of harm's way.

I should follow him, but bloodlust screams at me to eliminate the threat. And the fucking threat is right in front of me. Swinging from the hip, I punch my fist through the panel separating the back of the van from the front. I grab it and yank it toward me, and then I leap into the cab. I go for the pegasus first—he's the more dangerous of the two.

Gripping him by the wing, I shove him toward the door and out, landing on the ground. We tumble over one another in a tangle of legs and wings. I hear Shepherd's battle cry and a roar from the naga.

The pegasus draws knives from somewhere and slashes at me, but my vision drips with rage. I scream my fury at him, hitting him with an uppercut that knocks his head back. A sharp tooth goes flying, and then I'm pummeling until blood sprays me and the pegasus squirms to get away.

I punch until my muscles turn to jelly and my fists are coated with blood.

I punch until the Keeper drops down next to me, careful to steer clear of my onslaught.

"Brother, he's down." The Keeper's voice is calm, but it does nothing to tamp down the rage boiling in my stomach. I can't see past the fury. I punch his side one more time, reveling in the grunt he emits.

"Ohken, he'll be dealt with. Check on your mate." The Keeper's voice goes hard and insistent.

Wren. Mate. He called her my mate.

I look down at the pegasus underneath me. He's bloody and battered, one eye already swelling up dark as blood flows from a dozen wounds. His eyes have rolled back in his head. He's done wreaking havoc today.

I shove away from him, my thoughts turning back to my

sweet witch. Scrambling up the slight embankment, I sprint across flattened grass. Miriam and Morgan are untying Catherine and Wren, who's still slumped over and lifeless. Shepherd drops out of the sky with the naga in a headlock, his long coils dangling.

Alo holds his tail spade under the naga's throat.

But all I can focus on is Wren and how pale she looks. Blood trickles from a wound along her hairline.

I skid to my knees and carefully pull her up into my arms, rising to bark at the Keeper. "Call Slade. We need a doctor."

Morgan lays an arm on her sister's brow, her own furrowed into a concerned vee. She huffs, sounding frustrated, but looks up at me. "She's just out, Ohken. She'll be okay. I don't have the power to heal her, but I can sense she's coming awake."

The Keeper joins us, jerking his head over his shoulder. "Alo, help me bind the pegasus. I've got some fucking questions." He looks toward the wall of trees to our left. "Shepherd, fly the wards to see if you can get a sense of where they were going."

"It was Wesley." Catherine coughs as she stands up, holding on to Morgan's forearm. "They were taking me to Wesley, and Wren just happened to be with me. She saved us."

The Keeper's look goes thunderous. I clutch Wren tighter to my chest, hopping up into the back of the truck. I give the Keeper a look. "You deal with these assholes, I'm taking Wren to Slade's. Find me later?"

He nods. Alo gives me a final understanding look before following his brother and the Keeper toward the fallen pegasus.

Morgan, Miriam, and Catherine get back in the truck, and Morgan drives us back to town. I hold Wren in my arms, careful not to jostle her. Her eyes shift from side to side behind her lids, but she doesn't wake up even by the time we pull up in front of Doc Slade's cottage. He's standing at the front door with a concerned look on his face.

He swings the front door wide and gestures me in, black eyes falling to Wren as even darker brows slant in anger. "Who did this? Thea mentioned an attack?"

Catherine fills him in as we follow him through the seating area and down a short hall to an exam room.

I lay Wren down on a raised table, worry rising in my system. But then those beautiful green eyes start to flutter. She opens them fully, pink lips pulling into a smirk.

"Guess Catherine and I badassed our way out of the van, huh?" Her voice is throaty and broken.

I'm too overcome with relief to answer.

Slade steps to the other side of the table and looks down at her. "My dear, you've had a whack to the head. Let me take a peek at you, and then you can go home, alright?"

Wren nods and allows him to check her out, but her eyes don't leave mine. There's mischief in them even after what happened to her.

The sound of a door slamming echoes back to us and Slade straightens with a frown. Growling, I place myself between Wren and the door. Morgan and Thea move to my side and Morgan raises her fists like she's about to throw down.

Wren sits up and peeks around me. "What's happening, baby?"

"Absolutely not!" The Keeper's angry voice reaches us.

Then Slade backs into the room with both palms in front of his chest. "My patient is not ready for visitors, Evenia."

The three vampires sail into the room past Slade. The Keeper rushes in after them and stops in front of Wren and me. "There's nothing you need to learn right this second. Give Wren a chance to recuperate."

Evenia waves him away and looks at me. "Step aside, troll."

I cross my arms. I'm not about to let Wren be interrogated by these asshats.

But Wren hops off the table behind me and slides an arm around my waist, looking at the vampire. "Sounds like you're here about the attack?"

Evenia's head dips in confirmation.

Wren sighs. "And you are…?"

Irritation flashes across Evenia's dark gaze. "The Hearth, my dear. It's in the welcome packet." She glances over at the Keeper. "Did she not even receive that?"

The Keeper growls and steps protectively in front of Wren, who pats him on the side.

"It's okay, Keeper. I'm happy to answer questions. It's a little stuffy in here, though. Can we find a little space to stretch out?"

There's a momentary pause before everyone moves, leaving the exam room and heading back toward the front of Slade's bungalow. I pull Wren into my arms to follow.

"I can walk, you know." Her hand slides into my jersey and she strokes at my chest hair.

"Let me carry you," I say, dipping down to kiss her lips. "I was so terrified for you. I'm going to have a really hard time letting you go anywhere alone for the rest of our lives."

Wren's green eyes light up. "Oh, so you're keeping me then?" She props her chin in her palm.

"Yes. I'm keeping you." I'm still too hyped on adrenaline for a more poetic admission of love. But as soon as I get her home, I'll show her with my mouth and lips and tongue.

We meet everyone in the sitting room and I lower Wren and myself into a chair. She stays in my lap, but I don't miss the way Evenia watches us.

She speaks first. "Tell me everything about the attack. Don't leave out a detail."

Wren starts from the very beginning, explaining how she

and Catherine were abducted. Evenia questions her about the two males, and it takes everything in me not to go find them and rip them to shreds. Wren shares how she and Catherine peeled the covering off a window so she could see the forest, and she called it to weave into an enormous wall the van couldn't get around. She knew it would ping the Keeper and the castle's ward monitoring system.

My smart girl.

By the time she's done, Evenia and her husbands look incredulous. The vampire frowns over at Catherine. "You really need to come with us, Catherine. Ever isn't safe for a being with your extraordinary power. I'd like to—"

"No thank you." Catherine's tone is brusque but firm. "I've never felt as safe anywhere as I do in Ever. I trust the Keeper implicitly, even now." Her gray eyes flick to him, but his expression is carefully neutral.

Morgan looks over from her spot next to Wren and me. "Why did they want to kidnap you, Catherine? Can you tell us?"

Catherine sighs and folds her hands in her lap. "Very few beings know anything about my power because it's so exceedingly rare. The Hearth knows, and the beings in this room know. I'll tell you three, but you cannot utter a word of this to anyone. The only other person who knows is Wesley."

Morgan presses on. "And that's why he's trying to get you back now?"

Catherine nods. "When he attacked Ever the first time, he was trying to take me from here. It didn't work, of course." She looks around Morgan at Wren. "Wren, my darling, you saw my room with the paints and canvases."

Wren nods.

"I've always been a painter, but when I was younger I began to notice that sometimes the things I painted became real."

Someone hisses in a breath, but Catherine continues.

"I have to focus to make that happen, but I'm able to paint things into existence—homes, situations—"

Evenia breaks in with a hiss. "The haven system itself."

Wren jolts in my arms, sliding to a stand between my legs. "Catherine painted the haven system into existence?"

Evenia nods. "The wards, the system. All of that was created after the Cerinvalla Act. It is only because of Catherine's power that we were able to protect ourselves." She cuts Catherine an irritated glance. "Which is why she should really come stay on Hearth property where we can better guard her. If Wesley were to take her, he could make her paint anything" She shudders. "Or unpaint it…"

"She doesn't want to go with you," the Keeper reiterates, pulling Catherine to his side.

Evenia laughs, but it's cruel. "Well, it won't be your job to protect her any longer. This is the third attack on your watch, you know what that means."

A tic starts in the Keeper's jaw, but Catherine slings her arm around his waist. "Oh, I don't think so, Evenia. When I wrote the Cerinvalla Act, I made it clear that the Keeper rule of three only applied to attacks upon havens, not from within havens."

Evenia's face goes dark purple as blood rushes to the surface of her skin. She stands, fists balled. "You cannot tell me that after the initial attack, and now three subsequent attacks, you believe your Keeper should remain at his post."

I stand behind Wren, wrapping an arm around her chest to hold her to me. "That's exactly what we mean, Evenia. There's not a monster in town who would get behind you sending us a new Keeper."

Catherine waves a hand at the vampires. "We're splitting grammar hairs here, but you set the precedent yourselves when you didn't allow Wesley's first attack to count toward our Keeper's three. Furthermore, you're duty bound by the same act to take extraordinary measures to find Wesley, as he's now attacked the same haven four times."

Evenia sputters. "Of course we want to find Wesley! Our team is already—"

"Best of luck in doing that," the Keeper interrupts her. "You've questioned my people as much as I'll allow today. If you need to talk to Catherine or Wren any further, you'll have to wait until tomorrow. They need rest."

"And I need to get home to Annabelle," Catherine demands. "She must be distraught."

Wren turns in my arms. "Can you help fix her? They blew a huge fucking hole in the third story."

I can, but all I want to do is get my woman home and check every inch of her to make sure she's okay. But the eager look in those emerald eyes tells me we'll be making a stop first.

The Keeper shoos the vampires out the front door, but I hear them mention the Hectors registering with the Hearth again. We won't be able to get away with them not registering for much longer. Not with Thea and Wren's power. If they're any indication, Morgan will be incredibly powerful too. And who knows what will happen when their Aunt Lou arrives in town.

Doc Slade cautions Wren to be careful for a day or so, but as long as she's not dizzy, she can do her normal things.

I thank him and then carry her all the way back to the Annabelle. The inn is still swaying from side to side in a panic, but the moment Catherine runs around the corner and toward the home, it visibly shudders in relief. The front doors swing open, and when Catherine gets to the steps, the house shuffles her up and through the doors.

Wren laughs as I set her down. "I think they're hugging. That's pretty much what's going on, right?"

Thea and Morgan link arms with Wren as we walk around the side of the inn. I take a peek at the giant hole blasted in the poor building, and then I place my hand on the inn's pink siding and work my magic. I feel Wren's hand come over top of mine, her magic twirling and tickling against me. I sense the inn knitting back together under our touch, and when I step back, it looks perfect. Except now there's a vine of trailing clematis that crawls up a lattice on the siding, all the way to Catherine's window.

"That's fucking gorgeous, Wrennie," Morgan murmurs, squeezing her sister tight. "I'm so glad you're okay." Her voice breaks a little bit. Wren turns and pulls her sister into her arms for a big hug. Thea shoves her way between them. Shepherd gives me a look and smiles at the girls.

When they part, Wren turns to look at the Keeper and me, her face serious. "Did we win the game?!"

The Keeper slaps a hand over his face and groans.

CHAPTER TWENTY-SIX
WREN

The Keeper gives me an apologetic look. "The game is still going on, Wren. When I left, we were winning."

I rub at Ohken's big chest. "Wanna go back, baby? I could stand to see you running around in those short shorts a little while longer."

Ohken's hand comes to my throat and lightly squeezes. Russet eyes burn a hole through me as he shakes his head. "Not a chance in hell, Wren. I'm taking you home right now."

Thea snickers and makes the classic porno bow-chicka-wow comment, but I'm not fussed. I shoot her a wink and thread my fingers through Ohken's. "I'm ready to go."

The Keeper reaches out and places a hand on my shoulder, his dark red eyes focused on me. "You were amazing, Wren. Ever owes you a huge debt. *I* owe you a huge debt."

I rub the back of his hand. Just like Thea has said, I'm beginning to understand our surly pseudo-mayor a little better after being forced to protect Ever too.

Morgan pulls Thea and I in for another hug, and then they decide to go back to the game. I can tell they're on high alert, but I have to trust they've got it handled.

Shepherd comes to my side when I turn to leave, holding up his three-fingered hand for a high five.

"You kicked ass and took names, Mary."

I laugh at his use of my Sanderson sister nickname.

"If I'm Mary, who are you?"

He scrunches his nose up. "I guess I'm one of Sarah's many boyfriends, but all wrapped up in a better boyfriend she can't get rid of?" Thea laughs behind him.

Ohken lets out an impatient growl.

My man is ready for privacy.

The Keeper stands in the street and watches us go with his arms crossed. I get the sense he'd rather trail us home to make sure I'm safe, but I assume he doesn't want to step on Ohken's toes or hint that my man can't take care of me on his own. So he stands in the middle of Sycamore and watches until we cross Main and head for the bridge.

Ohken insists on carrying me the whole way, and I don't bother to ask him to put me down.

By the time we reach the trail, there's a change in him. He's focused on getting home, his hands tight under my legs and my back. Black pupils eat up the amber of his iris and his lips are slightly parted, white teeth peeking out behind them.

I slide one hand into his tee and brush my fingers over his nipple.

He groans and stumbles a step, then surges forward with a growl.

Hot dog, I do believe I have myself a rut.

When I pinch his nipple lightly he snarls and throws me over his shoulder like a sack of potatoes. He swats my ass, then leans over and bites it.

I yip. "I was so excited about the whole rut concept that I never bothered to ask if you do it once or...."

"Few times a year for mated trolls," he purrs. "You ready for it, Miss Hector?"

"Ready as I'll ever be," I mutter, pressing my hands against his back as I try not to flop around.

He chuckles low and devious, slipping his fingers into my ass crack and stroking. Big strides eat up the path until we're at the bridge. He opens the door and we enter the dark hallway. We're down it in moments, but the cave already has the second door open wide. The hall lights blink on and off. She's laughing at us; I can tell.

Reaching out, I stroke the cave's walls and whisper a thank you as Ohken sails through the second door. He stalks quickly down the steps and into the cavernous living space, past the kitchen and through the door to the bedroom. I'm unprepared to be thrown onto the bed, so when he tosses me, I bounce ungracefully, flailing against the soft pillows.

A rumbly growl causes me to tense. My body recognizes a predator. The hair on my arms lifts, my muscles going tense and still. The room is dark, but he's outlined at the foot of the bed by the lights in the living room. Sconces flare to life one by one, illuminating Ohken where he stands. His eyes are narrowed slits, both meaty hands poised on the edge of the mattress as he looms over it. His chest rises and falls with ragged, shallow breaths.

"I'm losing control, Miss Hector." His voice is so low I can feel the vibration of it against my skin.

"Yes," I whisper. "Fucking finally."

His upper lip curls back into a sneer. "Say 'river' if you need me to stop."

My heart kicks up a notch, galloping in my chest. A safe word? I can't wait to see how crazy he's about to get. I feel like I've been waiting for this my whole life.

"Understood, plant daddy." I shoot him a saucy wink.

The chuckle that rumbles out of him is devious, promising retribution for my teasing.

"I'm not your daddy, witch," he says. "But you can call me

mate or sir." He waits for my assent, casting a glance down my body.

There's a momentary pause before he stands, pulling his shirt over his head. Buttons pop and fabric rips. His frilled cockhead pokes out of the waistband of his pants, pale green cum dripping from the head and slicking his folds. My mouth waters looking at all that gorgeous dusky skin.

I slip to the edge of the bed, kicking my pants off as I kiss my way up his muscular stomach. He's burning up with heat. He tosses the shirt aside and collars my throat, pushing me back on the bed before crawling his way over top of me.

I gaze up at him in absolute wonder. Big green muscles quiver slightly. There's no amber brown left to his iris, he's all black pupil and focused intent. He brings both hands to my tee and rips it down the front, shoving it off my breasts. Heat flashes between my thighs as his focus drops to my chest.

Ohken dips down, bringing one hand to my breast and squeezing. He shakes his head from side to side, rubbing his tusks over my sensitive skin. Warm lips come to my nipple, sucking hard and then biting until I cry out. It hurts, and it hurts so damn good.

I arch my back to get more of that sweet torture. He moves lower, scraping his tusks along my soft stomach, planting hot kisses as he goes. With a knee he nudges my thighs wide, one hand slipping between them to gather moisture. His touch is a gentle tease, his fingertips trailing along my slit. He slides one finger deep inside me, groaning when I cry out. His fingers alone fill me, and when he curls them to hit my G-spot, I can't help humping his hand.

"So fucking tight." He snarls as he continues the slow pump in and out of my pussy. I'm aching for more, reaching up to cup my own breasts and tug at my nipples as heat streaks through my body.

He slides farther down between my legs, one finger

circling the pucker of my ass. When it slides in, a scream rips out of my throat at how fucking full I am. But he doesn't stop, he never goddamn stops. In. Out. In. Out. His thumb rubs gentle circles on my clit until I'm heaving and rocking against his hand, desperate to come, desperate for something to break the dam inside me.

Ohken moans, and it's the sound of a man who's lost his cool somewhere between lust and ecstasy. "I need you wet and desperate, Wren. I need you wild, witch."

My breath turns into heavy panting as I cry out and hold onto his muscular forearm. I'm so fucking close. Nearly there.

With a laugh, Ohken pulls back and sits on his heels.

I shoot upright with a scowl. "What in the hell, sir? You're supposed to be in a damn rut and losing your mind. I expected feral. Give it to me." I crook a finger in my direction.

Ohken grins, but it's the grin of a madman with the way it splits his face. He looks unhinged, but not nearly as out of control as I'd like.

"I will never *not* want to take charge of you, Miss Hector," he murmurs, shifting forward and pressing me back down to the bed. "Even lost to lust the way I am, I'm still your Dominant, my sweet."

I plant my hands and shift backward, but he chases me across the mattress and straddles me. His fingers twist through my hair and he groans, rocking back onto his heels. His enormous cock pokes through the air, seeming to strain toward me as he drips cum like a faucet.

I don't bother trying to hold back. Instead I surge forward onto my knees and open my jaw wide. The magic of his potion helps me, and I suck him all the way to the back of my throat and farther. He fills me until I can't breathe, but the desperate whine he lets out urges me on. I grip his heavy balls and knead them gently, tugging on the skin between them as I suck my way around the frills lining his cockhead.

His stomach muscles flex, his dick bobbing against my lips as I attack it again, nipping and tugging at the extra skin around his tip. His whine rises into a desperate cry, his hand coming to the back of my head. He fists the length of my long waves and guides me up and down his dick. I'm thankful as hell for the magic, because without it there's no way I could take his sheer size.

Sugary sweetness bursts across my tongue as his precum comes harder and faster. My man's gonna blow, and I want it.

I go wild on him. Sucking, nipping, lapping at the slit in his tip where all that sweet nectar stems from.

Ohken snarls and yanks my head back.

"Not yet, witch."

I snarl back, smearing precum over my lips.

"Dare you to stop me," I snap.

With a bellow, he shoves forward and tosses me up against the wall, sliding his forearms underneath my thighs. He reaches down and lines himself up with my core, then thrusts in with a feral growl. Unlike the first time we fucked, he doesn't wait for me to catch up or adjust to his immense size. This time, his core curls over and he jerks his hips, slamming me against the wall with the force of his heavy weight.

I'm impossibly full, split apart by a cock the size of my damn arm. Blistering pleasure slaps me every time he shoves back in. His pace is rhythmic and fast, his balls slapping my ass as he fucks me.

"Ohken," I gasp. "Oh God." That tidal wave of pleasure is building and rising, crashing into me as heat rages and curls, dragging me to the edge of a cliff I can't wait to fall over.

He roars and slicks his mouth over mine, swiping at my tongue with his. And that does it. Ecstasy yanks me into oblivion, the swift pounding of his cock shoving me harder and harder into bliss. I lose track of how many times I come, but when he joins me, I'm so full I can barely breathe. He lets out a choked roar that shakes the wall behind me, cum dripping out of me to coat our sheets.

I suck in a breath, desperate to fill my lungs. Ohken's big chest heaves against mine, his forehead pressed to my neck. He breathes gently against my skin, like he's memorizing my very scent and can't get enough.

When big lips come to my ear and bite, I jerk in his arms, my pussy squeezing tight around his cock.

"More, witch."

With a demanding rake of his tusks against my neck, he throws us backward. We hit the mattress and roll, falling to the floor. He holds me so I don't hit the ground, conveniently parting my thighs around his middle.

"Ride me, Wren." It's a command I'm only too happy to carry out. Rocking my hips, I slide my pussy along his incredible cock, up and over the frilled folds around his head. Pleasure builds again, because he feels so impossibly good.

When he snarls at me and shifts to his elbows to watch the show, I rake my nails down his stomach. He bucks underneath me, and I use the motion to grip his cock and slip back down on top of him.

We both cry out, my voice already hoarse from screaming. I roll my hips, watching the way his gaze locks onto my tits, traveling down my core. His mouth falls open at seeing where we connect. Dark green flushes across his cheeks, and his head falls back. He's too big for me to lean forward and bite my way up that muscular neck.

With a savage roar he shouts, falling to his back and gripping my hips as he unloads inside me. For the second time, I'm filled and dripping, panting and covered with sweat.

Ohken rolls forward and stands with me in his arms, lifting me like it's nothing. I cry out at the loss of connection with that beautiful fucking dick, but he tosses me facedown over the edge of the bed and parts my asscheeks. He slides back into my pussy in one swift move, sloppy sounds echoing around the room as he rails me from behind.

Long minutes of ecstasy later, we come again before flopping to the bed.

I'm used and exhausted and that damn safe word never crossed my mind a single time. He's so much bigger, so much more powerful. And I've never felt safer or more cherished in my whole life. He's my favorite person in the entire world.

Ohken rolls me gently onto my side and kisses his way up my spine.

"Don't move, Miss Hector. You'll be sore."

"I've been abused." I let out a playful wail, throwing my arm over my head.

Ohken laughs and nips hard at the back of my neck.

"I'm just beginning to abuse you, my love. I hope you're in for a lot more of that."

I shrug. "I've already forgotten the safe word."

He rolls me over, whiskey eyes narrowing. "Not funny, sweet witch. It's important you be able to stop me if you're not—"

I silence him with my lips, shoving against his much bigger frame. He falls back to the bed, allowing me to crawl on top of him and slide my hips over his face.

"Too much talking," I murmur, running both hands into his hair. I use my grip for leverage to rock my pussy over his soft, warm mouth. "Not enough eating."

Enormous hands come to my thighs and spread me wider, and he feasts until I explode a fourth time, coating his neck and lips with slick.

When ecstasy fades, he rolls me onto my back and kisses his way up both thighs, spreading me wide to clean me with his tongue. When he's done, he shoves off the bed and disappears into the living area.

I look around at the room.

"Where's he going?"

In response, the door opens wider and I hear the faint sound of trickling water.

Ohken returns and hands me a glass of water and a bowl of noodles. They remind me vaguely of ramen, but thicker.

"Eat and drink something," he commands. "You need your strength."

I shrug and take the water, downing half of it before I snark back.

"Oh I dunno. You said rut and I expected you to be like a wild man, incapable of words and such."

The corner of his lips tilt up into a smirk, and he grabs my ankle, tugging it up to his mouth to bite my instep.

"We've been at this for an hour, Miss Hector." He laughs. "I told you it would be days of nonstop sex. You're going to be begging me to quit by the end of it."

I slurp down a noodle. It's like a miso egg drop combo, fucking delicious. I give my man a saucy look.

"I'm not a quitter."

"No," he murmurs, tucking my hair over my shoulder. "You're not."

I smile. We both know he doesn't mean right now. And I'm fucking proud to have saved not only myself, but Catherine too.

But then Ohken's breathing goes short and heavy, like he can't wait for me to finish. I set the meal aside just in time for him to tackle me, and we do it all over again.

∽

Days later, Ohken's passed out in the bed next to me and I'm reading a romance novel I got from the historical society on Main. It's fucking hilarious to me that the "human" section of books is mostly romance novels, but hey, I'll take it.

Every one of my muscles is quivering. I'm fucking exhausted, but somehow feeling elated and amazing all at the same time.

I set my book on the table and flip onto my side to look at my man. Amber eyes gaze back at me in the low light.

"Back to whiskey, I see." I reach out and stroke a lock of auburn hair away from his forehead. "You don't look quite so predatory."

He rolls onto his back. "I don't feel it either. I've never been this sore. We need a bath, Miss Hector."

I push on his shoulder. "Roll over."

One brow travels up, but he obeys, moaning when I crawl on top of his back with a thigh on either side of his broad waist. I lean over his shoulder and bring my lips to his ear. "Good boy, troll."

"Fuck," he bites out. "I'd never have thought that would be sexy, Wren."

I grip his shoulders and begin to knead the thick muscles. He groans as I make my way from one side of his beautiful back to the other. His skin flushes darker green under my touch, his moans rising in appreciation. It's not long before he's humping the bed, rising up onto his forearms to give me access to his neck. I slide an arm around his front, pinching a nipple as I yank his head to the side with my hand and bite his neck hard.

He snarls and rolls, gripping my hips and dragging us both upright. He rocks back to his heels and pulls my pussy to his mouth, lapping at my core. I scream and he stops. A low growl rumbles from him, and then he spits. I jerk in his arms as slick spit hits my clit and slides down. I'm so fucking shocked, but he buries his tongue inside me and eats until I've come twice, and I'm officially drained of fluids and in desperate need of water.

When I can't take any more, he lays me gently against the pillows before straddling my legs. Ohken grabs one of my arms and kisses his way up the inside of it.

Amber eyes flash to mine, and he smiles. It's breathtaking, his smile. It's confident, teasing, and authoritative. It's absolutely perfect.

"I'm in love with you," he murmurs. "This thing between us is more perfect than I could have ever imagined." His gaze comes to mine, but he doesn't stop kissing the inside of my wrist. "Do you agree, Miss Hector?"

"It's pretty damn good."

"Excellent. I want you to be mine forever, Wren."

I shuffle forward, watching as he drags his tusks along the inside of my arm. "What are you saying, Ohken?"

"Marry me." His voice carries with confidence. "Take vows with me. Let me bind us together in the ways of my people."

I swear the cave around us goes perfectly still. There's not a single whisper of noise in the entire place.

"I will." My eyes fill with tears as I stroke his cheek with the back of my hand.

Pale eyes flash open. "I want to bind you now, Wren. I don't want to wait."

I throw my arms around his neck and pepper his face with kisses. "Do it, mate."

Ohken growls and grips my wrist, holding it between us. He strokes his way along the back of my arm.

"Troll males alone possess the magic to bind a female. I'll say the vows, and you simply have to accept them with your heart. The magic creates a binding tattoo that'll connect us. We'll feel each other through it, tease each other. It's beautiful."

I look at him, really look at him, and it brings a huge smile to my face.

"A month ago I couldn't have imagined you were out there just waiting for me to show up and make your dreams come true. And now here we are. You're finally complete."

"Wren," he groans. "This is serious."

"As a heart attack," I agree. After a pause, I press a soft kiss to his lips. "Bind me, plant daddy."

Ohken laughs, and it's heartachingly beautiful the way it's so deep. His laugh tumbles around in my stomach like butterflies.

He takes my wrist and begins to murmur soft words. I don't understand any of them, they must be in his native tongue. But as he speaks, blue lines appear in the air. They overlay on top of my forearm and his, wrapping around us both. Then with a moment of intense heat, they imprint onto my skin, glowing a faint blue.

I gasp.

Ohken lifts my arm and says a final piece of the binding spell, and then he brings my wrist up to kiss it.

"Bound," he says, his voice brimming with pride. "We belong to each other, Wren Elizabeth Hector."

I rub my cheek along his tattoo, smiling when a zing of heat streaks down my spine.

"I always belonged to you," I whisper. "I just didn't know it yet."

There's a sudden flurry of movement, and a cacophony of noises echo into our bedroom from the living area.

Ohken laughs.

"She's happy for us."

"Good!" I clap with the cave, because I know that's what she's doing. "I'm happy for us too, Mister Stonesmith."

CHAPTER TWENTY-SEVEN
OHKEN

Wren jogs past me to the corner of Sycamore and Main where Thea and Morgan stand. Her sisters pull her in for a hug, and then they all turn to look at me with barely contained grins. Oh, I'd love to be a fly on the wall for Wren sharing what the rut was like. I'm under no illusion that her sisters won't hear all about it.

It was absolutely glorious. *She* was glorious.

When I pause behind Wren, Thea shoots me a fake scowl and untangles herself from her sisters.

"I hope you thoroughly enjoyed your days of rut heaven, because we got the pleasure of being grilled by Evenia on our powers. She's a real gem."

Wren slides her arm around my waist, hugging me close. "Sorry, girlies. I'd love to say I regret missing out on that, but the only thing I regret is not watching Mor verbally spar with those Hearth assholes."

Morgan huffs out a breath and crosses her arms. "She literally made us fill out the registration paperwork in front of her. I thought the Keeper was going to lose his shit, but Thea's mated, Lou's on the way and you two are..." She pauses and cocks her head to the side. "I don't know what to call it. Dating seems too low-key. Do trolls take mates? What's the right verbiage?"

I bend down to kiss the top of Wren's hair, basking in the floral fragrance she dabbed on her neck.

"Mated works," I murmur. Wren turns her face up to look at me, and the look of pure happiness has me soaring with pride. My tattoo glows faintly under her long shirt. Her sisters haven't noticed yet, but I imagine she'll tell them all about it soon.

Alo walks up with Iggy perched on his shoulder. His brows are furrowed; he looks frustrated. Iggy pushes off his dad and swoops over to Morgan, landing on her shoulder and wrapping his long tail around her neck. The tip snakes down the front of her shirt. She laughs and rolls her eyes, but puts a hand on his outer thigh to hold him carefully in place.

"There's a meeting, you guys. We've got to go listen to the Hearth-holes say some—"

"Ignatius Zion!" Thea and Alo shout at the same time.

I scoff and glance at Alo. "Hearth-holes?"

Alo rubs sheepishly at the back of his neck. "He might have heard me complaining to Shep about our beloved representatives. Not my finest parenting moment."

Iggy crosses his arms, preening under the attention. "Dad, you said to always tell the truth, and those people seem like jerks."

Thea thumps his wing and gives him a stern look. "We're gonna have to talk about the sort of stuff you can say in front of people, and the stuff you have to keep to yourself. In this case, let's make sure not to call the Hearth people Hearth-holes when they can hear us, okay?"

Iggy rolls his eyes and waves his hand toward town hall, sighing. "Let's just get this over with."

I look at Alo. He's barely holding back a laugh, one hand clapped over his mouth.

Wren swats his arm, but a chuckle slips out.

We walk together to town hall. The gazebo creaks and shifts, widening to make space for us. Extra chairs appear out of thin air, and we walk to the back and find seats in the back row.

The Keeper comm'd me early this morning, but I'm still a little surprised to see Evenia, Aberen, and Betmal standing at the front of the gazebo. The Keeper stands off to the side, his big arms crossed and a thunderous look on his face.

Evenia stands in front of her husbands, thin hands clasped together as she stares imperiously at the gathered townsfolk.

Wren looks up at me, a wry expression on her face. "Why does this feel like a shitstorm about to unload on us?"

I lean in close, wrapping an arm over the back of her chair. "You're not wrong, my love."

"Can't wait to see where this fucking goes," she mutters. Next to her, Thea sits, but Shepherd stands behind her.

It takes a minute for the remaining seats to fill, and then Evenia spreads her arms wide. Dark red lips part on a smile, but she reminds me of a spider about to cocoon its prey. There's nothing friendly in the way she looks at us.

"Deepest condolences on your loss in the skyball finals," she begins.

Someone groans in the audience. In the seat next to me, Wren shifts and presses closer to me. I already know she feels partially responsible for our loss, but that's bullshit. I would pick her over a godsdamned game any day of the week.

Evenia drones on. "You're probably aware by now that there was an attempt by two males to kidnap Catherine and Wren Hector. The pegasus and naga responsible were captured by your protector team and delivered to the Hearth for interrogation. While we're still gathering information from them, we do know they're affiliated with Wesley."

Concerned musings rise from the crowd, but Evenia silences everyone with a harsh look.

"This is Wesley's fourth attack on Ever, three of those happening within the last month." She casts a disparaging look at the Keeper. "Unfortunately, due to the unusual verbiage of the Cerinvalla Act, we cannot replace your Keeper with a more experienced option." She grins, not taking her gaze from her son's. "However, we are going to send a second Keeper as well as a hunter team. Ever will become their home base as they search for Wesley and any of his associates."

The Keeper says nothing. This isn't news to him, so they must have talked about it before this meeting. But it's obvious from the tense set of his shoulders and the way he's clenching his jaw that he's furious. He's between a rock and a hard place, though.

"What if we don't want hunters here?" someone shouts.

Evenia whips around, dark eyes searching for whoever asked the question.

"There is no choice," she hisses. "We cannot allow Wesley to damage the haven system. Our lives and the lives of all monsters who reside in havens rely on the system's magic remaining intact. We must protect it at all costs."

"I stand in solidarity with our Keeper," a second voice calls out. Catherine stands in the front row, chin lifted and shoulders straight. "It is *our* Keeper who protected this haven four times from our greatest threat. He's the best Keeper I've ever had the pleasure to know. Anyone you send will pale in comparison."

The Keeper's mouth purses into a thin line, his brows furrowing. He looks desperate to say something, anything.

Next to me, the triplets rise as one. I stand the moment

Wren does. Alo comes to my side, and then the whole town rises in one swift motion.

I can just see Evenia over everyone's heads. She looks around in fury. Betmal comes to her side and whispers something in her ear.

Someone starts clapping, chanting out for the Keeper.

"Keeper! Keeper! Keeper!"

The whole town takes up the rallying cry, stomping and howling as we cheer for the man who sacrifices so much of himself to protect us. The Keeper looks out over the crowd. His hands have fallen to his sides. He slips them into his pockets and gives Evenia a carefully neutral look.

She waits, her gaze narrowed on her side, until the shouting dies down. Then she turns from him and faces the crowd again.

"That's all for now, Evertons. Remember that the Hearth's only goal is to keep you safe. We'll continue working with your Keeper for now."

She falls silent after that, and most monsters rise to leave. Nobody wants to stick around to chat with the Hearth representatives.

I wait for the crowd to dissipate, and then I head to the front of the gazebo. Alo, Shepherd, and the triplets trail me up there. We stop next to the Keeper, and I hope Evenia sees it for what it is—a further show of support for him.

Morgan rounds me and sidles up next to the Keeper, slipping her hand in his and holding onto his arm with the other. She bats her lashes at Evenia.

"Much as we've loved having you visit, I imagine you're needed back at Hearth HQ, or wherever you spend your time?"

Evenia sneers at Morgan, dark eyes dropping to the hand Morgan has wrapped around the Keeper's bicep. He glances down at Morgan, the ghost of a smile on his face.

"Yes, Mother. It's high time you three left. I'll wait for a comm about what's next."

Evenia grins, but her fangs slide down from behind blood-red lips. "Don't think for a moment that a second Keeper will make things any easier on you, my son. I fully expect you to comply with whatever he or she deems necessary to keep Ever safe." She waves her hand dismissively at us. "Don't forget that if Ever falls, so too will the rest of the havens. I cannot allow it."

The Keeper's fangs descend, red eyes flashing at his mother. "That is the only thing you and I have ever agreed on, Mother. Now if you please, Richard is here to take you to the train station."

Evenia's dark eyes fall to Morgan again, but Morgan gives her a neutral smile. The vampire clasps her hands together and looks around at the rest of us, pausing when she sees Wren.

"Ah, the third Hector triplet. Your sisters have told me all about your green magic. You'll register of course, now that you're mated." Red eyes flick to me and back to Wren.

I let out a growl. "We're well aware of the need to register, Evenia. We'll get to it when we get to it."

"See that you do." She smiles at Wren before snapping her fingers at her husbands, who join her side.

"You're really mean." Iggy's tiny voice echoes in the now-empty gazebo. Alo claps a hand over his mouth, but Evenia whirls around, narrowing her eyes at the tiny child. I take a step closer to Alo, who flares his wings wide.

Evenia steps into Alo's space and reaches out, poking Iggy in the stomach. Alo snarls and swats her hand away, stepping back and out of reach. "Don't, Evenia."

She laughs, the sound cruel and heartless. "My my, Ignatius. Your mother would be mightily disappointed at your lack of manners. I'll mention it to her when I return home."

Iggy's lower lip quivers, and he glances at Alo before looking at the vampire woman, his blue eyes wide with unshed tears. "My mother? You know her?"

Evenia crosses her thin arms. "Of course, child. She protects Hearth headquarters. Her job is quite important."

Iggy gasps in surprise. Alo roars, spines appearing along his shoulders and arms. Miriam pops into large form and he presses Iggy into Miriam's arms. "Take him, please."

Miriam nods and tucks a shocked-looking Iggy against her neck, jogging out of the gazebo and toward the garden.

I move forward, but Morgan and Wren step in front of me at the same time.

"Listen here, bitch," Morgan starts. "I don't give a flying fuck what you rule. I don't care who you're related to. I don't care if you send ten more Keepers and a hundred goddamn hunters to Ever. But you don't get to be shitty with a child."

"In case that's not clear enough for you to get through your thick head," Wren snaps, "it's time for you to go the fuck home."

Evenia reels backward. Betmal grabs her by the back of the neck and pulls her close to him. "Let's go, Ven."

The three vampires step away from us and skirt the group.

"Let me make something else clear," Morgan calls out. Evenia stops and turns, glaring at us as Morgan continues. "If you hurt that child or any of my friends, I'll find you and you'll have to deal with me."

"Safe travels!" Wren shouts. "Hope your train doesn't derail and kill you on the way home!"

The vampires turn and scurry to the car. The silence inside the gazebo is deafening. Morgan turns to the Keeper. "I'm sorry if I overstepped. I'm sure you were about to rip that bitch a new one, but I just could not stand by."

The Keeper's gaze softens, and he smiles. "As you noted, Miss Hector, not needed, but still very much appreciated."

Morgan clears her throat and steps back, sliding an arm around her sisters. "Well, okay. Just so you know I wasn't trying to steal your thunder or anything."

The Keeper dips his head, then turns to Alo, who stands there seething with his fists balled. "I take it Iggy was unaware of his mother's role at HQ. Would you like me to speak with him?"

Alo snarls but unballs his fists. His big wings flutter, but he tucks them behind his back and lowers his head. "I'll handle it. I can't believe she mentioned Keira."

The Keeper nods. "It was a dick move. My mother loves to get under a being's skin. Go home. Hang with Iggy. Let me know if you need anything."

The Hectors stare at the Keeper like they don't know him, and I suppose they haven't seen much of the caring side of his nature.

"I think we should all go see Iggy." I look down at Wren. "Make a big fuss over him and how much we love him. What do you think, mate?"

Wren's green eyes flash with fierce determination. "Perfect," she whispers. "Misfits unite."

"Indeed." I laugh at my gorgeous, wondrous woman. "Indeed, my love."

CHAPTER TWENTY-EIGHT
WREN

It's been a few days since the extra visitors cleared out of town, and life is returning to a new normal. I close my eyes, relishing the sun's warmth on my face while I wait in the garden for Thea and Morgan. We're continuing witchy lessons with Catherine, even though Thea and I more or less have the basics down. Morgan doesn't, and that's okay, because we're here to support her until she does.

Glancing at the journal in my lap, I mull over the last few weeks. A breeze dances through the garden, and the moonflowers flutter wildly in the warm air. They're finally looking healthy again, crawling up the lattice I built with my magic.

There's a zap, and Miriam pops into large form and sits across from me with a cup of coffee. "Wren, we need to talk."

"Hoboy," I deadpan. "For humans, that saying always makes us want to barf."

She laughs and sips at her coffee. "Humans are so weird. That new double-sized gourd you grew for Kiril is amazing, and I need one. He's the talk of the A-frame! I need it. I want it. Grow me one please?"

I might as well be ten feet tall with how proud her request

makes me. I'm not the girl who blew up Kiril's house anymore; I'm the powerful witch who works alongside my friends to keep our home safe. I fit here in Ever, and I've never been more sure of that.

"Of course I will. Draw me up what you want and I'll build it for ya."

"Perf." She gives me a thumbs-up and glances toward the garden's opening, her smile falling. I suspect I know why.

Reaching across the table, I rub the back of her free hand. "How's Iggy since that bullshit with the Hearth?"

Miriam shrugs, staring at her coffee. "I don't know, to be honest. I've barely seen him or Alo since. Alo came home from that meeting, thanked me, and whisked Iggy to their nest. I haven't talked to him since then."

My heart's a little broken for her, because it's obvious that it kills her not to spend time with them. I'm firmly in the Alo-should-heart-Miriam camp, because they're perfect for one another. But something's holding him back, and I've got to respect the idea that he knows what he wants.

Or doesn't want, maybe.

Thea and Morgan stroll into the garden arm in arm, holding matching cups of coffee.

I smile when I see the green foam piled high on Morgan's order when she sits next to Miriam.

"Well, well, well." I cross my arms. "Guess somebody got over the main ingredient to troll whip?"

Morgan shrugs. "Listen, I'm trying to be a good neighbor, to really lean into the whole monster town thing."

"Gee," I snark. "Didn't realize that meant drinking purified troll jizz but you do you."

Morgan slams her cup down. "Listen here, my hair is so soft since I started drinking it. Ohken told me all about its restorative properties, and so I'm just going to overlook where it came from. Kinda like Ohken's mead. It's better not to ask or think about the ingredients."

Thea snorts. "We got some bangin' mead from him last night. Tasted like rhubarb but he said it was made out of centaur hoof clippings." She shrugs. "Camp don't-ask is fine with me too."

I smile and close my journal, setting it on top of the table. Morgan's pale eyes fall to it, then crinkle in the corner when she smiles.

"Mom would be really proud of you, Wren."

Tears fill my eyes, but I nod. "I know she would. And also I think she'd have a few choice comments about my husband."

"Definitely the size of *said husband*." Thea cackles and slaps her thigh.

Two more figures duck through the hedge. Shepherd trails behind the Keeper, who stalks up the gravel path with both hands tucked behind his back. He smiles at us when they get to the table, but doesn't sit.

Morgan peers up at him, shielding her eyes from the sun. For the first time in a long time, she's not glaring at him like she hates him.

Hmm.

When Shepherd stops next to him, they share a glance.

"You want to share the good news or shall I?"

"You do it." Shepherd winks at Thea and rounds the table, sinking down onto the bench next to her. He pulls her into his lap while we stare.

The Keeper clears his throat to get our attention.

"I've confirmed that your Aunt Lou is close. She should be arriving in the next week."

"Fucking finally," I say. Across from me, Morgan beams. She and Lou have always been close, and I know she'll be glad to have another single girlie to chill with. Thea and I have been a little less available, although I know she understands.

The Keeper smiles at us, and it's breathtaking to see under his prickly exterior. When he grins, a dimple pops up on one side of his mouth. "I'll let you know when she's at the gas station so you can be there to greet her, unless you'd like Shepherd and me to do it."

"No!" Morgan shouts, then seems to think better of it. A pink blush coats her cheeks. "I just mean we haven't seen her in a while. I'd like to introduce her to Ever gently. You know, because our arrival wasn't all that easy."

The Keeper's smile falls, and he nods. "Of course, Miss Hector. I'll let you three know when she's close. The glamour will be up for her until you let me know it's time to pull it down."

I give him a thumbs-up, but when Morgan says nothing else, he turns and walks back toward the garden exit.

"You hurt his feelings, Mor," Thea mutters, slapping Morgan on the shoulder. "Be nice, he's pining for you."

Morgan rolls her eyes and shrugs. "That man is pining for no one. I don't want Lou to get terrified like you were. Remember when Alo roared at us? I almost crapped my pants."

"He's done roaring," Shepherd says agreeably. "He's not allowed to be the first face people see anymore, on account of his past bad behavior. And Lou is part of your family, so I'll be there with snacks."

"Snack up, shack up!" Morgan hollers, bumping Shepherd with her shoulder. "Amiright?"

He snickers and slings an arm around her neck, pulling her close. "Yes indeedy, sis. I snacked up, now we're all shacked up. It's absolute perfection."

Their voices fade as I close my eyes again, letting my head fall back so I can feel the sun. Magic thrums in my veins, beautiful green magic that shows me the ground underneath my new home. Every leaf, root, branch, and limb is visible to me now when I focus. And when I reach down and touch the tattoo that swirls around my wrist, a hot curl of pleasure strokes between my thighs.

I grin.

Ohken's on his way, called to me by the magic that binds us together.

I didn't expect to find happily ever after in a hidden monster town, but I wouldn't have it any other way.

++

Wanna know what happens when Wren ties Ohken up under the stars? Sign up for my newsletter at www.annafury.com to access the spicy bonus epilogue where all that (and more) transpires.

If you can't wait to see how Miriam and Alo's love story unfolds, preorder Partying With Pixies!

CHAPTER ONE

UNEDITED DRAFT

MIRIAM

"Let me get this straight." I cross my arms and sit back in my chair, trying to understand what my soulfriend is telling me. "You carve the pumpkins with scary faces and then you put them on your front porch, and they just *sit* there?"

Wren scoffs and opens her arms wide, looking to her troll mate, Ohken, for assistance. "Well yeah, Miriam. It's meant to be creepy."

I look over at the enormous bridge troll sitting to her left. "Humans are so weird. Do you get this Halloween holiday?"

Ohken laughs, a deep rumble that causes Wren to nip at her lower lip.

"She brought me a book about Halloween to help me understand. I can give it to you, if you like?"

"Yes, please." I snort. "Who ever heard of scaring people with pumpkins?"

Wren's eyes go gleefully wide, and she lifts her arm to point at me. "You know what? I haven't gotten to the best part. And you're gonna love this part. This part is right up your alley."

I flutter my wings at my back, shifting forward to pay attention. Wren looks utterly delighted about whatever she's about to share.

"The best part," she chirps, "is each house prepares candy and treats for the kiddos, and they go from door to door yelling "trick or treat!" and you get to give them candy!"

"Trick or treat?" Ohken looks skeptical.

Bright joy fills my chest. "Candy, you say?"

Candy I can do.

Wren sits back with a triumphant hand slap on the table. "Yep, a shitload of candy. The holiday had far different origins, but the candy is sort of the main thing now for your average human. That and the dressing up like monsters and characters from movies and such."

I cock my head to the side. This human holiday seems to have a never ending litany of rules. Glancing over at Ohken, I thrum my fingers on the table. "I'll take that book, friend."

Ohken laughs and shoves back from the table, turning to head into the depths of his cave.

Wren watches him go with a wistful expression. "I swear, he's got the best ass on the planet. Look at that thing Mir."

Dutifully, I follow her gaze, but all I see is a male who isn't the one I want. Big bouncy troll asses aren't my thing.

High and tight gargoyle muscles? That's what I want. I compare everyone to Aloitious Rygold. He's fucking perfect.

Wren snickers. "You've got the sappiest look on your face, Mir. Lemme guess, you're fantasizing about Alo's ass?"

I rub my wings together to dissipate the slew of butterflies that rocket around my belly. It's no secret I've got the world's biggest crush on one of Ever's two gargoyle protectors. I've known Alo for five years, since he left another haven and came to live here with his newborn son, Iggy.

"It's complicated," I mutter.

Wren's expression goes soft and understanding. "I know he's just as nuts about you as you are about him, Mir. He stares at you all the time. I wonder what holds him back?"

Duty.

His child.

Not wanting to ruin a stellar friendship.

I don't say any of those things, though. Wren's only been in Ever for a month or so. She hasn't watched me pine over Alo for five entire years. She still thinks there's a chance we'll end up together. I'm starting to give up that hope. No matter what I do to show him I'd be the perfect partner, he doesn't reciprocate.

The blue leather band around my wrist shimmies, and a name hologram pops up just above it. I groan when I see it.

"Gross," Miriam snarks. "Ezazel?"

The head of my pixie order is my least favorite person in town. But he's in charge of ensuring we stay on track with pixie dust production, and we fell behind after a recent thrall attack on the community garden. There is nothing more important than making pixie dust.

"Miriam?" Ezazel's voice is as gruff as always.

"Yes, I'm here." I roll my eyes at Wren, whose brows furrow. She doesn't care for Ezazel's brusque manner, especially when he directs said brusqueness at me.

"You're on the schedule to stir the dust this evening. See that you're on time, Miriam." Without another word, he clicks off.

Wren scoffs. "Jesus, he's condescending."

It's on the tip of my tongue to remind her how important

pixie dust is to maintaining the protective wards that surround Ever and keep us safe from the outside human world. But Wren's well aware. When she and her sisters arrived, they accidentally punched a hole right through them.

I rise from my chair. "I've got to stop by the shop and check on a few things before my shift, so I'd better go. See you tomorrow, soulfriend?"

Ohken emerges from a back hallway with a book in his hand. He hands it to me with a smile. *"On the History of Halloween.* Wren confirms it's an excellent primer for the non-human among us."

Laughing, I take the leather-bound book and tuck it under my arm. I gesture around with my free hand. "Thank you for the lovely breakfast, friends. And your renovations to add plants to the living area are genius. Now Wren can be thinking about plants during all your activities instead of just in the bedroom."

Wren groans and throws a hand over her face.

One of Ohken's auburn brows travel up to his hairline. "Thinking about plants during activities, huh? Hmmm." He strokes his chin softly. "I suppose I'll have to try harder to keep your focus on me, Miss Hector."

He grins devilishly, and that's my cue to leave. They're newly mated, and they're still in the fawning over one another phase. Although something tells me they'll be fawning for a while.

Wren stands from her chair and rounds the end of the chunky wooden table, opening her plump arms wide.

Hugging all the time is such a human thing, but I've quickly come to love it. I sink into her arms, squishing our cheeks together as I hold her tight. Wren's heartbeat is a steady, comforting thud, her chest pressed to mine. We hold the hug for a long minute before she steps back.

I've decided I love being hugged. And I think I love it

because there's really no other physical interaction in my life. Pixies aren't huggers. Nobody wants to accidentally touch wings and be awkward. It's a mates-only thing.

Wren walks me up a few stairs and out their first door, following me up a long hallway lit by glowing blue troll glyphs. Ohken's cave was always beautiful, but she seems so happy now that he has Wren. The glyphs never glowed before Wren came along.

She presses her hand to the wall just inside the cave door and grins. "I can't wait to hear all your questions once you read about Halloween. It's the best holiday ever. It's Thea's favorite, too!"

I smile at her mention of one of her triplets. Thea mated Alo's brother Shepherd not that long ago. She is wonderful—bubbly and hilarious and just so lovely.

Also, I'm incredibly jealous of the Hectors and their relationships. They've been in Ever for just a month, and two of the three girls are now mated to monsters. The third sister isn't mating anyone any time soon, but that's another story entirely.

The bridge entrance's black stones crack and slide out of place, tumbling to the ground outside. I wave one last time at Wren, then step out, emerging under the troll bridge. The creek is quiet at this time of day; the merminnows who use it to get to school have already done so.

Sighing, I soak in the sounds of the verdant green forest. It's so quiet and peaceful here by Ohken's bridge. I duck out from under the aged stones and head along the river before taking a right onto the path that leads back toward Sycamore street. With Wren's book in-hand, I can't switch to my small-form and zip back to the garden—the book will be too heavy and I don't have any dust with me to tiny-fy it.

I walk quietly along the forest path, flipping the book open. It's a lot of small words, causing my eyes to immediately glaze over. I've always had trouble focusing on reading, so I'm grateful when I flip a page and there's an illustration. A woman wearing striped stockings, a black tattered dress and a conical black hat with a wide brim smirks at me from the page. In one hand she holds an upside down broomstick. In the other, a vial of purple liquid.

Small text below the image indicates she's a witch ready to go flying on Halloween and steal children.

Oh my word. Witches don't steal children. It's preposterous. Witches are protectors. Don't humans know anything about us from myth? There was a time before the monster haven system was put into place when monsters lived in hiding. Surely the humans had enough random interaction to get some parts of our lore correct?

I flip through a few more pages as I walk. When I come to a page with a black cat staring into a cauldron as a "witch" dumps toads in, I cackle aloud. By the time I reach the end of the path and Sycamore street, I've made it through all the book's illustrations and come to one conclusion—human Halloween in its current form is utter nonsense. Absolute made-up bull crap.

Hooking a right on Sycamore, I head for Main Street. By the time I get there, my brain buzzes like it often does when I ingest new info. Ideas start to come to me, floating lazily around inside my mind like fireflies.

Main Street is busy this time of day. Like always, there's a line of monsters out the door at Higher Grounds coffee shop. Two centaurs meander down the sidewalk hand-in-hand. As I head toward my store, Miriam's Sweets, I wave to Richard, the pack alpha of the shifter pack in Ever.

"You're not usually in this part of town." I laugh and clap his muscular shoulder. "What brings you to Main Street?"

Richard smiles, pearly white fangs glistening in the midmorning light. "Meeting with the Keeper and protector team."

His smile falls a little. "After a lot of arguing from the Keeper, Hearth HQ agreed not to send us a secondary Keeper, but they're sending a hunter team sometime this week."

My happy mood falls flat as a pancake. I lift my hand to nibble at my thumbnail, then lay it back down. It's a nervous habit. "Do you think they'll bring hellhounds?"

Richard nods. "Absolutely they will." He runs one hand through perfectly slicked back salt-and-pepper hair. "I haven't told the shifters yet. They won't be pleased."

Hellhounds and shifters have a sordid history. I'm not surprised he isn't anxious to have the creepy dogs here in Ever.

"On the other hand," he continues. "Wesley has attacked us three times in the last month. Something's got to give—he's too powerful a warlock to allow him to continue what he's doing. The Keeper's job is to keep Ever safe. He can't be expected to go out and hunt Wesley, but someone needs to."

I nod but I'm lost in thought. Richard notices, intuitive shifter male that he is. He rubs my shoulder before striding past me.

I lived here for a long time. I've never felt unsafe here until the last month. Even now, I don't feel unsafe necessarily, but I do feel like we're in a spiderweb of Wesley's making, caught and struggling, and he's crawling across the web to wrap us up for dinner.

Shaking my head to ward away the jittery sensation in my chest, I walk past Scoops Ice Cream and shove my key in the lock at my store, Miriam's Sweets. The glossy red wood front always brings me peace. Well, most days it does. When I open the glass front door, the scents of spun sugar and vanilla fill my nose. It brings a smile to my face.

I freaking adore candy. More than that, I love making people smile. And my candy does that. Most of it is just plain candy, but I've got some magical candies that make things happen—like turning your hair another color or making your voice go high and squeaky.

We don't open until lunchtime, but I'm rarely on the schedule myself. My work with the other pixies making dust to power the protective wards is too important. The sweets shop has always come second. And it's been successful despite my torn focus. I'm really proud of that.

I walk through the customer area toward the back. Two of the four walls are floor-to-ceiling jars of various candies. Walking past the glossy red checkout counter, I enter a short hall and go left into my office. We aren't teaching any classes tonight, so thankfully I don't have to get the classroom ready. I don't have enough time for that before my shift.

Breathing out a sigh of pleasure, I look around my office. One whole side is a long storage area with ingredients, but the left is my desk. It's where I get all my best thinking done.

Setting the Halloween book down, I round the desk and drop into my chair. There's a stack of paperwork from my assistant Celset. She's a harpy and she's fairly reclusive. She comes in to do the books and paperwork overnights, and on mornings after she's come, there's always a neat stack of papers on my desk awaiting me.

I glance at my comm watch. It's 9:45 a.m. Ever-time. I've got forty-five minutes until I need to be at the factory. Plenty of time to whip through this stack of purchase orders and send them off to my supplier in Vizelle. The Swiss monter haven is the very best place for recreational pixie dust. Most dust is used for ward protection, but Vizelle has developed a type specifically meant to enhance pixie magic.

Grabbing a pen, I get to work, but my mind is still distracted by what I saw in Wren's Halloween book. The inklings of an idea that came to me earlier stretch and move in my mind, forming into a full idea so tangible and exciting, I can't help but grab a sheet of paper and start jotting everything down.

Lost in ideation, I sketch and draw and make myself notes. With a triumphant purr, I sit back and stare at the paper.

The Hectors' birthday is coming up soon in human-world time, and I don't want them to miss it simply because Ever works on a different timeline. I'm going to recreate Halloween for the Hector triplets. Yes! It's going to be amazing.

My comm watch pings, and I notice it's nearly eleven a.m. Groaning, I slap myself on the forehead, not bothering to answer Ezazel. It'll be another sermon and I'm too excited about Halloween to deal with it. Snapping my fingers, I transform into my small form and zip out of my office, through the store, and out the small pixie-hole next to the door handle.

BOOKS BY ANNA FURY (MY OTHER PEN NAME)

DARK FANTASY SHIFTER OMEGAVERSE

Temple Maze Series

NOIRE | JET | TENEBRIS

DYSTOPIAN OMEGAVERSE

Alpha Compound Series

THE ALPHA AWAKENS | WAKE UP, ALPHA | WIDE AWAKE | SLEEPWALK | AWAKE AT LAST

Northern Rejects Series

ROCK HARD REJECT | HEARTLESS HEATHEN | PRETTY LITTLE SINNER

Scan the QR code to access all my books, socials, current deals and more!

@annafuryauthor
liinks.co/annafuryauthor

ABOUT THE AUTHOR

Hazel Mack is the sweet alter-ego of Anna Fury, a North Carolina native fluent in snark and sarcasm, tiki decor, and an aficionado of phallic plants. Visit her on Instagram for a glimpse of the sexiest wiener wallpaper you've ever seen. #ifyouknowyouknow

She writes any time she has a free minute—walking the dog, in the shower, ON THE TOILET. The voices in her head wait for no one. When she's not furiously hen-pecking at her computer, she loves to hike and bike and get out in nature.

She currently lives in Raleigh, North Carolina, with her Mr. Right, a tiny tornado, and a lovely old dog. Hazel LOVES to connect with readers, so visit her on social or email her at author@annafury.com.

Printed in Great Britain
by Amazon